THE INCOMPARABLES

Also by Alexandra Leggat

Animal (stories)
Meet Me in the Parking Lot (stories)
Pull Gently, Tear Here (stories)
This is me since yesterday (poetry)

THE INCOMPARABLES

Alexandra Leggat

A NOVEL

Copyright © 2014 by Alexandra Leggatt

All rights reserved. No part of this book may be reproduced by any means without the prior written permission of the publisher, with the exception of brief passages in reviews. Any request for photocopying or other reprographic copying of any part of this book must be directed in writing to ACCESS: The Canadian Copyright Licensing Agency, One Yonge Street, Suite 800, Toronto, Ontario, Canada, M5E 1E5.

Anvil Press Publishers Inc.
P.O. Box 3008, Main Post Office
Vancouver, B.C. V6B 3X5 CANADA
www.anvilpress.com

Library and Archives Canada Cataloguing in Publication

Leggat, Alexandra, 1964-, author
    The incomparables / Alexandra Leggat.

ISBN 978-1-927380-62-8 (pbk.)

    I. Title.

PS8573.E461716I53 2014   C813'.54   C2013-904804-9

Cover design by Rayola Graphic Design
Cover images: Photos of fabric © Claudia Botterweg; Noh mask © kvap
Interior by HeimatHouse
Represented in Canada by Publishers Group Canada
Distributed by Raincoast Books (Canada) and SPD (USA)

The publisher gratefully acknowledges the financial assistance of the Canada Council for the Arts, the Canada Book Fund, and the Province of British Columbia through the BC Arts Council and the Book Publishing Tax Credit.

Printed and bound in Canada.

For my dear brother Graham
In loving memory

The Drive to the Country

IT'S DAWN AND the rising sun drapes a yellow veil over the city. It's hot, too hot for spring. Lydia watches the rows of passing brownstones emerge through the dirty dawn. Residences she has passed by for years and never thought about or pictured the people inside. On the other side she imagines a yellow-hued man, pollution ridden, attempting to rise in the city, getting ready for another day in the arms of a woman he'd die for.

Rosa grips the steering wheel. "What are you dreaming about?" she asks Lydia without taking her eyes off the road.

"If the couples in those brownstones are happy — no, not happy — faithful, are they faithful..."

Rosa taps Lydia's knee.

"...if while shaving, pulling on stockings, eating oatmeal, drinking coffee they're already looking forward to the end of the day... if right now at the break of the dirty dawn they're thinking about the person they're coming home to."

"Lydia, really..."

"...or someone they'll see when they walk out the door..."

"Lydia, stop."

"...if the habit of being with someone day in, day out leads to the indiscretion. Is it boredom? Tedium? Habit? The getting up to the familiar face, watching it over coffee, oatmeal, brushing teeth, it's there in the mirror, in the hallway, on the couch, in the coming home, eating, sleeping and waking up to it again and again, drives..."

Rosa turns up the radio. Yo-Yo Ma plays the *Cello Suites*. "No one plays Bach like Ma," she says.

"What if Charlie's in there, starting the cycle over again with her face?"

Rosa ups the volume loud enough to say, *take your mind off things, Lydia. Bach wouldn't have wasted his time wondering about strangers in passing brownstones; think of the music that never would have happened.* Lydia listens to the depth of the cello, its yellow-veiled hue, a dirty dawn. Maybe he did, maybe those thoughts created the music.

The further from the city they travel, traffic loosens, the sky stretches out, breathes. The veil dissipates and the lilac moon lingers in the west. Lydia complains about the heat and pushes what she can of her newly cropped hair behind her ears. It feels cool, and unlike herself, a relief. Her breathing slows. Her chest remains tight.

"He had nine children."

Rosa fixates on the horizon, wills it closer.

"Bach had nine children. Did you know that?"

Rosa opens her mouth then closes it a few times, no idea what to say. She resorts to asking, *Are you okay? You good?* and pats her friend's knee.

Lydia doesn't nod or shake her head. She rubs the hospital band on her wrist and stares at the open road. How should she answer that? *Look how long the sky is?* There's something unnerving about an endless empty road and the way the clouds drift across the crescent moon. *Why's the moon hanging around? Rosa, you're a doll for driving me to the country.*

"I read about this French pianist who left Paris to live with wolves in South Salem."

"What?"

Lydia stares at her hands. They're rough, chafed, rubbed sore. Rough hands are an awful characteristic for a woman to bear. Hands can't be hidden like feet. Gloves, there's gloves. Gloves aren't an everyday thing like shoes. She wants to cut off her hands. Sever them at the wrist for all the trouble they cause. And the faces, the difference in ten years. Lydia places her hands on the dashboard, they're white and blue like Rosa's, all bone and veins, gripping, gripping.

"Imagine balancing a career as a concert pianist *and* raising wolves."

At work, Rosa and Lydia compared themselves to the porcelain surfaces of the actors, polished and pristine. Fit them into their costumes, and sent them on their way to the world they thrived in, the same turn of events day in, day out, scripted, and when they skipped away, Rosa and Lydia were left looking at themselves in the space in the mirrors. Dishevelled, the signs of wear and tear, the long hours written all over them, lines that remained after the laughter, blue and purple pooling beneath eyes, and veins of red around their noses. Crumpled clothes they wore day in, day out, painter's dungarees and cotton T-shirts or men's shirts hung loosely over their large bones hidden beneath baggy jeans. They were average size for women their age but seemed so much bigger than the minute actresses, sculpted and miniature as jockeys. "We look like mothers," Rosa once said. "Their mothers. I don't want to look like someone's mother if I'm not a mother. Give me a kid, I'll gladly look like a mother."

"I imagine it wouldn't be much different than being Bach attempting to compose in a house with nine children."

"Why are you telling me this?"

"I don't know."

Gripping, gripping.

Faces are much harder to hide than hands. Lydia touches her hair, the hair she can no longer let fall over her face, hiding it, closing it off from the outside, like curtains. Her hands crawl under her cashmere cardigan. Masks are acceptable only in the theatre or on halloween. A trio of turkey vultures floats above them. There's no explaining this, the journey home, back to a place she spent her entire youth clawing her way out of. She rubs her hands. They'll never look young again. Hands like weathered soles, her feet smooth and soft, *peau de soie*: "silk skin."

"These could never play a piano."

Shut up, Rosa thinks, *shut up, nothing you're saying makes sense*.

Yellow stalks, naked and erect sway in a field by a roofless barn.

"Cashmere, bury me in cashmere," Lydia whispers, "in a field of yellow, by a roofless barn."

"What did you say?"

"But wolves, these hands could raise wolves."

"Lydia."

"Imagine wearing a mask like people wear wigs."

"What do you mean?"

"I mean getting up in the morning, getting dressed, brushing your teeth and placing a mask over your face and leaving the house like that. Why didn't we do that? Why didn't I? Then maybe there wouldn't have been the tedium, the boredom, a different face to wake up to every yellow-veiled day. I mean, how many masks would one need?"

"Why don't you try to sleep?" Rosa says.

"I guess it would depend on the husband."

Rosa reaches for the radio.

"On how many masks you'd need."

She turns it up and says, "Sleep, the doctor says you need to rest."

Lydia grabs the volume button, turns the music down.

"I can't sleep in cars." Rosa sticks her head out the window to smoke, somehow managing to not veer off the road. A trick she mastered when she swore she'd never give up the one thing in life that remained pleasurable. She buys her Japanese cigarettes in Chinatown. They come in a silver tin with Kanji lining the top, and beneath it in English, the word *Hope*.

Lydia wonders if the Kanji say more than the name of the cigarette. If, like regular cigarettes, they have multiple warnings across the pack, but *Hope* says:

"Smoke, enjoy yourself, life is short and if these kill you look on the bright side, you'll be reincarnated into something better.

So smoke, smoke, be happy, relax, take a puff, there is hope in every inhalation, in every exhalation."

For Christ's sake, loosen up, would you, have a goddamn smoke, everyone dies in the end.

"Hélène Grimaud, that's her name, Hélène Grimaud, the pianist. Special, she's special, wouldn't you say. Unique. There's no one like her."

Rosa grips the wheel with her right hand; with the left, she inhales, exhales *Hope*. "How do you know there's no one like her?"

"Do you know anyone like her?"

"I don't know her, or of her, okay, she doesn't exist for me."

"Right, she's no J.S. Bach, although she plays him really well. But there's no one like him, right?"

"What's your point?"

"I don't know, maybe you are one of his nine children, there's no one else like you and you said you never knew your dad?"

Lydia envisions the car door flying open; she'd roll at first, then run. Run until she reaches an unknown village, where she can start again with a different name, a different job, work in a convenience store wearing a peacock-feathered mask and gloves. Sell Japanese cigarettes in silver tins, raise wolves, nine, and smoke until she dies. She grips her hands.

"Are you tired, Rosa?"

Rosa shakes her head, hangs onto the steering wheel. She looks younger from the side, her round face in a constant state of smiling even when sad or frustrated. The road remains empty, not a soul coming or going except for the turkey vultures hovering around them. In the city everyone comes and goes. It makes you wonder. Out here, people are happy to remain wherever they are, avoiding the vultures.

The sky melds with the road like a drive-in movie screen. Lydia's mother appears, but not like in the films she's made or on the familiar stages. She's smiling, holding out well-rehearsed hands. Everyone approaching her wears black and says, "We're sorry Constance, so sorry Constance, our condolences." When they take Constance's outstretched hand they also grip her arm, or touch her shoulder, embrace her. Constance remains still. She isn't acting — or maybe she was that day, more than ever.

She clutches her black silk shawl, grits her teeth, the way to be strong at a husband's funeral. White knuckles against black silk, her aging mother's veins like eels beneath rice paper. Lydia wants to drown in her work. She will keep her mind off things, make her mother proud, keep her mother's mind off things — that thing — the thing she had no idea how to talk to her mother about. She hadn't been home since the funeral, and her mother hadn't come to the city to see her since Henry passed away. She said she had trouble leaving the house. The city was too big for her now, the noise, the crowds, and the memories of when life was happier are too painful to recall, a time when she was a porcelain actress being dressed in the mirror, like the ones Lydia dresses for a living.

Rosa turns off the throughway and veers left onto the concession toward the Templar estate. When the car wheels squeak, Lydia realizes she *can* sleep in cars.

"How are you doing?" asks Rosa.

Every thirty kilometres or so Rosa asks how Lydia's doing? She's worried, unsure if this is right, if she's doing her friend a favour or not. *How are you doing? How are you doing? How are you doing?* And every thirty kilometres, give or take, Lydia wonders, *How am I doing? How am I doing?*

"You'll get through this," Rosa says. "In a month you'll feel like a new woman, strong and ready to tackle the world again."

In a month, one month.

She agreed to drive Lydia to her mother's only if she promised to hang onto her already-paid-for apartment in the city for one month. "You can't let go of everything at a time like this. It's a bad time to make life changing decisions."

Vultures, vultures... where are the doves, the starlings?

"Hang on, see how you feel in a month."

Rosa agreed to stay in the apartment and look after it. Not let it decline in the way a furnished empty dwelling does, becoming stale and musty in a tenant's absence. They'd been in too many abandoned homes, estate sales, bartering for antique fabrics and furniture upholstery. Charlie moved out. In the melding of belongings, he found and packed up the last eight years of their life, quickly, too efficiently. Who knew he could do that for himself? Incredible how a spouse can divide what one assumes is "ours" into "mine" and unhinge themselves from the foundation when another woman's waiting with food on the table, different habits, foibles, new lines, a brand new face to live the routine with — masks.

In one month Rosa figures everything will go back to normal but there's no "normal" in their realm of things, and Lydia isn't sure she wants to go back, not now that an open road's luring her away. And how does Rosa think that in one month, or every thirty kilometres, Lydia will be okay? A month, four weeks, thirty dirty dawns.

Lydia reaches for her once-long hair, grips the ragged remains. In her palm the memory of pinking shears and rage, surging and snapping. Her waist-long yellow tresses veiling the apartment floor she promised to hang onto for one month. The shears crunched through her hair like teeth biting into an apple, she hears it over and over. What would a new woman feel like? A new woman's just as likely to experience the same thing at some point in her life. Her grandmother once said, the difference between a good haircut and a bad haircut is one month.

The road twists and the still water of the Chase River is close enough to leap out of the car and into it like so many before. It's teeming with drowned souls. Lydia senses her mother, imagines her face in the river, one eye smiling, the other calling, begging her, lithe arms reaching up and out of the water. Lydia shudders and turns away. There's no guarantee that smiling eyes and open arms will greet her at the door. She rubs her hands, touches her own skin: sad, it feels sad, tired, old paper holding together the words of some book for too long, faded and dry. Her mother's greatest joy was raising her children, she told them, and until Henry died her greatest sorrow was having no control over them growing up and leaving.

Pine trees line the road, blocking out the sun and casting a dusk-like hue between them. Lydia pictures her sister, tall and poised like the pines. Sophie smiles and waves to her from the river bank. Rosa watches her friend, her fingers out the window, fluttering in the wind. *What does she see?* "Why do mothers have children," Lydia asked Sophie after the funeral, feet dangling over the edge of the bridge that their grandfather had built in the woods across the Chase. "Why have children if the leaving's so troubling, why not have pets? Pets don't grow up and leave. Pets always need you."

Sophie thought about it for a long time and said, "Do you think some of us are mothers before we have children?"

Lydia stared at the side of Sophie's head, the angle of her nose, chin, her skull, her petite ears, the perfect profile like Lydia's favourite phase of the moon.

"Yes. I do. Born mothers."

Her mother's face blends into the dandelions lining the edge of the road. In school, she learned that the flower heads of the dandelion open for several days, then close for a fortnight before opening to release its seeds. The "period of quietus" she read, is when *"the yellow rays of the flower metamorphose into a delicate ball of fluff,"* the evanescent stage. She imagines plucking her mother from the side of the road, her head the fluffy ball of a dandelion, the evanescent stage, dissipating across the corn rows when the wind blows. Lydia's left staring at her hands and through her hands the feeling of the uneven road ahead of her.

"When all of the seeds are gone, the bare knob at the top of the stem resembles a tonsured head of a monk."

Lydia slumps in her seat.

"What are you thinking about?" asks Rosa.

"Nothing. I'm not thinking."

Lydia's hands run back and forth and back and forth across her jeans. Back and forth and back and forth, touching, always touching.

"You sure this is what you want?"

"I can't answer these questions anymore."

"You haven't answered. You said, 'nothing.' That's not an answer."

"That's not an answer because your questions are rhetorical. There are no answers, Rosa. There are no answers." She thumps the dashboard.

"Hey, not the car. Do not take this out on my car. You think it doesn't feel that."

"It feels this?" she hits it again.

Rosa glares at the open road, the insipid paleness of the sky, her thoughts stream across it like subtitles. *This is shit for me too. I don't think you're considering how your actions have affected me and my career. How the hell am I supposed to do this without you? This was it for us, a chance to move up, make a name for ourselves. We've worked years and years for this.* She bites the inside of her cheek, reaches for another cigarette; she wants a drink. Envisions the twist-top bottles of Shiraz she keeps in the trunk for frustrating drives, dates, the nights she drops off deadbeats and *Hope* won't cut it alone for the lonely drive home.

"Rosa?"

She doesn't answer.

"Are you okay?"

She draws on her cigarette.

"What are you thinking?"

"Nothing."

The estate's been in the family for years, handed down from generation to generation like a wool coat and a pair of sturdy shoes. The sprawling acreage is home to the Queen Anne, a now crumbling barn, and a small house through the woods built for her grandfather's employees who travelled in search of work. Men who worked for less than the educated and licensed, happy to have a place to sleep, to be fed, a few guys to hang out with on weekends, and be free of the babies and wives they were brought up believing they had to have and had.

When Henry retired from teaching at the local high school, he converted the extra wing of the sprawling home into a bed and breakfast for Constance and him to run at their leisure. Henry honoured the home, his father's and grandfather's craftsmanship, but he refused to follow in their footsteps. That was not the kind of architect he was going to be.

He wanted to share the home with outsiders looking for comfortable vacation dwellings. To make them feel like family. "Being around and meeting new people keeps you young," he'd say. *Who wants to stay young*, Lydia wondered. *Growing up was where free-*

dom lay, as long as you didn't have children. "Honey, I don't mind if you play in those woods," said Constance, "but run straight home if you see a stranger."

But strangers are everywhere, even in our home. The day that Constance and Henry smashed a bottle of champagne against the bed and breakfast's front door and welcomed their first guests, Henry said, "Honey, we are all strangers at some point in our lives and it's important to make people feel like family. Some people don't have families and we should be grateful for what God's given us and open up our home and our hearts to those seeking a warm and safe place to stay on their travels."

God. She didn't grow up with God. He wasn't a member of their family until the bed and breakfast opened and Henry's health changed. God was a stranger until they began frequenting the old cathedral in town, kneeling on the concrete floor, praying to the silhouette of Christ that remained after the sculpture came down. God was a stranger until they all came back from the cathedral one night and Henry acted like God was a VIP guest at the B&B. Lydia spied on Henry talking to him and kneeling before the end of the ballroom on the top floor. The floor that Henry never rented to other strangers. "He's here, I can feel him," said Lydia to Sophie one night when she was roaming the halls touching things to try and fall asleep. "What does he feel like?" whispered Sophie. "Fire," said Lydia. "Ew," she said, "you sure Dad didn't bring home the devil?" Lydia shook her head, "No."

God became one of the guests that never left.

Henry could never let go of the little white house through the woods. He loved that in the winter he could see it peeking through the leafless trees. There's something comforting about its presence, like a good cousin, one who's there if you need them but doesn't impose. Family you like. Without Henry, Constance worries about the extra upkeep and costs, and has recently contacted a local real estate agent about putting it up for sale. She would be relieved to see it go. She knows Henry would never forgive her but the Queen Anne itself is becoming too much to maintain. She has no idea where she'll go or if she can even bear to live in a different place, but she has to be realistic.

LYDIA ROLLS DOWN the window, breathes the morning air. She should have remained in the anonymity of a medical institution. Allowed a resident doctor, not some on-call student, to look into her eyes and say, *I see it. Not to worry. There is a light at the end of the tunnel but it's not coming from the direction you think.* Then the pills, a sensation of cream being poured over her body, limbs losing the heaviness of bones, draped at her sides like *peau de soie*.

There were visions, she agrees, but everyone sees things when they're tired, the nightmares, exhaustion, stress, the pressure of the job. The doctor squinted, unsure. "It's the occupational hazard of the theatre," she said to him. "I work in a made-up world. You should see what I see every day — witches, soldiers, imps, murder. I dress them, create those peoples, those personalities, I'm responsible for what they feel, their traits good and bad." The doctor didn't wear a white coat. His face was expressionless, devoid of any lines, age or otherwise. He wore tight indigo jeans — Lydia could see by the weave that they were not cheap — and a plaid shirt. She swore he was no older than when she fled to the city to fulfill her dreams. *Was this your dream, Doc? To listen to a broken woman tell you that everything she was brought up believing is a lie?* And what was she brought up believing, hard work pays off? That God is a squatter?

"Do you believe in God?" Sophie asked one night, legs dangling over the bridge, the moon leaning in to listen.

"I don't believe in anything I cannot see."

"But you see everything."

Lydia noticed her legs passed Sophie's for the first time. She was determined to touch the water before her sister's toes did, to be taller and wiser one day. Her mind goes blank, dark, she's tired. She touches the window, hands pressed against the glass like a child wishing to reach through it and stop her sister from leaving. She misses Sophie; death and marriage bring out the worst in people.

"Bananas," says Rosa.

"What? Me?" Lydia pulls her hands away and shoves them under her thighs. "Leave me alone."

Rosa laughs, "No, no, I forgot I brought bananas. Let's eat them, they're good for us. They alleviate pain. I heard it on the radio, bananas and grapefruit are good for pain."

Lydia looks at her, "Bananas?"

"They're in the back."

"Don't believe things you hear on the radio."

"Why not?"

"Because you can't see the person's eyes."

"That's ridiculous."

"They can tell you anything on the radio because you can't see their eyes to see if they're lying."

Rosa grips the steering wheel harder.

"Bananas," says Lydia and reaches for the clear bag behind her, eyes the freckled fruit and shakes her head.

"Fine," says Rosa. "Go hungry. Remain in pain."

Rosa lights another stick of *Hope*, and blows the smoke out the window. She should have left Lydia in the hospital. Her own mother's voice echoes in her head, always telling her to stop thinking, she knows better. It was the smells, the moaning emanating from behind drawn curtains, expressionless nurses moving like ants, in and out of the curtained partitions with needles and pills. Helpless, she paced back and forth. Her hands grasped long flowing auburn hair. She took Lydia's limp hand and said they had to go. All the on-call doctor was going to do was advise her to call her family doctor in the morning. He'll set up an appointment with a psychiatrist for the latest antidepressants they receive payback for prescribing, and veil the source of the problem. The psychiatrist will refer her to a therapist who'll say she's depressed and broken down and they'll ask mundane questions she couldn't possibly know the answers to in this condition.

Rosa reminded Lydia she'd been through this before, discovering the husband with someone else, the deceit, the stress of moving, starting over. "And I wasn't married to Posthumus Leonatus, my dear. I was married to Emilio Escobar's bad understudy. But you'll realize, sweetheart, you don't start over, you start back up again — you move on."

She mouthed the words, *move on*. Then she left and returned with a wheelchair.

She babbled on about how she couldn't leave her dearest friend in a dirty inner-city emergency room with a bunch of crazies, drunks, and mugging victims, have them force Diazepam down her throat and ship her back to her place of bad memories.

"I'm taking you to your mother's."

"Now?" Lydia said. It had to be at least four in the morning.

"You know, maybe it's the best place to go. If my mom had still been around when this happened to me, I'd have run back there too. The fresh air, the open spaces, you can walk this off. Screw the doctors and the drugs they'll drown you in. Walk it off."

Rosa draws on *Hope. Screw the pills and the doctors?* She thinks. *Walk it off, Lydia — walk it off? What the hell was I thinking?* Rosa lifts her foot off the accelerator, wants to slam on the brakes and turn around. She takes a few deep breaths, counts to ten. "What do you want, Lydia?"

"I just don't feel like a banana."

Rosa hits the steering wheel, grumbles. "You had everything. I don't understand."

"What do you mean? This is not my fault."

"Maybe it is your fault."

Lydia grips her pale blue cashmere cardigan. She wills Rosa to shut up and stop asking questions. So she can listen to the sounds she loved as a kid, the music of lakes and rivers, the hum of sky and road blending into one, wide and endless as water, corn stalks swaying like a gospel choir. She has no idea what she wants. Rosa's right, she had everything she wanted, was one grasp away from what she thought was her ultimate desire, and now what?

A glint of white appears through the trees. The final stretch of the journey, the bell lap, she whispers, a term she clung to since hearing her father say it a few weeks before he died. Doctors counting down the days until his death with confidence, precision, like New Year's in Times Square, everyone waiting with bated breath for the ball to drop. He took her hand and said, "It's okay, Lydia, I've been waiting for this, for the bell lap, the final stretch then I'm free."

What did he mean by free — of us? Of this? The disease? Life, mom, what?

Henry's life ending, dropping second by second like the ball in Times Square, ten, nine, eight, seven, the years of struggling, six, five, the bell lap, *four, three, two, I'm almost free, almost free,* one.

"Dad."

"You okay?" Rosa pats her friend's knee.

Lydia's life was rising, rising, the years of struggling, rising to the top like the ball in Times Square, rising, rising, rising. *Charlie? Charlie? Is that you? Are you alone?* Rising and it stops. "Jesus," she says. Rosa touches the cross that hangs around her neck, born with God. Lydia clutches her hands, makes a fist, resists reaching for the velvet swatch in her pocket, stares at the sky. Her father's face appears in the saffron-tinted cloud, backlit by the sun. The turkey vultures circle beneath it. She pounds the passenger seat door. *Fucking, Charlie!*

"Hey," says Rosa, "take it easy on the car."

Framed in the white fence her grandfather created by hand, every panel and post, the vast lawn glistens, pristine, as if Henry had just cut it for the second time that week, a green that defies nature, the blades jewelled. Lydia's head lightens, like it's deflating and about to flop onto her shoulders. Rosa pulls into the long driveway leading to the ornate Queen Anne resting in the valley. The Palladian windows peer through the wraparound porch, the ornamental spindles and decorative shingles stand out like decorations on a house-shaped birthday cake. The turret looms on the west side; it always reminded Lydia of a prison watchtower, and the steep roof gleams like sateen in the sunlight.

Henry spent the last few years of his life restoring the family home. A home Lydia believed had a mind of its own, an all-knowing one. Greater than her grandparents, her own parents, special, there was no one like them, the family, no one like her, the Queen Anne. "This particular architectural design is known for having an element of surprise," her grandmother told Lydia when she found her curled up and quivering in a back stairway, unable to find her way down to the main house. Lydia swore voices echoed from the other side of the walls. "Nonsense, dear! It's just the house creaking and cracking — growing pains. We all age, darling." She watched Lydia retreat into herself, turtle-like, eyes glazing over, arms crossing and hands hiding under armpits. She held her close. "That imagination of yours will get you in trouble one day."

When they built the house, her grandparents gravitated toward lavish touches. They were aging, unable to do the things they'd always done themselves. Their own lives were turning grey and lifeless, but the opportunities that came with the industrial age were endless. They could build the ornate, character-filled home they desired more quickly, the young workers, like Lydia's great-grandparents, came with machines, but the factory-made materials didn't stand the test of time. "We'll build a home for you and your children," Henry's father said, "with a personality. This house will keep the meaning of family alive, goddamit, even if I die creating it." When the test results from an aching side came back "terminal," Henry spent the last few years of his life ensuring the home his parents adored was as solid as possible, and God joined them at dinner and in conversations on long walks through the woods. If he couldn't keep his wife, his family, and their guests protected, Henry made sure the house — so much bigger than any ordinary home — and its presence would. "I was wrong son, his own father told him. I got greedy, lazy, enticed by speed and volume, quantity over quality, damn machine robbed work from human hands, the home ...always work with your hands, son."

Always work with your hands, Lydia, she hears her father saying to her, like he did for years. Encouraging the use of her "talents." She stares at her hands, hands that could never play the piano, hands rough like feet, hands that could raise wolves. "Like the house, my bones, the structure, are all good," Henry once said. "But there's something wrong on the inside." His words resonated to the core. The car approaches the house. *The bones, the structure are all good,* she grips her hands, *but there's something wrong on the inside.* Lydia received her promotion the morning Henry was given six months to a year to live. He called with his news before she had a chance to call with hers. "I think I'll be done by Christmas," he said.

"The house?" she said.

He was gone before the leaves fell, before there were any signs of Santa Claus.

ROSA PARKS THE car, leaves it running. She taps another cigarette on the side of the miniature silver tin.

"You smoke too much."

"So what."

Lydia's tempted to ask for one, to pick up smoking *Hope* now she's back in the country and every nerve beneath her skin's begging for a vice. "You want to come in and rest before heading back?"

We shouldn't be here, thinks Rosa. She watches Lydia unload her sewing machine and bags from the car. She stops and rubs her palms with her fingertips. Rosa shakes her head, stares at the house.

"It's so extreme what happened."

"My mom will be happy to see you."

Rosa holds back tears. She feels sick. Lydia picks up her sewing machine and bites her bottom lip. *She's about to kiss it*, Rosa thinks, then she shoves it away from her, arm's length.

"Ten years you devoted to that place."

"I'm sure she's baked something for us, made tea. A hot cup of tea before you go? I know it's not wine but..."

"Ten years."

"Stop."

Lydia slams the sewing machine onto the gravel driveway. "It's over, Rosa. Let it go." Stones fly up from the toes of Lydia's sneakers and her sewing machine rolls across the gravel like an old can. She bites her tongue, pretends her foot doesn't hurt from the impact.

"Why didn't you fight for this," she throws her arms out in front of her, "for your job, for your husband, the family? We were a family. Why?"

Lydia steps back and studies her friend in the bright country light. The woman with whom she's shared a decrepit, damp sewing room, worked with for a decade, side by side like two kids in wonderment of what they did; hands gliding back and forth over antique lace found at old estate sales, brocades, kilim-style chenille, linens, watching them transform before their eyes into layered sculptures that brought to life even the dullest humans in the cast. They bonded over a love for period pieces: velvet, damask weaves, silk, ornate flowing headdresses, masks.

"Maybe, that's what I'm here to find out."

"Lydia, this..." Rosa spreads out her arms and looks up at the house looming over them, "isn't permanent. I'm coming back to get you in one..."

"I'll never pick up a needle and thread again."

Rosa stomps out her cigarette. "Bullshit. It's what you live for."

Lydia glances at the turret then back at her friend who, she decides, looks smaller in this setting, less menacing.

"The things we live for change."

Rosa jumps when three crows caw and land on a branch above her. "Jesus," she says and clutches the gold cross, its glow dulled years ago. Under the circumstances she thinks Lydia should go in on her own. She has to get back, try to sleep for a bit before heading to work. The house frightens her as much as the country.

Lydia reaches for the patch of velvet she keeps in her pocket to calm her. Her fingers know it well, bury themselves into its short dense pile like a child into a mother's chest.

Constance always said she wished Sophie and Lydia could go back to the age when they needed her, little did she know needing a mother has nothing to do with age. Rosa throws her arms around Lydia. They've been inseparable since they first met ten years before on the concrete steps of the theatre, in the good snow, snow that came and went when it was supposed to.

Lydia has no idea what the right thing to say is, so she says, "I should have married *you*."

Rosa holds her breath and sucks in her stomach, everything she can do not to cry. Lydia says she's sorry and this she means. Rosa is losing the thing she worked so hard at not losing and she cries. To uphold her part of the bargain, Lydia hands Rosa the keys to the apartment. Rosa throws them up and snatches them out of the air. "One month," she hollers, scaring the crows, hesitating before getting into the car and driving back to the place where she will always feel more comfortable — the city.

A SHARP PAIN shoots through Lydia's eyes. She sees red. She looks at her palms, the suffocating fabric she worked with for weeks and weeks gnaws at her skin like rats. She shakes and shakes them, then shoves them in her pockets and glances around in case somebody's watching. The grounds around the Queen Anne are empty, quiet, but the back of her neck tingles. *Maybe it's a city thing,* she thinks, *even in your own little world some stranger's watching, staring.* "God?" she whispers. *Oh stop it, you didn't bring any strangers with you, they didn't follow you here like the noses of dogs.*

Chickadees flitter around and the sun looks like it does in fairytales, golden and liquefied, caramel, nothing dirty about it. She listens for cars on the open road that runs alongside the property. She wants to hear traffic, movement, something calling her back, but an open road's not the voice she longs for. She wishes Charlie would soar up the driveway, imagines him leaping out, begging her to come back, spewing apologies, all the rehearsed words he's memorized from the mouths of made-up men, generals to imps, all the classic roles he's mastered. She presses her eyes shut and pictures someone else driving up and leaping out of the car, begging her to come back, someone she hasn't met. It's the wanting of her, the yearning for her, she thinks she needs. She jams her eyes together, focuses on their back cover, opens them, envisages a car with no one in it. Red. Sporty, sixties. No, that was then. Black, long, four-door, a silver emblem protruding from its bonnet. She gets in, it drives off, leaving the shadow of herself standing on the driveway, conscious of her dead relative's ghosts hovering in the turret windows, gazing down, wanting to know what the hell went wrong.

She reaches for her bag, and the sun catches a tongue of yellow cotton lapping at the zipper. *The sash that fell from the monk's waist.* He had rushed into the temple across the street from the theatre. She watched it float to the ground like an orphaned kite, and ran down the fire escape to grab it. For years she watched the monks coming and going to the temple. She clung to that sash every night hoping the wisdom would seep through its pores into hers, to have something else to cling to — other than fabric. She pulls it from the bag and loops it through the belt loops of her jeans. *One month, thirty days, thirty figurative kilometres.* She knots the sash at her left hip and picks up her bag.

The front door stares at her *come on, welcome me home.* It doesn't, just waits for her to make the first move. She doesn't let herself into the house. She waits, then grabs the round copper knocker from the lion's mouth and knocks twice. She listens for the familiar clip-clop of Constance's "indoor" shoes and fears the absence of her father's footsteps that normally follow his wife's. She presses her ear to the thick black door. Listens for the "Who is it?" in a singsong manner, even though Constance always knows who's on the other side of the door.

Lydia knocks harder. She steps back, smoothes her hair — the hair Constance made her promise she would never cut. *Look strong,* she says, *do not to show weakness, not to a horse, or a mother. Hide it.* Mime-like she reaches into her head and drags out the itching and scratching materials she believes are weakness and fear, hands moving through air, dragging, dragging, dragging, yards and yards of the stuff out, wrapping it in a ball and rolling the unwanted sensations into her purse. She wipes her hands clean of it and grabs the door handle. The door's locked. In all the years she lived there it was never locked. She reaches into the head of the concrete horse and pulls out a key, rusted over time. The door creaks when it opens, it always did. One of those doors that came that way, her grandfather said and that's what he liked about it, *but it's the hinges that creak, not the door, right Grandpa*, Sophie said and he dismissed her, saying she knew nothing about doors. And Lydia agreed with him because doors were always open for her, she never had to open them, find the key, hear them creak, she just walked up to them and they were open. This door would be open for Sophie, the door to home. Into the long dark hallway, Lydia makes her way. The twelve-foot ceilings feel higher than she remembers. *A daughter my age should not be coming home like this. A woman my age is too old to be running home to her mother, too old to be a daughter.* She shoves the key into her pocket, afraid to be locked out again.

The bright white kitchen tinkles with cutlery and plates sliding across each other. She continues down the long hall. An echo of her mother's laughter and the faint murmur of a low voice follows. *Mom?* The familiar sound of the kitchen's screen door slides open then closes. Lydia makes her way through the narrow hallway lined with photos of her late father, her sister, and the long-gone relatives that once constituted her successful family.

The house isn't warmed by the smell of scones and melting chocolate like she expected. Singed bacon, burnt toast. On the kitchen counter, china plates; a drop of water remains on the rim of the one on top. Two teacups sit on the sterling silver serving tray, remnants of an unfinished mouthful of tea in one, a scrunched napkin on its saucer. The other shines like it has never been used. A door closes. The one she knows leads to the back stairwell of the bed and breakfast.

"Mom?"

The back stairs creak but not like the door, a lower pitch, like agony. Outside on the interlocking stone patio, Constance stands waving toward the woods. Lydia can't see who her mother's waving to. She looks tiny from behind, more thin than usual. Her always erect posture sloped. Lydia jumps when footsteps pound above, followed by the sound of another door closing and water running. She forgot there might be strangers in the house. She flips through the reservation book lying on the table by the phone. The month of April is crossed out with four red lines and "The Counselors!" written in blue through the middle of the page. The Counselors, Mr. Counselor, welcome. When said that way, it has a ring to it. She hears her father's voice greeting the family at the door. Mr. and Mrs. Counselor, nice to meet you, please come in, make yourselves at home. She needs her mother to herself. It took a long time to get used to strangers sharing her home. It took more time to get used to sharing her mother. *It's like she wants to be everyone's mother,* she told Sophie. Sophie didn't care. That's fine, she said, let her. To Lydia it was like she was never good enough, her mother kept meeting better daughters in the people that stayed. "What's wrong with us?"

"There's nothing wrong with us," said Sophie, "we're just not *enough.*"

"Not enough?"

Even though the back stairwells and separate entrances enable guests to come and go without accessing the main home directly, Lydia never felt comfortable with the arrangement. Large homes in the lake counties are often turned into bed and breakfasts. When the girls moved out, Constance and Henry agreed they had to occupy the space with family. It's what his parents believed a house of this design was for: the marriage of idea and functionality, to preserve the architecture of family. Henry wanted children, a yard full of children. Every bedroom in the sprawling home full of happy, sleepy children. He was an only child. Constance couldn't have another child after Sophie. Her health weakened in childbirth. Lydia loved reminding her younger sister, *you almost killed Mom when you were born.*

Yeah? Well, you're killing her now, she imagines Sophie saying.

She slides open the screen door and steps out into the yard.

Constance turns around and takes a step back, her hand slapping against her chest.

"Oh, Lydia, you scared me!"

Lydia pulls at her hair.

Constance walks over to the small wrought-iron table and dusts it off with the handkerchief she uses to wipe away tears. She fiddles with cut flowers in a crystal vase, mutters to herself, "Lilac, yellow, red, blue... lilac, yellow." She presses her hands on the table, "Your father would have known how to make this work."

"Mom?"

It's as if Lydia stepped out of the house on a regular morning when she lived there, like her presence is nothing unusual.

"Is that a wig?" Constance asks. "You aren't feeling well at all, are you?"

"Hello, Mom."

Lydia opens her arms and Constance walks into them but doesn't open hers, they remain at her sides as Lydia pulls her mother into her then puts her back in the upright position. Constance reaches for her daughter's long thin arms, arms like the spindles of the house. She holds her at arm's length, looks her up and down like her grandmother used to do. Constance admired and feared her mother-in-law. She said she was never really sure if she was being a good mother, she never had one to compare herself to and a mother-in-law is more like an aunt. She looks and acts like the woman she never wanted to become. Lydia tries to make her hair appear longer by tilting her head forward and allowing the fringe to fall over her eyes.

"You're too thin."

"I've always been thin."

"Not this thin. First you need a cup of tea," she pinches Lydia's taut face. "That's what you need, and after 2 PM a shot of single malt and a steak to knock you back to your senses, right Henry?" She drops her daughter's arms and elbows the space to her left, grips the handkerchief to her chest.

Lydia watches the spot her mother elbowed. She waits for her to make a joke but she doesn't. When Constance turns away, Lydia runs her hand through the space. Constance waltzes past her daughter and into the kitchen, leaving the screen door wide open. She never does that, *always close doors behind you.*

Something red shimmers between the still trees, glinting in the now risen sun. Lydia's palms tingle, "Silk..." she says and takes a step forward, her hands reach out and she slaps them back against her thighs. Turns to see if her mother's watching. She shoves her hands into her pockets. She shakes her head and reaches for the kettle. Red silk floats in the woods. The fabric sways between the trees like two graceful flags. Then disappears. Lydia presses her eyes shut. Everything spins, whirls around like a game show wheel. She prays the wheel will stop on last week, if she could just go back a week, or even two — a month, one month and undo the damage that's been done.

"Lydia?"

She grabs the velvet swatch she's carried with her for years, her comfort, given to her by her grandmother.

"Lydia?"

Along the edge of the lilac Rose of Sharon, Lydia claws a hole in the dirt. "Enough," she whispers. "Enough," and plunges the velvet into the hole; it lies there like a pool of blood. The dirt went back easier than it came out.

"There," she says, "it's a start." She turns and bumps into her mother. "My God, you scared me."

"What are you doing?"

"Burying the past."

"You shouldn't do that, dear. It's going to grow back twice as big and haunt you. You've got to face it now before it becomes unmanageable."

Lydia imagines a red velvet tree pushing its way up from the moist soil, every branch a suppressed memory, Charlie, Henry, her grandfather, her grandmother, the mother she feels she doesn't even know anymore, all the unborn children her and her parents never had. It keeps growing and growing. She feels too small, small like toes and all the weight they carry.

Constance points to the tea and cake laid out on the table between the Edwardian wicker chairs Lydia salvaged from one of the many theatres closing down in the city. They walk arm in arm to the chairs. Constance doesn't ask about Charlie. She doesn't broach the subject at all. She gazes over the glistening grass her husband cared for with pride and tells her daughter about the lovely young man who moved into the house through the woods, who's been helping her with the grocery shopping and maintaining the grounds and other odd jobs around the place now that she's all alone.

She swings her arms out in front of her. "You didn't think I kept this up on my own, did you?" She reaches down and runs her hands through the carpet of grass. "And it's not like your sister or you come out on weekends to help." Lydia almost jumps in to defend herself but excuses are futile. She hasn't come home to help. She hasn't been home since the funeral. Constance would call and call and leave messages on the daughters' answering machines, like, the house is so big now she's all alone in it and she's tired of hearing the echo of her slippers on the hardwood floors and waking in the night disoriented and cold, even in the unseasonably warm weather. Lydia listened as her mother left the messages, watching the phone. When she knew her mother was going out, she'd call back, and after hanging up felt good that she at least called.

Every message opened with, *I know you're busy*. She was busy, so busy, the busier she was the less chance there was to think about the breathless father, the lonely mother and the man on stage in the arms of a woman he'd die for. The special ones, the ones she had to keep busy to attempt to be as special as. Henry was gone. Things would never be the same. Lydia stopped returning the calls. She had no idea how to comfort her mother, had no idea how to talk about the loss they shared. Constance kept telling the girls she was fine and Lydia chose to believe her. If that's what she says, that's what she means, said Sophie from the chrome kitchen of her successful bistro she called Cymbeline, in the west side of the city. They shared something so alien to Lydia, she had no idea how her mother felt beyond sad, they were all sad, but Lydia's sad was different from her mother's, she knew it but she didn't know what that difference felt like: tweed, gabardine? Her sadness was like splinters of moon-bone, small scratchings at the walls in her veins. She wasn't brave enough to ask. She wondered if she assumed mothers don't need their children in the way their children need them. She lost her father, the first man she ever loved. Constance lost her husband, the first man she ever loved enough to marry. She needed to be cut off from the outside, to concentrate, or else she wouldn't be able to create the way she needed to. She needed to have no obligations, or guilt-riddled afternoons, and up until now, she hadn't realized how selfish that was.

THE TEA BURNS her throat, and the cake soothes it. She holds the sweet and sour lemon mouthful in her throat hoping it might end up choking her, and she'll die right here on her father's perfect lawn, the weed, the dandelion after all the seeds are blown away and the monk head drops. She wants to believe the healthy flowers, the groomed grass, the clipped hedges, are a sign he is still there. Tells herself the illness and death were a bad dream. Henry will run out of the barn, gripping a garden tool of some sort and greet his daughter with the deep embrace she longs for and talk to her. He'd say, *What happened, tell me everything, are you okay? What can we do to help? We'll write things down, the pros and the cons.* Lists, he swore lists solved everything — order, order. Order in the different sense of the word used by Constance — he didn't mean control, he meant semblance. Get it out of your head and onto the paper in front of you and you can see it all clearly. She never wrote anything down, no idea how to put things into words. His singing, low and melodic echoes from the house, his humming drifts across the backyard, and down the path into the woods.

"There's something about Raiden and his associates that feel like family. He's been so kind and helpful..."

"Raiden?"

"And just when I was about to sell that house he came knocking at the door."

"Sell the house?"

"Just like that, like an angel. They're like angels, sent from your father, I think."

The cake sticks in her mouth. Tea burns her throat. *Is it 2:00 p.m. yet?*

"Not the house through the woods?"

Constance turns around and faces her daughter. She takes Lydia's hands, meets her eyes. "It's just nice to know it's never too late to start a new family."

Lydia's hands burn, she doesn't grip back. Rosa's voice resonates in her head, *don't go back, don't run home, it will never be what you want it to be.*

"What exactly is the definition of family, Mom, because I think I may have the wrong impression?"

Constance looks too small, detached, a stringless marionette. Was she thinking about it? She's off somewhere, unblinking, focused on the end of the yard. There's nothing out there, not even a fly.

"I read somewhere that your own children don't necessarily make a *family*."

Water rises up Lydia's throat, in her eyes.

Constance grips her daughter's hands. "They're counsellors, dear, from the city. Isn't that a coincidence?"

"That they're from the city?"

"No, that they are..." she slows down and enunciates her words with wide eyes, "...counsellors. Counsellors." She nods her head. Lydia wants to miss her point. *The* Counselors she thinks and pictures the reservation book in the kitchen, not Mr. Counselor, *a* Counselor, *the* Counselors, in the bed and breakfast, in the little white house through the woods, everywhere counsellors, and all she wants to do is escape.

"Mother, please. I just need fresh air, I need to walk this off."

Constance squeezes her daughter's hands. "Raiden has rented the bed and breakfast for his associates' wedding party. They've also decided to have the wedding here darling, isn't that nice and..."

"What wedding? A wedding? Here?"

"...and the bride is a little sensitive, so it's best we keep things quiet. She needs a lot of rest, poor thing's been through a lot."

Lydia squints, hard, balls her fists. *Deep breath, Lydia, deep, deep breath...count to ten, backwards. She needs rest, this bride-to-be? She is a little sensitive? She's been through a lot? The bride? A bride? One of the strangers in my house is a bride?* Her phone vibrates in her pocket: Rosa. She can't share walls with a bride, with counsellors.

A THIN HAND, fingers like bleached branches, black-stained nails, overgrown and curved like boomerangs push apart mercerized cotton curtains. A blaze of orange slices through the dark room. Junko gasps. She catches a glimpse of the daughter she's heard so much about, the one in common. Pipit watches from the striped slipper chair in the corner, unsure what her charge will do next. Pipit places the newspaper on her lap, "Why not open the curtains all the way? Let the light in."

"Quiet, it is death to be lit by that ball of fire. We will wait for the moon's bulb to read our futures by."

Pipit shakes her head, not out of disagreement, but confusion, for weeks she's been trying to make sense of Junko's incomprehensible lines and wishes Junko would allow her to open the curtains all the way. She's tired of reading by candlelight, or when Junko sleeps by the small light attached to her book, when outside the world is golden and glimmering, warm, alive. She feels herself drying like a prune, next week she will be old and have missed her youth in the back room of a bed and breakfast in the country.

"She is a waif," says Junko.

Pipit observes the curve of Junko's spine, counts the visible vertebrae from the collar of her nightgown, up to where her clasped bale of dry black hair begins. *She is a waif?*

"We should go for a walk today, Junko, get some fresh air."

"Go and walk the waif. Leave me. I am capable of walking in my sleep."

She thrusts the curtains shut. Pipit leaps up, certain that the rod and the curtains are about to crash to the floor. Junko spins around, and giggles. "You are jumpy, little one. Fly away, fly away little songbird with the wagtails and longclaws."

LYDIA LOOKS BEHIND her and up at the closed, curtained windows of the guest wing of the house. It's unusual for it to look so dark when occupied.

Constance dusts her hands off on her apron, "I told the guests that you would help sew their wedding gowns for them. Will you do that, darling?"

"What?"

"They don't have a lot of money and I said why spend a lot of money on something you'll all wear once when my daughter's on her way home and can whip you up something for half the price of store-bought."

"What?"

"Stay calm. I think it will be good for you to get right back on the horse."

"Mother, you've got to be kidding me. I just got home, I haven't even slept. What horse?" She leaps to her feet. Constance's eyes remain on the same spot at the foot of the yard, "I still see him out there, you know. Preening the rose bushes, cutting the grass, caring for the fish in that pond he struggled to build for the two of you."

Lydia's mouth opens and for a moment she thinks of hurling the words she's biting at her fragile mother, *why don't you get back on the horse, what about you Mom, are you moving on?* But she swallows them.

She rubs the bottom of her cotton T-shirt, worn thin from the gripping, all the gripping and rubbing. Her mother looks at her hands, then back up at Lydia. "See," she says. "They need a job."

Lydia shoves her hands behind her back, imagines cuffs clicking and the sound of the key whooshing through the air and landing in the Chase. She's hot, so hot and itchy, the nerves beneath her skin prickling, prickling, burlap.

"Lydia?"

"Mom, I'm sorry. I can't do it. I can't."

"Your father looked after those fish like children when you and Sophie left."

"For God's sake Mom, I've come here for help and it's really heartbreaking to realize you have other things on your mind, strangers whom you're more interested in than me. Volunteering my services? For a wedding? I'm ill, broken down. I've been deceived, betrayed, lost the only thing that ever mattered to me. I don't know who the hell I am anymore and you've hooked me up with a sewing gig?"

She makes fists, has no idea what to do with the hands, the sensations. Constance watches her and has no idea how to help, she never did. Henry, she needs Henry. She gets up and holds her daughter's hands, rubs them. "Lydia, listen to yourself. Get a grip." She bites her tongue. "I mean..."

"Get a grip? Listen to myself? I can't *feel* myself. I've never been able to feel myself." She tears her hands away. "Get a grip, Mom?" Shakes them, tries to cover her eyes, her lips, with her hair, *grow for God's sake grow.* A wig, she'll get Rosa to mail her a wig, Rapunzel's.

"I can't, I can't do this anymore." She runs toward the woods.

Constance takes a step, then hollers, "You can't keep running away, Lydia Templar. What goes around, comes around, my dear. Raiden will tell you that."

Raiden will tell me that? Raiden?

The Counselors

RAIDEN PARKED THE car on Main Street. He passed Kaito the map lying across his knee and asked him to fold it and put it away. "We don't need this anymore. We're here."

Through the rearview mirror he watched Little-Nan and Pipit peer out their windows like children do when they've arrived somewhere they didn't want to go, church or camp. Their shoulders hunched, eyes solemn, no smiles. "It will be okay," he said.

Junko sat up for the first time on the journey. She peered through her wooden mask, grunted, and lay back down. "Good," she said, "the closer you are to nature, the closer to death. We are in the right place."

Little-Nan gripped her granddaughter's hand. Pipit lowered her head, eyes straying over to the interlocking limbs, the gripping hand of the woman who has become like a mother to her and there was nothing in the grip, in her skin that was reminiscent of her own mother's. They had the same faces, still beautiful, even more so with age, but such different hands. Little-Nan's were smooth and soft as silk and Pipit was unsure if not feeling the roughness of her own mother's was liberating, a sign to let go. She looks back out the window, *one month*, she said to herself.

"Well, this is it then," said Kaito and clapped his hands together. His smile radiant.

"Thank you," said Raiden. He stepped out of the car and looked up at the cathedral spire alone in the empty sky. He smiled. "We are here," he whispered and told his associates he needed to pick up a few supplies and walked over to the hardware store first.

Pipit leaned forward, grabbed the headrest. "What are you thinking?" she asked Kaito. He kept his eyes focused on the road in front of him, didn't turn around. He breathed a deep breath. "I don't know, but I like what I see."

"Now, now, little ones," said Junko, her voice muffled, she could have been talking in her sleep. They didn't respond. Just waited for Raiden to return.

MUSIC STREAMED THROUGH the cathedral walls. Mr. Randal watched a man he'd never seen stop and listen. "Johann Sebastian Bach," he said. Raiden turned around. "Concerto I in D minor, allegro," Mr. Randal continued. Raiden entered the store.

"That harpsichord, imported from Germany in 1967. Templar's the man who designed the damned church."

"The damned church?"

Mr. Randal pointed out the door, "Look at it?"

Raiden laughed.

"There's nothing like it," said Raiden.

"The cathedral?"

Raiden rummaged through the bins of nails.

Mr. Randal followed him, "The harpsichord?"

"Bach," he said, "Johann Sebastian Bach."

Raiden strolled up and down the aisles, his hands reaching in and out of nail bins, picking up handfuls and letting them fall through his fingers, like clumsy steel waterfalls. His gait slow and measured, *posture straighter than a plank* thought Mr. Randal.

"You looking for anything in particular?"

Raiden halted, he didn't turn around. "Yes," he said.

Mr. Randal waited, *well*, he wanted to say.

Raiden continued meandering up and down the aisles and returned to the counter with nails and a hammer.

"Can I order plywood and beams from you?"

"Building something?"

Raiden smiled. "Trying."

Mr. Randal hadn't heard of any developments being erected in town, or new homes being built. He supplied the vicinity with lumber, power tools, concrete. He'd know if there was building going on. He sat in on all the town meetings, was on the development committee, boards. No new developments.

Mr. Randal followed Raiden out and stood on the front steps of his crumbling hardware store.

"Who's playing the harpsichord?" asked Raiden.

The cathedral spire loomed over Main Street. Its wrought-iron doors resembled the backs of medieval guards. Mr. Randal had no idea who was playing the harpsichord. The cathedral had been abandoned years ago when the bishop stormed out over a dispute with the city council; over money, the newspaper reported, but locals suspected it was something much deeper than money. When a bishop leaves, a cathedral's relegated to a church. The cost to run it became too high and economical and environmentally sound buildings were erected. Congregations were taken over by local ministers. For the last twenty years, it housed town meetings, community events, dances, bake sales, stags and does, bingo, non-denominational weddings, and funerals. It hadn't needed a resident organist in years, so who was playing the instrument — and so beautifully —

was a mystery to Mr. Randal, but not something that seemed all that out of the ordinary. The place was like a second home to some of the older locals. Volunteers maintained the grounds and opened and closed the building each morning and evening for those who still sought comfort in its original purpose. It had a caretaker, paid for by the Templar estate.

It was slated to be torn down and replaced with a hotel. The last Constance heard the town was divided in their decision, the final say came down to the Templar estate. If Henry were here, he'd make sure the original structure was maintained and they'd be adapting the inside to some new incarnation. In the city they were turning churches into condominiums on a regular basis. Constance last stepped foot in there at her husband's funeral and until someone came along with a plan not to tear it down or alter the architecture of the forsaken structure, it would remain as it was.

"My grandfather played the organ," said Raiden.

Mr. Randal wanted to say, *well, I don't think that's him if that's what you're thinking*, but didn't get the impression that a man like Raiden would find it that funny. He was certain he'd come from the city; he had that air about him, all in black, his shoulder-length hair tied in a ponytail. Mr. Randal was tired of the city folk coming into the town he'd spent sixty-five years in acting like they were superior to him.

"It's a beautiful structure."

"You an architect?"

Raiden thought about it. "No."

Mr. Randal thought about the nails Raiden bought, the type used for wood. "I'm looking for somewhere to stay," said Raiden. "My associates and I . . ."

Mr. Randal walked around the Volkswagen Westfalia parked in front. "This yours?" he asked.

Raiden nodded.

"What's he looking at?" asked Pipit.

Kaito and Little-Nan took no notice, their heads down, reading the notes Raiden had prepared for them. Mr. Randal walked around the second-hand vehicle. The reliable campmobile home had taken good care of them on their travels and Raiden wondered why Mr. Randal was inspecting it so closely.

Junko remained still, eyes closed, breathing a sleeper's breath. She listened to shoes crunching against gravel. "He's old," she said.

"Doesn't he see us?" said Pipit. "He's looking into the windows like people do at zoo animals but his eyes are like a blind man's, still and milky."

"That's disgusting," said Kaito.

"I like these vehicles," said Mr. Randal, hitting the side.

Junko jumped.

"What was that?" asked Kaito.

"That man," said Pipit.

"Hippies drove them. Hippies and gypsies."

"Gypsies?"

"Yeah, gypsies."

Raiden laughed.

"They still exist. I get a feeling you know what I mean."

Raiden glanced at his associates through the windows, at their cotton robes, the ebony hair tied up in balls on the tops of their heads and thought of Junko in the very back, out of view, hands gloved, a wooden mask over her taut face and said, "No, I don't know what you mean."

He'd drive back to the tourism shop he passed on the way into town and find somewhere to stay. He glanced over at the cathedral again, realized the music had stopped. He waited for a few minutes to see if someone would leave the building from the front.

"The Templar's place is your best bet for lodgings, just left here onto Concession 25, along the Chase, beautiful place, lots of history. It's Tyrone's old place, the architect who built that cathedral, the man who adopted the harpsichord."

The man who adopted the harpsichord, thought Raiden. He sighed. Mr. Randal watched him grip his hands and drop his head. Then compose himself in an instant.

"We will check it out," said Raiden. "Thank you, sounds like exactly the place we're searching for."

The Fabric

LYDIA PACES IN her room. It feels dollhouse small. She lies back down on her bed, stares at the ceiling, it churns. She wills a set of arms to emerge through the cloud and hold her, then pull her up and into the sky where she can float for a bit. She sits up, looks around, sees little Lydias in the corner, at the vanity, sitting on the floor, in different phases of her youth, those hands, touching, feeling. She shoos her old selves away with a few blinks and a shake of her head. The room is still but she senses breathing, presses her ear up against the daisy-laden wallpaper. Junko runs her fingernails down the wall of her room, senses the waif. Pipit asks her to stop, to mind her own business. Junko hits the wall. Lydia jumps, grabs a hanky from the top of the chest of drawers and runs downstairs.

"You're up?" says Constance. "I was just about to bring you some tea."

"How long have the Counselors been staying here?"

"Not long, pet, a few weeks."

That's long. She grabs an apple, it's red and marbled like raw meat. She puts it back in the glass bowl.

Constance struggles to lift the teapot. The fragility of Constance's wrists, the knotting long fingers — fingers Lydia once admired — are startlingly old. Lydia steps in to help. "It weighs a ton, Mom." But it doesn't. Constance flitters from counter to counter, picking things up, putting them back down, staring, putting finger to chin, opening a drawer, closing it. "Have you lost something?"

"Lost?"

"What are you looking for?"

"What are any of us looking for?"

"What do you mean?"

She reaches into the drawer and pulls out a steak knife, "There," she says and places it by the newly baked Madeira cake. On the other side of the counter, next to the stove, is the cake knife.

Lydia glides her hand over the barn wood harvest table, the backs of the handcrafted chairs. "Do you think Grandpa died happy?"

Constance sighs and touches Lydia's forehead with the back of her hand.

"Did you sleep well?"

She clutches the chair back, *to think he made all this, and now look at it, sitting empty.* "I slept really well, it's good to be back."

Constance smiles and reaches for the kettle. "It's full, Mom."

"It is?"

"You just filled it."

Lydia turns on the burner, the blue flame erupts into orange. She stares at her mom, "This is dangerous."

"It's been like that for years. Did you sleep well?"

"Yes, Mom, I slept great."

Constance smiles, and knows by Lydia's pallid skin and the purple beneath her eyes that she's lying. All she wants to do is sleep, she can't stop sleeping, but they are fitful sleeps, restless, tossing and turning and dreaming, the dreams. Now she's home she lies awake and listens to footsteps on the creaking floors, to the movement on the other side of her bedroom wall, where she knows the bride-to-be spends her days in a dark room lit with candles. She stares at the ceiling, wondering if Junko is lying on her bed staring at the ceiling.

She walks around every room of the house brushing her hands against the peach herringbone-weave silk curtains, velvet curtains, the *fleur-de-lis* muslin sheers, brocade chairs and tapestry tablecloths. Anger, calm, confusion, elation, captivity, freedom. Too many sensations at once, all jumbled in her hands.

Constance watches her daughter run the lace doily through her fingers. All the years she made excuses for the behaviour, to friends, guests, teachers, store clerks. "Is she blind?" One saleswoman asked. Constance stepped back, shocked, and turned to see Lydia reaching, touching, sniffing, running every garment she was drawn to across her cheeks, sniffing, touching. Constance grabbed Lydia's arm and rushed her out of the store. "How can you embarrass me like that?"

She dragged her to the doctor, Henry in tow, "Is she blind?"

"No," the doctor said, "No, she's not blind."

"Then what is wrong with her?"

Lydia kept her head down, hands still on her lap, clamped together in an attempt to prove there was nothing wrong with her, that maybe there was something wrong with her mother.

Constance left dissatisfied. Lydia left wondering, *is there something wrong with me?*

Lydia stormed out of the car and into the house, clomped upstairs and upstairs and upstairs into the turret and slammed the door. It had been her grandmother's sewing room, rolls of fabric and boxes of a mishmash of unused pieces, filled the old room.

Lydia organized the lot by texture, each type categorized by an emotion, a sensation, a mood.

Constance ran into the house after her. Henry stopped his wife and looked into her eyes, "She's fine. She's simply incomparable, just as you are, in your own way my love."

Constance took an actor's breath. Sophie wandered into the lounge, "Well, what did the doctor say?"

"She's not blind," said Constance and poured herself a Cinzano on the rocks and fell into the *chaise longue* without spilling a drop of the liquid.

"Go and see where she is, would you dear?"

Henry sat down by his wife, "She's safe, we're all safe, not to worry."

Sophie ran upstairs and upstairs and upstairs, "Open the door." The lock clicked left. Sophie peeked into the room, slammed the door, the lock clicked right, then downstairs, and downstairs and downstairs, "She's in the turret, wrapped in velvet."

Every time they couldn't find Lydia she was upstairs buried in old fabrics. Sophie said, "I think she has head issues."

"Nonsense, dear, she's..." Constance had no idea how to explain what it was. "She's tactile..."

"Mom says you're a reptile."

"Go to hell," said Lydia.

Constance said, "Don't you think it's strange Henry, how she touches everything?"

"No. She says it helps her feel."

"Feel what?"

"I don't know."

The old sewing room had been abandoned and became the

place to store junk and other sundries thrown to the wayside — paintings by nameless artists, tainted silver beer mugs, chipped crystal, and much to Lydia's amazement old Victorian garments that her great-grandparents had worn throughout their lives, including school uniforms and baby gowns. It seemed that everything was salvaged those days, even old underpants or drawers, long johns that had yellowed and frayed over time. Lydia tried everything on, pretended to be from another time, felt different the moment she wore what felt like costumes. The turret was her own world, a place where she believed the people who had once worn these old clothes, came to life when she wore them. It was her secret, one of many buried in boxes in the small round room at the top of the house. What comes around goes around.

CONSTANCE TAKES THE doily from Lydia's hand and places it back on the serving plate.

"We have to move forward, we'll make a plan."

"What kind of a plan? I'm not helping the guests sew."

She grabs the newspaper lying on the table. She wanders through to the dining room, glances behind her. Her mother's not watching. Her fingertips glide across the brocade chairs. Gritty, exactly. She stops in front of Degas' solo ballerina. She always felt they had similar thoughts by the pained expression on her face. She admires ballerinas, the strain beneath grace, those elegant feet. She strolls into the lounge located at the front of the house. The ceiling rises higher than she remembers, the large bay window welcomes half the country that sprawls before it. The aged, yellowing wallpaper draws the garden into the house, and the flowers on it bloom in its warmth: rose bushes, topiary, blue bells, magnolia.

The original hardwood floors peek out beneath expensive cream throw rugs that devour bare toes. Periwinkle slipper chairs Lydia reupholstered for Constance a few years ago flank two oversized beige couches. The glass tabletop never shows fingerprints. Through the bay window, the Japanese maple she planted with her father flutters.

It isn't quietness, but emptiness shrouding the house. She can't bring herself to look at the mantelpiece where her mother placed her father's remains. "One day, I'll scatter him in the garden like he wanted, but for now I can't let him go," says Constance, her eyes pale and damp. "I can't bear the thought of him not being in one piece."

Lydia wants to dissolve into dust like him. She isn't ready to talk about it. She has no idea how. The phone rings. Lydia sneaks into the library across the hall. The door whines when it opens. She wills her father to appear in his favourite chair, healthy, doing his crossword puzzle, the pipe he never lit, between his lips. The aroma of the leather furniture and remnants of her grandfather's pipe tobacco permeate the room. She sits in his chair, flips to the back of the paper. Jobs at the bank, the pharmacy, landscape businesses and the dry cleaners.

Outside the window she sees a glimmer of blue, Little-Nan bends over the fish pond. Lydia looks closer, a small woman in a dark blue robe feeds the fish. Her silver hair hangs down her back, woven into a tidy braid. She looks up and takes a slight bow, she smiles and reaches out her hand. A tiny woman, a doll, with the face of a pearl takes her hand and drops her head, shakes it. She is young, black hair falling over her shoulders, shiny but tired. Lydia gets up and walks closer to the window to get a better look at the woman she realizes must be one of the counsellors. *Is the young, beautiful one the bride?* Pipit glances toward the window Lydia's staring out of. Lydia grabs the curtain and hides in it.

They're strangers, Lydia tells herself, *I have no obligation to be friendly. They're paying guests in my house. I'll be cordial, professional, help Mom with the bed and breakfast upkeep, wash sheets, clean bathrooms, vacuum,* "You ever clean for a living?" an old man once asked her in a laundromat. "No," she said. She peeks out of the curtain, Pipit and Little-Nan are gone.

She scrunches the paper. Tomorrow she'll find a task. Tomorrow she'll venture into town. Tomorrow she won't sleep for the greater part of the day, tomorrow she'll see about visiting the family doctor as advised — she'll begin again. For now she'll allow herself to sit in her father's chair and stare at the walls, the window, the books, the floor, and the curtains, to stare at the past.

Persian rugs cover the hardwood floors in deep blues and burgundy. A gift from Sophie and her husband Rupert, shipped back from one of their vacations. Sophie never liked Charlie. She thought of calling Sophie but didn't want to give her the satisfaction of saying, "I told you so." Sophie hasn't called. Lydia wonders if her mother's told Sophie. She's told the Counselors, the strangers she now considers family. She was punishing Sophie too perhaps. Annoyed that her two daughters are so consumed with their own lives they don't come to help, not like her new family.

When the rugs first arrived from Persia, they smelled of cloves and angelica, spices her grandmother told her were used to ward off evil spirits. She lies down on the rug. Its texture like a strange land, the smells of witchy spices long gone. She gazes up at the books her father and his father spent hours immersed in. Books by and about people who built things, all things, from wars, to empires, to libraries, bridges, rockets, cures and life itself. Sun Tzu, Louis Kahn, Le Corbusier, Mies van der Rohe, Marie Curie, God. Names flung across the kitchen table at dinner, Henry and his parents conversing in long, lagging sentences about people she felt she should know but never met. People who didn't come to dinner but joined them at dinner, who unlike God, didn't feel like strangers.

Light filters through the Palladian windows in two thin lines between the almost closed curtains. The first pair of curtains Lydia made, the fabric chosen for its weight and hue, a deep olive. She fights to keep her hands from diving into the plush velvet. From one of the many books Henry shared with her and Sophie, she remembers, *Windows are the connection to nature*. At the time it didn't seem as obvious. There was something magical about that connection, that a window was far more significant than people gave it credit for. As a young girl it seemed like windows were the looking glass, crystal balls, the connection to things beyond nature.

Sophie used to watch Lydia run through the house throwing open the curtains, Sophie's eyes rolling, Lydia's gleaming as she imagined an unreal world on the other side of the windows. The grass, the pines, the sky, the squirrels, the man who played her father, her mother, the little house in the woods — she created a whole new life for them out there beyond the window on the other side of the curtains. Sophie knew Lydia was different, happier when she observed them through the windows of the house.

At night the performance ended for another day and it was her job to draw the curtains. This carried on into her teenage years, the storylines changing, the material, the textures, she used to create her own curtains, changed all the time. Sophie found her sister's behaviour embarrassing. "It's passion," Henry said. "Passion," said Sophie, "more like madness, Dad, madness." Sophie rarely invited her friends to the house because she never knew what Lydia would do, like appear from behind curtains, lying on the floor face down smelling the rugs, or emerging from the turret dressed in old Victorian undergarments pretending to be some dead child from long ago. "Darling, the house is meant to have friends in it," Constance would say. "It's what your grandparents wanted. A home where friends and family converged." Sophie said that if she did invite her friends over, could someone invite Lydia to their house at the same time.

How windows are dressed impacts the character, mood, and style of a room. That line she read over and over and over again. *Just like people*, she thought. She presses her palms into the soft curtain, and touches the window through it. *What is out there now?* She began dressing windows, and costumes naturally followed. "Why not make clothes instead of costumes?" Constance once asked when Lydia walked downstairs in a misshapen attempt at a Harlequin's attire. Her face painted white and feet clad in a pair of little black shoes she'd found in the turret. "Because it's far more fun to bring people to life who don't really exist, Mom, like the pictures on the wall, the books on the shelves. Look, I'm him," she said pointing to Picasso's Harlequin.

The house had more curtains than windows to display them across. Curtains became emblematic, specific materials her amulets. There were so many variables affecting how fabrics hung, their weight, texture and drapeability, like people. "We are, after all, a type of fabric," she stated at dinner one night, turning the heads of her grandparents, with smiles. "How we hang, our texture, our drapeability, how we feel to the touch."

"How much light we let in," Her grandmother said and she never forgot it.

Lydia walks around her father's library, eyes half-closed, laughing as she relives walking around the house with her grandmother, Constance in tow, wishing Lydia would take that kind of interest in her vocation, jotting ideas down, conveying every characteristic of the space, its function, aesthetic; hands on chins, deciding whether the room needed complete privacy or sun control. Lydia advised a pleated draw drapery so that they could close it during the hottest part of the day, or at night when people could see in. Sophie shook her head and said, "We're in the country. Who the hell's going to see in?"

Constance said, "You never know."

Stripes do not make pretty draperies — stripes do not hang attractively when gathered or pleated. Variables such as these Lydia related to everyday life, people, eyes, obstacles she'd come across. Stripes rarely hang well on people. Sophie took offence when Lydia tugged at the sleeve of her stiff cotton blouse and said that she should be more like a swag than a roman shade. She explained that swags have body but are soft. Roman shades have a great deal of body but are hard because they have to be stable. Sophie stormed off and complained to their mother that Lydia was cruel and why did she have to touch everything she wore.

Lydia leans her head back and gazes up at the library ceiling. It churns. If her arms were as long and elastic as they felt she could reach up into the churning clouds and grab her father out of heaven. The doctor said she would feel disoriented, it was natural. Rosa was convinced that shock does that to people and there's no pill more effective than a good walk — screw the pills and the doctors, walk it off, walk it off. *What if the mind goes past a point of no return? Keeps walking.* Sleep, all Lydia wants to do is sleep on the Persian rug praying the clove and angelica will keep her safe from evil.

THE KITCHEN SCREEN door slides open. Constance lights up and grabs the bottles the thin woman hands her. "Sorry, the milk is late, Constance, this early heat is affecting the cows, if you can believe it."

"Not to worry," says Constance and asks Jane if she'd like a cup of tea and a scone. Jane always eats the scones, she leaves the Templar Estate last on her route for that reason, tea and sweets.

"How's she doing?" she whispers.

Constance shrugs.

"It must be so hard to watch your child go through this kind of thing. And what can you do but let it run its course, I guess."

"It will be good for her to see you. When she's feeling better."

"Oh, it's okay, I don't know what to say, anyway. It's been so long. She didn't even acknowledge me at Mr. Templar's funeral."

Jane dreamt of following in Constance's footsteps, which pleased her very much since Sophie and Lydia had no interest in acting. They had planned to go to the city together to get jobs in the same theatre. Jane the actress, Lydia in the wardrobe department. Their whole lives they planned that future, together. Before they graduated from high school, Jane's belly was unnaturally round for a young woman with dreams and talent and so much to do before the boy inside changed everything she thought she lived for.

Constance reaches for a mug and knocks over the milk bottles. They crash to the floor. Jane jumps. Lydia's startled awake.

"I'm so sorry," says Constance. "I've been so careless lately."

Jane grabs a cloth from the sink and wipes the spilled milk. "Don't be sorry. You've been through so much. There's more in the van. I always bring extra."

"I have no strength in my hands anymore."

"You do, you do. You're just tired."

Pipit hears the crash and runs downstairs to see if Constance is all right. Junko leaps out of bed. She locks the bedroom door behind her and fishes through Pipit's bag sitting at the side of the chair. She finds the matches she knows she keeps in there. She pulls the curtains even tighter shut and lights the beeswax candles she insists on having in her room. "You cannot light these when you are unsupervised," Little-Nan and Pipit warn her. She cannot bring these types of obsessions into other people's homes.

Jane blinks a few times when Pipit appears in the kitchen. "Watch your feet," she says. Pipit sways her bare feet up to tiptoes and stops. She places her hands together in front of her chest, and bows. "I've known many that say striving for the pure life is like walking on glass." She laughs and lets herself down onto the balls of her feet like a ballerina.

Jane recognizes her from the cathedral. "You're part of that new program for the kids, right?"

Pipit nods.

"I signed up my son," Jane chuckles and places her hand on Constance's arm. "You should have seen his face when he walked in the door with a lady's bathrobe over his arm."

She bends over laughing. Can barely get the story out. Pipit remains straight-faced, hands pressed so hard together in front of her they look glued. "He got all grumpy and said, 'Before you say anything, it's my homework, okay?'"

Constance laughs along with Jane. It was good to laugh, to watch someone laugh.

"I thought, my God, if Glen could see him right now, learning to be good by sewing what looks like my bathrobe, he'd have left town a lot earlier than he did."

"Kimonos," says Pipit. "They are kimonos, not bathrobes."

"Don't get me wrong, I think when I was leaving schoolboys started to take home economics and girls took shop classes, and he says he's learning to play a type of drum too, but jeez it was just a funny sight, you know."

Constance nods. Lydia tiptoes out of the library, follows the voices down the hall and presses herself tightly against the wall, listening. Above her Junko peers between the banisters, unnoticed, like an owl.

"I think it's great. I really do," Jane says to Constance, her back slightly turned away from Pipit. "It's just not what you'd expect, you know, not your typical parks and rec program."

Constance drops her head. She was instrumental in convincing the town council to at least give Raiden and his associates a trial run at introducing their counselling programs here. The old cathedral was wide open, no one was using the space and with budget cuts many of the other programs for young people were being eradicated. Young people need things to do to keep them out of trouble, Constance told the council, it was always Henry's vision to help the young. The loyalty to Henry won out and they agreed to give Raiden a trial run with his programs. After the wedding, they would reassess the progress and popularity of his vision.

"It's great though," Jane nods toward Pipit. "It's keeping Daniel out of trouble somehow."

"One learns a lot about oneself through the stories the kimono tells."

"Yeah, he mentioned that."

"He will learn from Raiden's program. More than from Boy Scouts, or reform school."

Jane spins around. "How did you know he was in reform school?"

"I didn't."

"You know it's tough for kids his age out here."

"It's tough for kids that age everywhere. It is one thing we all have in common. We have all been young. Some don't even know who their parents are."

Constance reaches her hand out to Pipit, the other to Jane. Pipit smiles and shakes her head, subtly flips her other thin soft hand to say, *it's okay. I'm okay.* Constance asks Jane if she wants more tea. She nods and helps herself to another scone.

Pipit excuses herself, lowers and lifts her doll-like head and goes back into the guest quarters. The door clicks behind her.

"She's tiny," says Jane.

Constance smiles, "There is much more to her than meets the eye."

LYDIA TURNS AND looks down the hall, the light beams in from the top of the front door like light at the end of a tunnel, *run,* she whispers to herself, *run. Go back to the city, figure it out.*

She takes a step toward the door.

"Yes, run," she thinks she hears, "run until you no longer feel your feet." Junko backs away from the banister so she cannot be seen, "fly, little one, fly." Lydia holds her ears. Junko giggles and ducks back into the guest quarters. Lydia looks up and around. She holds her head and retreats into the library, throws herself onto her father's chair. She swears she feels the scratchiness of her grandmother's hands on her cheeks, holding her face the way she used to, looking into her eyes and saying, *you listen to me, you don't let anyone bring you down. You be yourself and to hell with everyone else.* Followed by the tickling hairs of her grandfather's moustache when he held her close and whispered, *you follow your heart, Lydia, and don't let anyone steer you in their direction because it's all they know.* That crazy moustache her grandfather lived and died in, curled at the ends, grey since his teens the photos told her. She rolls herself in the hanging velvet dressing the windows.

Windows like eyes to her, the eyes to nature, the connection between worlds, inner and outer, curtains their lids, sometimes all she wants to do is shut her eyes, shut everything out, hide. Then there are the days, hours, the minutes, her eyes want to be wide open to see every detail, to connect with nature.

The ceiling creaks, footsteps of strangers Constance now considers family. Sophie's voice resounds in Lydia's head, *You came home too late, Sis, Mom's moved on.* Lydia wraps herself tighter and tighter in the curtain. When her parents created the bed and breakfast she resented being cut off from that part of the home, for not being able to open and close its curtains. Lydia believes her father saw more than what lay beyond the window he spent hours gazing through from this chair. He never talked about what he saw, what he wanted to see. The shelves beside her full of biographies of people her grandparents revered. Henry didn't want to be that kind of architect, he didn't want to be like them, the names talked about over dinner, and in the backyard and when Lydia hung her legs through he banisters, listening to her grandparents and parents talk in the lounge over clinking glasses and what she later discovered was Bach on the old turntable her father bought in town from a man with one eye and a guitar that never left his side like a loyal dog. Corbusier, Mies van der Rohe, Gehry, Wright and Kahn. She ran her hand across a book on Louis Kahn. After his father's death, Kahn's son discovered the father he barely knew had more than one family. Another family like Constance has now.

The door slowly opens, "Mom, I'm so sorry I wasn't..." Lydia unwinds herself from inside the velvet. She stops when the figure in the doorway is not her mother. He's holding Lydia's sewing machine. "This was on the floor in the hallway," he says. "One might question if it were coming or going." Raiden puts down the sewing machine and presses his hands together in front of his chest, introduces himself, "You must be Lydia. I've heard a lot about you."

She pulls her hair, tries to draw it across her face. She wonders if Raiden always lets himself into the main house without knocking, if he's become that much like family. His hair's pulled into a ponytail, wisps of it hang down past his thin chest. He's dressed in a black tunic and black, loose-fitting linen trousers that stop at his ankles. A small silver box with the head of what looks like a monkey weighting it down hangs around his long neck. On his feet, flip-flops. His eyes black like his shimmering hair, pupil-less. He stands in the doorway like a dignified pole.

"Do you always let yourself in without knocking?"

He remains still, as if he hadn't heard her. He bows slightly and steps back, face blank.

"I'm sorry," she says. "I'm not quite myself."

"Perhaps you are more yourself than you realize."

She reaches into her pocket for the comfort of the swatch, pictures the deep hole by the Rose of Sharon, and the buried velvet. She struggles for breath. "I've barely slept. I'm sorry, I'm..."

He lowers his head then raises it, more like an exercise than a nod. She twiddles the velvet curtain in and out of her fingers. Raiden picks up on her ill ease, her restless hands touching everything within their reach and explains that he came to see if Constance needs anything from town. "And," he says, "to ensure your safe arrival. I cannot imagine it was an easy journey." He drops his head, and raises it again, "I am sorry for your losses."

Her lips pucker. A barrage of words and images behind them. *This stranger, sorry for my losses, losses, plural?* She's naked, inverted, turned inside out. No one turns her inside out. She wants to wrap herself back up in the velvet curtain, tighter and tighter. Despite what Constance wants to believe, no matter how helpful, Raiden and his associates are not family. She doesn't want her own sister to know anything about her "losses" yet. *What kind of a journey did he think it was, across the desert, barefoot? She came from the city by car, a two-hour drive.*

She composes herself. Stills her twitching fingertips. "And your journey?"

He smiles, looks away.

Constance appears clutching a blue gingham dishcloth. "Oh," she says, "I thought I heard something. So glad to see you two have finally met."

"Mother..."

"This is Raiden, pet, isn't he lovely, such a help. Aren't you dear?"

She eyes Raiden in a way that shows they are familiar. It horrifies Lydia to think her mother was so lonely to ingratiate a stranger like this. It's hard to guess his age, fifties perhaps. He might not be that much older than Lydia, too young for her mother. Constance's eyes lit up when she realized he was there. *Could he mean anything like that to her?* Lydia will physically kick him out of the house if she has to.

Raiden asks if Constance is all right. He comments on the paleness of her face. His voice gentle, controlled. Lydia's incapable of speaking to her mother that way. It's different when it's not your own mother. *Raiden probably doesn't treat his own mother that way. And where is his mother?* Constance says she's fine and glances at her daughter who notices Raiden fills the doorway to the same point on the frame that her father had. His hair shimmers in the sun that makes its way through the window at the top of the door. *What is it about his face, the memories on it.* He looks like a man whose heart's been broken, and not by a lover — beyond that. Perhaps his mother broke his heart like her father broke hers. What did he want from Constance, from her family? *Leave,* she wishes, *move on.*

"Your mother is so happy to have you home," he says and exchanges nods with Constance.

"I wish it were under better circumstances, Raiden. All that hard work... she loved the theatre."

"Mom, please..."

Her mother shushes her. The atmosphere stiffens. Constance offers Raiden a cup of tea. Lydia prays he won't accept and he doesn't. There's too much to do. He's heading into town to help Little-Nan with the wedding preparations and there is a class in the afternoon to run and papers to be signed. The cathedral needs tidying, a few things to be built, the ceremonial robes need to be completed. "Which is what you'll be doing, dear, helping Little-Nan sew the wedding gowns." Constance follows this with the nodding head, the one that means you must nod with her, *nod Lydia, nod now and don't make a fool of me in front of the guests*.

Lydia's neck hardens. It is incapable of a nod. It's locked, along with her eyes, and jaw. Everything slammed shut, a prison lock down, slam, slam, slam. Raiden bows and adds how grateful they all are that Lydia offered to help. It's such a busy time, what with the program starting up and Junko's ceremony, isn't life like that, it rains and... Raiden's voice becomes rain in her ears, pouring, pouring. She stares at her mother. Constance hums and diverts her eyes, scrunches her blue gingham dishcloth that Lydia imagines is on the verge of bleeding red. She hasn't offered to help. She isn't going to help. Her mother better make that clear and soon.

"We feel especially honoured," Raiden says, "when we learned that you design costumes in the city." He pauses. "For Shakespeare himself."

"We never met."

"Lydia."

Raiden chuckles.

"I hear you are quite accomplished, have a special gift for choosing the right fabric to express much more than..."

"I don't do that anymore. It was a passing fancy."

"Lydia, it was your life."

"The things we live for change, Mother. Didn't you tell me that once?"

"Enough."

Raiden turns away. Lydia wishes she could disappear, draw the curtains. She apologizes between tight lips and asks if she could please be excused. Her skull itches. She imagines devils gnawing their way in. *Where were the angels?* Constance said Henry sent angels. Outside she pictures the turkey vultures circling the house, breaking into the turret and making their way downstairs. Constance said Raiden and his associates were angels. "Sent by your father, I think." She swore that's what she said, angels. Raiden seems more like a devil than an angel, shrouded in dark cloth, dark eyes, a weighty demeanor. Henry would not send devils. *I think God is in the house, I can feel him. What does it feel like? Fire.*

Constance walks into the hall. Raiden presses his back against the door frame, Lydia slides past him. He takes her arm, leans closer and whispers, "One who thinks one's insight exceeds others has no eyes."

"What did you say?" she yanks her arm away. He joins Constance in the hall. Lydia steps back into the library, takes a few breaths; she's warm, chest tight. She touches her eyes, her connection to nature, wants to slam the lids shut for good. She runs her hand across the distressed leather chair to garner support from the essence of her father. All she gets is a faint whiff of the gardener's hand cream he used, wafting into the air by the ghost of his shaking finger.

Raiden's grip was firm, intimate — not unlike the grip of someone who cared. Its daring familiarity bothered her. Constance and Raiden chat under their breaths by the front door. She tries to make out what they are saying, their darting eyes, turned backs, hunched shoulders conspiring to hide between them the words about her. She makes her way through the lounge, past the ballerina whose gaze is off to the side, not wanting to be involved. Lydia slips on her Converse runners to sneak out through the dining room and into the woods.

"Wait," Constance says.

"Shit," Lydia turns and idles toward her mother.

"I need you to take these towels and extra supplies up to the guest rooms for Raiden."

She points to a box on the hall bench.

"I can do it," he says.

"No, no, you're busy. Lydia has nothing else to do."

Lydia ignores her mother. They can say anything they want and it has no bearing on her state of mind. She feels nothing and doesn't reach for anything to help change that. She looks for support from the static ballerina, wonders what happened to her in life outside of the picture. If like Mona Lisa, she had any clue how iconic she'd become. How lucky she was to be captured in a good place in time, eternally youthful and pretty. Outside the bay window the Japanese maple sways in the breeze. Shadows dance on the white walls, oblong faces, wide-mouthed and screaming without sound.

Raiden apologizes for asking for extra towels and hangers. Junko wants two of everything, as if there is more than one of her, he laughs. "No trouble," Constance says. "I know what girls are like, especially brides-to-be." She winks at Raiden and he turns his head.

Brides-to-be, how sickening, what fools we are, Lydia says to the ballerina, then asks her if she had ever married and, for the sake of things, decides she did not — she knew better. Degas knew better and captured her in her prime, single and young and doing what she loved most. *What fools we are, marriage. Marriage.* She moves further into the room, grips the arm of the tapestry slipper chair, feels the knots in its weave, the grit of frustration, anger. The print of Picasso's Harlequin catches her attention from the far wall, his hands like a woman's, his face a young boy's. A harlequin knows better than to marry and yet a harlequin might embrace marriage with the right attitude, the pantomime, carnivalesque, the comic-tragic side of things. All these lucky beings captured in paintings, single, without a care in the world. *I'll find an old frame in the turret, step into it and hang myself on the sewing room wall.*

As soon as Raiden leaves, she'll call Charlie, tell him how she feels, let him know the extent of the damage he's caused. *Does he have any clue what he's done?* Her clammy skin threatens to slide off her. She senses beads speckling her face for everyone to see. She's turning dewy. Reptilian. The floor sways. She grips the back of the chair and gulps back rising water.

"Lydia, help Raiden."

"I don't feel well, Mom."

Her mother's shoulders drop. Lydia moves toward the box. "It's fine," says Raiden. "I can handle it."

He picks up the box of towels, extra hangers and beeswax candles. Lydia opens the door wide for him so he will use the exterior door and not feel like he can access the guest quarters from the main house. Despite what her mother allows, she doesn't feel he should get any more comfortable in their home. She wills the breeze to graduate into a typhoon and suck him out and far away. "I'm sorry," she says. "It really has been a rough couple of days."

His dark eyes scale Lydia's dishevelled painter's dungarees, her chopped and uneven hair. She steps away from him and says, "I just need a little time to let things sink in, you know." He closes the distance between them and whispers, "The sword that kills the man, is the sword that saves the man." He winks and leaves.

"What did he say?"

Constance attempts to grab her arm, Lydia storms out after him. "Hey, what did you say?" He doesn't turn around.

"Lydia, please." Constance pulls her inside and closes the door.

Lydia runs into the lounge where she watches him through the bay window, through the branches of the swaying maple as he makes his way along the wraparound porch toward the other side of the house. "Lydia, you have got to calm down..." Lydia presses her hands over her ears, she doesn't want to hear her mother's scolding or the echo of Raiden's haunting whispers, his riddles, or any of the other voices vying for space in her head. "Who the hell does he think he is?" she says.

Constance slams her tea towel onto the floor. "How could you be so rude? What's happened to you?"

She drops her hands, her ears sting. "What's happened to me? Everything. In one day I lost everything, Mom. I lost everything. Isn't that enough to happen to someone? I can't feel my body right now and you want me to carry supplies up to the guests like a child, for some stranger who has the nerve to spew crazy proverbs at me. Who the hell is he, the goddamn emperor?"

"How do you know about the emperor?"

"What? You..."

Constance picks up the tea towel and slaps it down again. "Who do you think you are?"

I don't know. I don't know.

"Your father would be so disappointed by your behaviour."

Lydia grips her cotton t-shirt, feels small and opaque. The wooden heels of her mother's indoor shoes clomp along the hardwood floors and stomp up the stairs; the sound of the horse Constance speaks of, in the house, it is here, ready for her to get back onto. When she was young she used to dream there was a little white pony in the woods, with overgrown hooves and teeth, and a gold halter with aquamarine tassels. The clip-clop of hooves fades. Constance stops on the landing and calls down, "Raiden is not the emperor." She marches into her room and slams the door.

"What the hell is going on?"

It would be such a relief to rip out her conscience and dump it in the compost at the bottom of the yard; Constance was right, the house is too big when you're alone in it. The dented sewing machine waits in the hall, yearning to be spun.

The Punishment Garments

LYDIA'S HEAD SPINS. She imagines herself marching up the stairs and into the sewing room, like she did so many times when she was young. She'd slam the door and lock it, catching the beginning of — "You listen to me young lady..." then dive into her bevy of cloth — *cushion covers, doilies, place mats, curtains, what do you want, anything you want.* If she was grounded for staying out late in the woods or for disappearing in the house and not answering Constance, she'd sit amidst her fabrics, fingers implanted in the pile, eyes closed waiting for the right vision to express the perfect feeling, which evolved into the most suitable garment to convey her apology, "Mom this is how I feel, can you see it?" Constance appreciated her daughter's gift and despite her stubbornness couldn't help but forgive. She never feared spending time alone in the turret then. The only thing she feared when she was young, like now, was Constance. But the thought of heading up and into the turret petrifies her. There's a different feeling in the house. It suddenly feels full, crowded. Lydia realizes the only way to appease her mother, to help her, is to sew again and she can't do it. She grabs a gabardine-clad cushion, smothers it over her face and screams.

Junko glides toward her bedroom door. "Do not do this to us," says Pipit, "Your door is locked. I've been worried." Pipit tries not to lose a temper she's recently acquired, tries not to cry, to rub her already rough hands even more. They are scarlet from worry, alive, painful but she ignores the pain like she's been taught. Pain is a state of mind. Through the banister, from a corner obscured by a curve, Junko had been watching Lydia, whispering to her through her wooden mask, "If you hold a grudge, you will not pass over to the other side. If you hold a grudge, you will remain on earth, a ghost." Pipit whispers as loud as she can to get her back into the guest quarters and like a dog that suddenly stops from running away, she saunters back, eyes averted, head angled to the side. "What were you doing out there?" asks Pipit.

"Keeping an eye on the waif."

"You must stay on this side of things, You don't have access to their . . ."

"World."

"No, you don't."

"I do not possess the key to unlock the barriers that lead to beyond."

"No, now stop it. Be serious. Give me the key."

"I do not have the key, you just told me that."

"Junko, please."

She lowers her mask and shoves her bare face into Pipit's, who places her rough hands over her face and cowers. Junko laughs and from under her tongue removes the key to her room and hands it to Pipit. The mask's replaced and Junko enters her room and slams the door before Pipit can enter. Pipit catches sight of the candles as the door slams shut.

"What are you thinking leaving your room with these open flames burning?"

Doors slam and Pipit chirps. Lydia heads upstairs.

Junko unlocks the door for Pipit.

"You worry too much, *Makoto no Hana*. I think better by candlelight. I can see into my soul by the flickering flame. But not yours, odd."

"But you weren't there?"

"The mirrors, dear, the mirrors hold the reflection in the flame."

Pipit grumbles. Junko begins to close the door, Pipit places her hand on it. Junko continues to press against the pressure Pipit applies, determined to peer into the closing space to see the reflections in the mirrors lining the walls. She shakes her head. There are no souls in the dancing orange and blue light that she can see, just flames — hundreds and hundreds of flames.

Junko releases the door and Pipit falls into the room. Junko holds her arms out to the side and leaps on her toes toward the wall she shares with Lydia. "Stop," says Pipit. Junko scratches her fingernails along the wall, presses her ear against it. She senses Lydia is in her room. She scratches and scratches.

Lydia presses her ear to the wall. *What the hell? Rats. Rats. Rats. Rats.* She grips her head.

"Stop," says Pipit.

Junko turns.

Pipit steps back as Junko circles her. Through the slit in the pale wooden mask her breath is a cold slap against Pipit's face. The static eyes drooping down at the sides, powdered face, milky and expressionless, lips a burnt orange and mouth open just wide enough to see the tips of carved wooden teeth — Deigan, the mask of the vengeful dead. Pipit steps away from her, keeps her head turned to the side, avoids eye contact. She knows not to look creatures like her in the eye. "We have to be at the cathedral this afternoon to go over the ceremony. You need to try on your robes... at least decide what you want to wear."

She leans into Pipit and blows her cold breath out of the slit in the mouth. "I will wear this."

Junko giggles and walks over to the closet. She slips out of her white nightgown, her naked body a sickly cream, parchment paper over bones.

Nails like talons scrape the air in front of her like a cat scratching an invisible pole. "I will wear nothing to the ceremony. I will have defied the claws and fangs of the dharma cave, this is my soul, naked and ready to go. I will leave like this."

Pipit walks away, there is nothing else to do but walk away, leave her, do not encourage her, it's what she wants. Little-Nan told Pipit Junko acts on instinct, "She isn't like you and I, she is unlike anyone we know or have worked with. You have to learn to work with her nature not against it dear, like a wild dog, a wolf — like a mother works with her nature, not against it."

At times it is too hard for Pipit to play along, this mother is not like a mother, not like Constance, the normal mothers out there. She is a wolf. Junko lies on the bed, closes her eyes and sighs. She has one goal left, the ceremony, she's waiting, just waiting for that day. She cannot be discouraged, they can't lose her now.

The door shuts and Junko leaps up from the bed and locks it. Pipit won't care this time. *Let her die in there. If that's what she wants, so be it.* She slides down the wall and grabs her knees to her chest. "Mommy, this is not where I envisioned myself. Give me strength to see this through, I want to believe that you are in there, Mommy, in the flames, in the mirrors." She whispers into her knees then up at the white ceiling, "Everything I've learned can't be applied to this case. It is the test." If she can help Junko, she too will certainly escape the claws and fangs of the dharma cave. Junko *is* the claws and fangs of the dharma cave.

THE SUN APPEARS through the trees in rippled slices. *Pineapple, freshly cut.* Lydia's nerves ricochet off her flesh, the tremors wake her up. She's beginning to feel like a constantly vibrating pod, the Mexican jumping beans her father kept on his desk. For years they never rested and that petrified Lydia. She'd stare at them and wondered, *What's the point? What is the point?*

Downstairs is quiet. No sign of Constance, there has been little creaking in the guest quarters this morning; the tap ran once, a toilet flushed, then quiet.

Lydia prays she won't bump into Pipit or Little-Nan in the kitchen. Constance has been serving their breakfast in the main kitchen instead of the bed and breakfast's. This morning the scents of bacon and baking are absent, the kitchen is too clean, airy, no dishes, empty jam jars or teacups anywhere.

"Mom?"

Propped up against the salt shaker is a note with her name written in bold black letters across the top. *Please pick up groceries on your way back from town. At an appointment, won't be too long. Love, Constance.*

Love, Constance. Constance. Lydia slumps into a chair. "How the hell did she know I was thinking of going into town?"

Rosa calls, "I never really asked how you are doing."

"I'm about to embark on the search, I'm ready to get out there, to walk it off, like you told me to."

"Great, walk here, by the time you get here, you should be cured."

"I'm serious, Rosa."

"I need your help, I can't do this without you."

"Nonsense."

"He's insufferable."

"Please, Rosa. I can't hear about him. I have to go, I hear footsteps."

"What do you mean?"

"The guests, I have to go before they come downstairs."

Rosa stares at the phone, she blows smoke in rings and through them she watches the monks coming and going from the temple. Each one dressed the same, blue robes and yellow sashes. Rosa recalls Lydia saying she wanted to be one of them, all the same, the same goals, the same clothes, the same eyes.

"The same eyes?" Rosa said.

"Imagine if we all saw things the same way," Lydia said. "The understanding in that. Amazing."

"What an awful thought," said Rosa and drew on *Hope*.

LYDIA STANDS AT the edge of the stone patio. She'll walk the path through the woods into town every day, morning, and evening, like she did in her youth until she discovers a different path, a sign, one that would have taken her into an alternate future. Raiden's words whisper through Rosa's. She feels his breath against her ear, *One who thinks one's insight exceeds others has no eyes.*

"The answer's out there, I know it. I have to keep my eyes open."

"Okay, whatever, Lydia."

"I'll move on by blocking out the past ten years. The only way to move on is to block it all out, like it never happened. Start fresh."

"You're crazy," says Rosa. "No one gets ahead that way."

You can't bury the past, she hears her mother saying, *it will grow back bigger*.

"I can't do this without you."

"I had no choice," Lydia tells her. "The sword that kills the man, is the sword that saves the man."

"What? I'm worried about you, Lydia. Who are these people?"

"My mother's new family."

"Great."

Lydia says she has to go, blows kisses into the phone and hangs up.

Rosa stares at the phone and takes a sip of her wine. Charlie watches her from the balcony, through the muslin sheers waving in the breeze. Rosa looks at him and shrugs.

LYDIA GRABS THE shopping list from the side of the fridge. Every time Constance and Henry walked past it they would add another item into the desire column: Licorice Allsorts, Neapolitan ice cream, crisps, rice pudding, ornate scribbling, sweeping and curly letters.

The right side of the page, the serious food column has significantly thinner, rigid letters, all upper case — CARROTS, POTATOES, BUTTER, BEEF TENDERLOIN, BRUSSELS SPROUTS, CHICKEN, METAMUCIL. Constance keeps adding Henry's favourite foods to the list. Lydia wonders if it is unconscious, a habit, or a way of always keeping him around. Henry peers at his daughter from a picture hanging on the kitchen wall. There is nothing he can do to help her.

The lock on the door between the kitchen and the guest quarters clicks, followed by a slow creak. Lydia holds her breath, hoping in some way she won't be seen. Pipit walks past her carrying a tray of dishes. She places the dishes on the counter and walks in front of Lydia and smiles. Lydia looks for the strings she swears must be attached to her unrealistic body. She is too minute, too perfect not to be some kind of puppet. Where are the lines in her skin, on her hands, her perfectly round red lips, her black eyes that don't move when she smiles. "Good morning," she says.

"Good morning."

"You and Junko have a lot in common. You don't leave your rooms and keep the curtains drawn on bright sunny days. You should meet by the stream and share tales of sorrow over *sake* in the sunshine." She presses her hands together in front of her chest and nods her head slightly, which Lydia finds herself doing in return, like when someone yawns and you can't help but yawn. Pipit turns to walk away.

"I made those curtains," Lydia says.

Pipit stops.

"Chose the fabric for that very reason, to keep the sun out. I'm proud of my curtains, especially the robin's egg damask in mercerized cotton."

She walks in front of Pipit and looks right into her sea-green eyes.

"The fabric and design was popular in the sixteenth century. It was a rich time in Europe and the fabrics reflected that."

"They are lovely curtains, Lydia."

"Men turned the other cheek at the effeminacy because the ornate patterns and bright colours reflected abundance. Those curtains are fit for a king," says Lydia. Pipit watches her. She doesn't blink, doesn't respond at all.

The phone rings and rings. Lydia ignores it. Pipit excuses herself. "I'm sorry, I'm..."

"Not quite yourself."

Pipit turns and fixes her gaze on Lydia. She tries to escape Pipit's eyes. *What is she doing? Stop looking at me.*

"If you are not quite yourself, then who are you?"

"Pardon?"

"You jumped like a cricket when the phone rang. Your knuckles are white. The tea towel you've been wringing is strangled. If that is not yourself, who is it?"

"Who is it? Exactly."

"You are the self you are now in this very moment, you are you, Lydia. Your white knuckles, the jumpiness, the strangling of the towel, is you."

Lydia's head lightens, she sits down. Pipit puts the dishes in the dishwasher and wipes the counter, she hums. Then she runs her hand across Lydia's shoulder and crouches in front of her and smiles. "Nice to meet *you*, we shall see each other soon, I'm sure."

She closes the door to the bed and breakfast and locks it from the inside. Lydia throws the tea towel in the sink. "This is not me? What does she know?" The door clicks and opens again. "Psst, Psst."

Lydia turns to the door. Little-Nan pokes her head out and waves Lydia over. Lydia looks behind her first then goes toward the sweet older lady. "Pipit means no harm, she is preoccupied with the rehearsal of the ceremony. Please take it in stride, dear. We are all trying," she pauses, looks down then up again, not directly into Lydia's eyes this time, "to do our best."

She backs into the hallway, closes the door, the lock clicks and her tiny feet pad up the stairs.

Lydia's cellphone rings, it's Rosa. Lydia stares at the phone and thinks, I'm done. I don't want to hear about the theatre, about Charlie, about the encroaching opening night. The night that was supposed to change Lydia's life, propel her into the next level of her career, the critics are waiting for the costumes. She answers the phone. "Rosa," she sighs, "I'm just about to start walking this off.

Rosa's breathless, but swears she isn't tired. She's been sleeping well at the apartment which she's tidied up a bit. "Charlie knows I'll be staying until you come back, in three weeks. Three weeks," she stresses.

"He says he needs to sort things out before he talks to you, but he will eventually talk to you."

"Sort what out? He made vows. He makes stronger vows on stage in his lines every single night."

"Give it time, Lydia. Take a sleeping pill."

"What?"

"I put some in your purse."

"You did? You said not to take pills."

"Sleeping pills are different. I have no clue how country folk sleep without them. It's so damn quiet out there."

She swallows what Lydia imagines is the espresso she lives on until she opens her wine. "Take the dog for a walk," she says. "It'll help heal you. The dog and the country air. You don't want to be here right now anyway... it's a mess."

"We don't have a dog, Rosa."

She's surprised. She thought everyone who lived in the country had dogs.

"You've called three times this morning, Rosa."

She says she has to go, "Just wanted to call back and see if you are okay and to tell you I love you, Lydia."

Lydia doesn't respond. She grabs the shopping bags, slips on her Converse and steps outside. *Walk the dog? Tell me you love me?* Lydia reaches into her purse and grabs a pen. She jots DOG onto the shopping list, in the serious column: EGGS, BUTTER, BREAD, A DOG.

She turns and looks up at the cloaked windows of the bed and breakfast. Through the slightest crack in their centre, Junko peers back.

The Large-Mouthed Pure God

THE WAGTAILS AND longclaws flitter from tree to tree busy with their routines. The wooden signs at the foot of the woods have faded and shriveled in size. Lydia brushes aside branches, peels the winding weeds tangled around them. She takes a step back. To Town is etched into the arrow pointing right. The one pointing left says, To the Owl. She spent hours in the woods searching for owls because one morning Henry said they were hard to find, elusive, "kind of like true happiness," he said, and that moment stuck with Lydia. Before she understood certain sentiments, tones of voice, profundity, she knew he'd let her in on something personal, a window into the man behind the dad they knew little about. The girls had the signs made for Henry's sixty-fifth birthday. He died a few months before. Nobody should give up the search for happiness, even when they are gone.

Lydia turns right toward town and disappears between the pines. The river weaves through the woods. The water echoes like dripping taps in abandoned homes. Her chest tightens. Pins and needles irritate her fingertips. The past few days she's felt light, see-through, like sheers on a window. Constance had seen her walking in and out of her room at times, trying to place where she is. She wrote her notes and left them on her pillow, in her underwear drawer, on the vanity mirror, encouraging her to get to work and help the guests. "You need to be productive, dear, wallowing won't help," or "think about your father, your grandparents, all that they instilled in you and your sister."

Lydia had been avoiding conversations with her mother, the guests, praying Raiden would not show up in the hallways whispering things about swords and killing and having no eyes.

She's been smashing her face into pillows, cushions so Constance or the guests won't hear her crying. Junko doesn't cry. Lydia doesn't want to be that woman one hears through the wall sobbing. She's lived in too many apartment buildings with a woman like that and when you see them on the street, you never feel sympathy for them, but a strange kind of loathing.

Lydia asked Constance why Junko is so unhappy.

"I heard it's because this is not how she would have wanted to get married, dear."

"That's awful."

"She's making a mistake."

"A mistake?" She can't believe her mother said that. It doesn't make sense in this day and age that someone should get married if they don't want to. "Why are they making her?"

"They're not making her, dear. She's doing what she thinks is best and doesn't know how to move on any other way."

"Well why doesn't Pipit or Little-Nan talk to Raiden for her?"

"Honey, when all is said and done, she will be happy. This is what she wants." Constance gripped the countertop.

"Mom?"

"I don't want to talk about the guests anymore."

She stops on the path, her breathing is too fast, heavy. She bends over and grips her knees, the denim instantly gives her comfort, makes her feel a little more strong, like she can do this, she can carry on but wants to be able to do it without the texture of denim. She peels her hands off the fabric a finger at a time like her mother did when she was young, unwrapping her fingers one by one when she clung to clothes in stores, or people's coats as she passed, fur coats, she could lose herself forever in fur. Constance told Henry they could never buy bearskin rugs, "we'd never get her off the floor." She skirts her fingers through the air, across the ground, grabs a handful of dirt, leaves, grass, rubs her palms up and down tree bark, across fallen trunks, the petals of straggly nameless blossoms.

She envisions herself as a child, running along the path, giggling. Her hair long and tangled dancing in the wind as if it were attached to strings, was being guided by the trees. She wonders what she ran to or from then, her future or nothing, she simply ran. Her mother pops into her mind, sitting thin and pale in the Edwardian wicker chair talking about the guests, and how the man who bought the house through the woods has brought so much joy to her life. Her father used to say Constance looked like Daisy from *The Great Gatsby* when she sat in those chairs. It was Lydia's intention to create a Gatsby-like garden setting. Henry was the man Lydia thought brought so much joy to her mother's life. She never imagined him being reduced to ashes and placed in a box smaller than the one she kept her jewellery in. He was too tall for a jewellery box. Tall like the pines, too vital to be reduced to ashes. Her heartbeat thumps through the woods, every clomping step, every breath booming, wanting to be the kid running free in front of her, laughing, hair blowing out behind her like dancing fingers.

She screams for her dad, screams for him to come back, to wake up. He was always there when she needed him. She looks over her shoulder, listens for footsteps on sticks like her mother taught her to do. Her throat hurts, head booms. You can do this. She continues along the path Sophie and her traipsed back and forth on for years. It isn't overrun with weeds or new trees like she thought it might be. This path untouched, their footprints captured in it like fossils. A strange kind of preservation. Maybe Constance has been trailing back and forth across it searching for Lydia and Sophie at the age when she said they were still good. Maybe she walks back and forth searching for Henry whose spirit Lydia imagines traverses it at night looking for the owl. Even in the city, nature's fighting back, trees punching their way through cracks in sidewalks, roads, reclaiming their territory, like a recurring dream.

Through the trunks of the pines and the overhanging branches of the weeping willows she sees the small white house that now belongs to Raiden. Little red lanterns dangle from a long lagging clothesline strung across the backyard. The bridge Lydia's grandfather built over the river is aging and bending. She questions its stability. In the middle, she sits down and hangs her legs over the edge.

FROM THE SIDE of the house a figure appears dressed in a deep blue smock and ankle-length loose fitting pants. His feet are bare. He marches on the spot, face beaming, a small harp-shaped instrument clutched to his chest. The red sash wrapped around his waist is embroidered in gold emblems. In the middle of the garden he stops, doesn't look around. Lydia moves behind the tree at the end of the bridge to watch the man she assumes is Kaito; her mother speaks of him with such affection, but like Junko she's yet to see him. They stay hidden like chipmunks.

On a small wrought-iron table, he places the instrument by a vase of lilacs. Wisps of long black hair fall from the bun on the top of his head. He bends his knees, holds his hands out to the side and stomps his bare feet on the grass. Eyes closed, knees bent, feet stomping. Lydia squints to try and understand what he's doing. His skin appears soft and peacefully pale against his deep indigo attire, *peau de soie*, silk skin. He stops stomping, opens his eyes wide and looks directly at Lydia. He waves, a huge smile spreads across his vast face. She gasps and instinctively folds her knees to her chest. He raises his arms, waves them in the air, his wide sleeves swaying like flags, "I'm sorry. I'm sorry," he says, chuckling. He prances toward her. "You caught me chasing away spirits."

"What?" she whispers, standing up too quickly. The woods spin. She looks up above the tips of the pines at the churning clouds and an eye of blue sky. She closes her eyes and sees red, lots and lots of red; the suffocating fabric; the needle gleaming in the eye of the poppy, her husband in the arms of that Imogen, her father's skeletal body lying still on a viewing table, Desmond throwing her an envelope, the walking papers, her tiny mother pleading with her to get back on the horse; the proverbial horse she's been getting back on for the past twenty years. It gallops toward her, black, thrumming, snorting, sweat foaming on its sinewy neck, full gallop through the woods. "No," she screams and the tears become sobs.

"Shit," says kaito. He rushes into the yard and grabs the lilacs from the vase. He runs to Lydia, plum heads nodding violently, and thrusts the flowers at her. "I'm sorry," he says. "I was attempting to chase away the spirits but in some cases the stomping lures them closer. I'm still learning, it's all so complicated." She weeps harder.

"Please, don't cry. Come, come," he wraps his hand around her arm. "Stand up, stand up." He lifts Lydia to her feet, and leads her toward the house. They stare at each other. He smiles, "You must be Lydia?" he says.

She steps back, smoothes down her hair, "Why?"

He frowns.

"Why must I be Lydia? Why? Because I look ill, broken down, betrayed? I look nothing like Lydia. I am not Lydia. I do not know who I am."

Kaito fumbles for the right thing to say, wishes he had a handbook to refer to. He inhales, raises his hands to his chest, presses them together and says, "For the same reason I must be who I am, I guess." She squints, waits for another explanation. He looks like he should be *full of them*. He shrugs, "That is all," he says.

You are a lost kind of beautiful, he thinks. Little-Nan was right, with a few weeks of rest, her crinoline skin will be ironed out. Yes, a lost kind of beautiful, like a butterfly stilled by death, pinned to cloth and framed is beautiful. *Not quite tragic*, he thinks, *certainly cracked, cracked in so many places; one wrong move and she'll shatter*. He holds out his arms to her. Lydia backs away, keeps walking backwards with her arms held out in front of her.

"Please," he says, "it's okay. You are safe. We are all safe."

She steps further away from him, "No, no one's safe, we're dangling from a goddamn precipice." She points back toward the edge of the river so many souls have sunk in. "No one's safe." She holds her head. The forest turns clockwise, slowly like when a carousel begins to move, and the black horse she swore barrelled through the woods turns gold, decorated in red ribbons with a pole making its way through its withers, rising and falling to the tinny sound of carnival music. "Stop," she says. "Please stop the spinning."

Kaito stops but she isn't talking to him. She's talking to the carousel, to the high-pitched carnival music, the gold horse. She holds her head to try and stop the spinning. She has to learn to curb the chaos another way and she has no idea how. Her father would know how. "No one's safe," she says. The spinning, she has to stop the spinning. She tries to breathe, there's no air. Kaito kneels beside her and looks around at the lingering pines, at the river that has no intention of stopping to help.

Every tear she cries feels like fabric. Hand-dyed Jacobean weave tears, wool tears, velvet tears, chenille tears dive into the Chase adding texture and colour to everything, but tears are colourless after all and to Kaito the river remains an antiquated yellow hue, like sun rising in the city, the dirty dawn. To him, her tears hit the water like bullets. "Let it out," says Kaito. "Shout, cry. Bellow to the vastness, the vacant woods, to the spirits. They will discard of it for you. Cry, howl, howl like the wolf. Let it all out to the large-mouthed pure god."

She wants him to disappear, for everything to disappear, to wake up in her apartment, go to the Tea Lounge before hopping on the Seventh Avenue bus to the subway and then to Prince Street, walk two blocks to the theatre to finish the final touches on her creations before opening night. This is a bad dream. Except when she opens her eyes, it's the Chase River beneath her not the East River. How many years has she cried into the Chase? "I spent my whole life planning my way out of here," she says. "And I'm right back where I started with nothing to show for it. Nothing." Her arms flop out at her sides. "I'm lost, done, I don't exist anymore. I'm finished. Finished. I've become extinct. Everything I lived for is extinct."

You know nothing about becoming extinct, he says to himself. He takes a deep breath, a few steps, spreads his feet apart and stomps one then the other, "Many years ago the Ainu people of Japan called the wolf *Oguchi no Magami*." He stretches up and presses his hands together in front of his chest and repeats, "*Oguchi no Magami*, it means large-mouthed pure god."

A breeze blows up from the water, moves Lydia's hair across her eyes. She tells herself, *take a deep breath, take deep, deep breaths, and go to the local doctor, give in, and like all the members of the theatre company succumb to a prescription with repeats. Add 'pills' to the list. Barbiturates.* As much as she loves Rosa, who can really walk these things off? Her mother's right, *you walk right into them.* Kaito stares up beyond the trees, "*Oguchi no Magami,*" he says, "The large-mouthed pure god." The red lanterns swing in a gust of wind. "The Ainu worshipped the wolf, they believed *Oguchi no Magami* was created from the wolf and a goddess."

"What does any of this have to do with wolves?"

"Extinction." He hopped onto one foot, then the other. "The Ainu people, like the wolf, faced extinction. Unlike the wolf, they did not defy it. Their large-mouthed pure god was resurrected; they weren't."

No matter how many times wolves have been obliterated, they do not remain dead for long, they are resurrected, they fight back, like trees through city sidewalks, they return, they are indestructible, symbolic, otherwordly, like tree roots, like family roots, it takes years for roots to die, if they die at all. Wolves were the closest thing to godlike. "I have to go," she says. Her stomach knots.

She glances around for a path to escape on that will lead to an empty road with no end. She'll run, keep running toward the national park and search for the wolf packs that have been returning there. She'll run into Hélène Grimaud, the classical pianist, and her large-mouthed pure gods. The month will come and go like ancestors, like the Ainu people and Constance will call Raiden and say Lydia never returned from town. Kaito will recount their meeting in the woods in detail, insist she was on her way to town; when notified, police will comb the forest, drag long poles up and down the riverbed, exchange hopeless glances while standing over the thick green water, everyone will eventually go back to their lives and Lydia will be running wild and free with the wolves, and the river will take the blame.

Kaito and Lydia are quiet, thinking of the things they revere. Both afraid of losing what they worship. She doesn't want to tell Kaito that the one thing she revered is what she can't bear to face now, for fear he won't understand her reticence to help sew the wedding robes. She throws a stone into the river and says, "Over the centuries, kings, queens, men and women of the courts, the layman, courtesans, revered textiles, the motifs, the dyes, the weaves." It's not that unusual to him. His ancestors come from a culture that reveres much the same thing, just differently. "Textiles represented status, were a reflection of the times," she says. "But I revere textiles because of the textures, the weaves, it speaks to me, lets me feel."

"And now, they represent...?"

"Nothing. I have to find something new to love." She laughs. "Or just be satisfied loving nothing itself."

"A good step," he says.

A good step, she thinks. She stares at the pines, at their thick steady trunks, wants to feel their skin, the rough bark, their breath seeping through hers. "Whenever I run my hands over silk, cotton, velvet, tapestry I feel something. As soon as I touch a certain fabric I can see what it's meant to represent, to be." Kaito squints his eyes. "It's stupid, I know. I am attempting to let go of it, to get over it."

"Why let go of the thing you love, what moves you?"

"Because it's paralyzed me."

He prances on his bare feet, stomps them once, then twice.

"What are you doing?"

"Doing?" He wiggles his large toes, "You can learn so much about yourself through your feet. Connecting them to the ground leads to great awareness of the body." She looks at her muddy Converse, wiggles her toes inside of them. "Really?" she says.

"One must do what makes them happy without justification." He bows and smiles. That's what her father believed; he stuck to his guns. He had no interest in notoriety. He was a simple man, Constance used to say, and Sophie said that always bothered their mother. She wanted him to be so much more. *You're flittering away your talent here in the country, look at your father, don't you want to be a great man like your father? He was a great man.* Constance is not simple.

She wishes Henry to appear so they can walk in the woods and she can ask him all the questions she was too young to ask when they lived together, when he lived. The tears rise again and she bites her lip. Her father was the only person she felt anything for without having to reach for cloth. She watches the trickling water.

"The world is so different than when our ancestors lived, don't you think?" she says.

"People were different," he whispers.

"Like the Ainu people?"

"Like the Ainu. The Ainu were special, the first people of Japan, they were forced to conform, to let go of their own way of life, to be like everybody else."

Lydia hears her grandparents, feels their breath on her skin, "That's so awful," she says.

"It is part of why we do what we do."

"Why you are chasing away spirits?"

"It is my role."

He pauses, squints his smiling eyes and glances back toward the house. Raiden has gone to town to begin preparations for the wedding. He is not there physically, but in spirit he is and Kaito feels like he has already said too much but he leans closer to Lydia and whispers, "It's part of Raiden's program?"

"And what is Raiden's role?"

He leaps from one foot to the other, arms held up, hands dangling from his limp wrists. "He is the teller of truths."

Kaito tips his head to one side.

"That is something from my world, or the world I just left. I only just completed his wardrobe. Except our soothsayer was a teller of lies."

"Well, then, good you left that world." He hops.

It was in the woods not far from where they stood, she met a shaman on a school trip. His name was Wolf-walker and he walked the children through the woods explaining the messages animals deliver, how nature communicates. The message can be deciphered by the direction the animal comes from, and the type of animal. He taught them how to determine their spirit guides. Hers was the falcon. When she got home she slept for hours. She hadn't thought about the shaman at all until then. She regrets that. He'd exhausted her, frightened her, but she'd desperately wanted to be like him, like them. There was something about Raiden that was similar to the man she met. His wife was Ojibwe, an artist. She told Lydia a few stories and then turned her eyes away and said, "I can hear my grandmother say, 'Don't tell her anything else, the white man doesn't deserve to know.'" No matter how hard she tried, or studied, she could never be like the Ojibwe, never be privy to what they know. Like the Ainu, they were not allowed to be who they were. "I have to go," she says and strides across the yard toward the path to town. Kaito skips after her. "I'm sure Raiden would let you sit in on one of the sessions we are conducting with the children. You can learn a lot from his teachings."

She keeps walking. "I'm fine, thank you. I just need time."

Kaito raises his large arms in the air and says, "Wait, Wait."

She stops and turns around. "Let us howl, howl like the wolf, purge our sorrows to the large-mouthed pure god." His mouth opens. His lips round, head bends back and he howls, howls from his gut, from the very depth of that perfectly round belly. Lydia looks around to see if anyone's approaching to find out what the hell is going on. She looks through the trees to make sure a pack of actual large-mouthed pure gods are not preying on them. The woods remains still. Kaito howls. It reverberates in her gut. He howls like a wolf, like a large-mouthed pure god. She turns around and keeps walking.

"Don't tell anyone we met," says Kaito.

Lydia marches back toward the little white house. Kaito smiles at her and waves.

"I'm sorry," she says. "I appreciate your help, I just don't believe in that kind of thing."

Kaito places a finger over his mouth.

Her eyes widen with questioning.

"I am Kaito." He holds his arms out to his side, bends his knees, and stomps one foot then the other. He picks up his instrument and begins playing as he sidles to the left, then sidles right, quick steps, little stomps. Swallows gather in the trees. She comments on the beauty of the instrument. She's never seen anything like it.

"It's a *biwa*," he says. "Created in the seventh century. I am learning to play it more efficiently for Junko's ceremony."

"I have yet to even see Junko."

"You are better to keep away," he warns.

She gathers her shopping bags. "You should drop by the cathedral when you are done your shopping. I have things to build there. You can keep me company."

Her eyes laugh.

"But there are things to build here first," he says, and thumps his heart. There's so much to do in preparation for the ceremony. Junko demands her visions come to life and it's up to Raiden and Kaito to exercise it. "It isn't coming together the way it should," he whispers. Lydia asks him why but he looks away at the house as if her voice was the breeze.

He bows slightly and tells Lydia it was a pleasure to meet her. He places his *biwa* on a garden chair, kneels on the grass, stretches his arms in front of him and rests his forehead on the ground.

JUNKO REMOVES THE mask from her face and sets it on her bedside table. She waits for a few seconds before getting out of bed to make sure that Pipit doesn't come back for anything. She locks the bedroom door, peeks through the curtains and watches the young woman being paid to watch her run across the backyard and into the woods. "She will be eaten alive out there, too sweet, too beautiful." She tiptoes back to the far wall and presses her ear against it. "Are you still out, Waif?" Her scratchy whisper barely audible.

Constance stops dusting Lydia's bedside table. Having spent so much time alone in the house she's constantly thinking she hears something, even snippets of conversations the house was full of throughout its lifetime; the laughter, she still hears laughter and Sophie's voice calling her for something, *Mom where is my blue blouse, my red sweater, my white T-shirts?* Henry's singing or laughter or calling her for something, *Constance where are my rose cutters, my gardening gloves?* Everyone, always wanting for something. *The mother*, she thinks. *The mother. They only call when they want something?* She runs her hands across Lydia's bed. Looks around at her quiet room. Except Lydia. Lydia never called to ask for anything. In the echoes, she doesn't hear Lydia's voice.

Junko listens to the creaking floor, the murmur of speech and then a pause and humming. She pulls her ear from the wall. "Humming." She raises the mask to her face, "You are showing signs of improvement, *Makoto no Hana*. Humming. Perhaps there is hope for you beyond your cheating husband's arms, beyond your mother's." She scrapes her bending black fingernails down the wallpaper. "To have been you, growing up in this house, with a loving father and this mother, a proud mother. What on earth will you do without her?"

She pulls a silk robe over her cotton nightdress. She glances into one of the many mirrors placed around her room, tousles her already unkempt hair. Unlocks the door and steps into the hallway.

Constance looks around her daughter's room, at the shelves of masks, and clowns. The myriad of faces staring back at her, the unblinking, empty eyes. Did she push too hard, not push hard enough? *This is my chance to set you on the right path. I won't let you down. Raiden assures me he will help you and I believe him. One helps themselves by helping others. Isn't that right, Henry? You sent me the Counselors and you sent our daughter home, I suppose this is your way of telling me to get back on the horse, to give me a job.* She runs her hand over the framed posters Lydia kept of her plays. Traces the smooth, painted face, the wavy golden hair, long legs, the wispy red dress and high heels.

The room went a different kind of quiet, the kind of quiet that is playful but reassuring, like a lover who answers a question with a smile. *Okay, Henry, maybe I am yet to find out the reason why, if this is one of your challenges you're putting me through, I am up for it. It shows me you are still out there, you still exist.* She pulls the door shut behind her and walks down the hall into her own room, closes the door, falls onto her bed and weeps.

Junko tiptoes to the end of the hall and stands in front of the locked door that leads into the main house. *The door you are never to go through*, Pipit and Little-Nan warned her. "They are such worriers," she whispers as she turns the lock and steps into the upstairs hall. "Dark," she says. "For such a light-hearted family." The hall is narrow, red and cream striped wallpaper lines the walls, and the long thin rugs that cover the floors are squint and worn. She steps onto the rug, eyes her choice of closed doors. She looks back to determine the proximity of her room to the doors on the right.

She moves lightly. No creaks from the floor. She hears a tap run and waits. She stands in front of the door she senses is Lydia's. "At last we meet," she says and throws open the door. Sunlight fills the room. Junko slams her eyes shut. Her eyelashes brush against the wooden mask. The mouth a pursed slit, lips painted red and cracking with age. She steps into the room and closes the door, walks directly to the window and pulls the curtains shut. She tiptoes around, arms held up, hands hanging like rag dolls from skinny wrists. "Come out, come out wherever you are." She opens the wardrobe, flips up the bed skirt. Stomps her foot. "Hmph."

Constance lifts her head off the pillow. *Lydia*, she whispers. Her eyes shutting, she places her head back on the pillow and gives in to sleep.

Junko plunks herself onto Lydia's bed and lies down with her head on the pillow. *So this is what your ceiling looks like to you. Do you see the demons in it at night as I do? Does yours churn with grey clouds? Do you dream of escaping through it and being pulled into the sky to sleep there forever?*

Lydia's breathing becomes heavy. She stops and grips a pine tree. The spinning grows faster. She lies down on the forest floor, eyes hooked to the sky. The clouds churn, and she wishes they would suck her up into them, where she can search for Henry.

Pipit runs across the bridge into the garden and startles Kaito. She falls to her knees beside her brother. "I can't do this, I can't watch her go through this anymore." He takes her hands and they both rise to their feet, "Howl like the wolf" he says, "let it out to the large-mouthed pure god."

Junko opens Lydia's door, taps her fingernails on it. She looks back and around the room, "Clowns," she says. "Everywhere." She closes the door and disappears back into her room.

RAIDEN WALKS JANE down the long corridor that leads to the cathedral's front door. It is warm inside, even though the structure hangs onto the cool of winter. He thanks Jane for coming to see him.

"He's a good boy," she says. "Deep down, he is."

"They are all good deep down. We will look after him. It takes time, not everyone takes to the program right away."

"I worry about him, you know."

Raiden nods. He's been working with boys in the city who are far worse than Daniel. The absence of a parent is hard on a young boy. No matter what arguments arise around the matter. Raiden has been that boy. Raiden joins Daniel and the others at the front of the church. He picks up a hammer and watches him for a moment. Daniel struggles with aligning the two planks of the bridge. He throws down the hammer and the two-by-fours slam onto the floor. Raiden steps toward him. Daniel flinches and holds his arms in front of his face. "It's okay," says Raiden. "Leave it for now. Work on something else."

Daniel drops his arms. He glances at his mother. She's walking down the aisle with her head down. "Even monkeys fall from trees," he says and shakes Daniel's shoulder. They laugh and the other kids drop their guards and laugh with them. A chorus of laughter in the old cathedral, bouncing off cracking walls and painted windows. "Take a break, kids. And when you come back, go to the task you are good at. Choose a task you are drawn to from the choices presented. Do what you are good at."

They nod their heads, exchange glances, some rub hands in excitement, then a couple of guys hit each other and they all start running out of the main hall toward the main doors. Except Daniel. "Sir?"

Raiden smiles, and nods. "Does the task have to be here, on this floor, sir?"

"No."

Daniel claps his hands together and runs after the boys. Raiden sits on the edge of the unfinished stage they are erecting for the ceremony. His hand rises to his chin and he leans on his knee, looks around at the church he wants to transform into a temple for one day, for a woman he'd die for. The bits and pieces of wood, candles, tools; for a moment he doubts himself, this, the whole cause. *Because we made a promise*. He answers himself, *because I have to*.

Little-Nan runs into Jane at the door. Jane drops her unlit cigarette and steps on it. "Nice to see you," she says.

"Oh," says Little-Nan. "A fortuitous meeting." She reaches into the satchel strung around her shoulder. "Daniel brought me this yesterday."

She hands Jane the yellow sash embroidered with daisies. Jane turns the long wide piece of floral material in her hands. She shakes her head. "I don't understand."

"It is the tie that goes around the robes we often wear. It is where we begin our lesson. The tie that binds, you see." She hands it to Jane.

"Sure, I get what you're saying. Thanks."

"He wants you to have it but was too embarrassed to give it to you himself."

"That's silly."

"He says you don't understand what it represents, yet the more he learns the better he'll be at explaining it to you."

She grits her teeth, and purses her lips, grabs her cigarettes in her pocket "He told you that?"

"Yes."

Jane envies her porcelain skin, even with its cracks around her eyes, at the top of her lip. Her silver hair glistens. No one has been able to get Daniel to open up and say how he feels since Henry passed away. Henry had a way about him that kids responded to, they became like dogs wanting to please a master, all wagging tails and panting. Daniel hasn't opened up to Jane since his father left. *Since you drove him away*, she hears him saying. She keeps telling him she didn't drive his father away and that is true. The man she "drove away" was not his father and she hasn't found the way to tell him yet. Maybe he'll discover it in the program. Maybe it's best he doesn't know the truth.

"He will learn from this."

"As long as it doesn't turn him 'girly' if you know what I mean."

Little-Nan smiles. "Girly?" She bows and says she has to get to work, "So much to be done for the ceremony."

Daniel watches her from the edge of the playground. She waves and walks toward him. He runs back toward the church with the other boys. He grabs Little-Nan's hand and they disappear through the large mahogany doors, laughing. Tears drip onto Jane's gripping hands. She wipes them with the floral sash and stuffs it into her purse. She sits on a swing in the playground at the side of the cathedral and lights a cigarette.

Lydia stands at the edge of the woods looking out at the town where she grew up. It doesn't look as small as it felt then. Or as dull. One foot on the sidewalk, one foot on the soil of the path, she's reluctant to step back in time. Jane stops swinging and watches her old friend. *She's so thin*, she thinks, *and her short hair makes her look like an adolescent boy*, but those pretty features stand out even from where Jane watches. *She looks like a deer*, she thinks, *how a deer hovers between safety and venturing into our world.* They're the same age, thirty-five but Lydia looks so much younger. She always did. Jane looks down at her thighs squished into the swing, her wrinkled hands, the cigarette smoke billowing through her knobby fingers. Lydia rubs her rough palms. Jane wonders what she's waiting for. A traffic light to change? *She had everything, that girl, and look at her, like a deer scared shitless to leave the woods. Welcome home, fawn, what the hell are you going to do now?* For a moment Jane considers lifting her hand and waving. She doesn't. *You walked away from me when I needed you, to hell with you.* She throws her cigarette into the sand and ducks behind the far side of the cathedral before she's seen.

LYDIA'S CELLPHONE VIBRATES in her purse. The dry cleaner's sign turns from a green neon CLOSED to a pink OPEN. She considers going in and applying for the job she saw in the paper. She'll press and alter clothes instead of create them. Constance speaks of reinventing herself but was her situation really reinvention when she'd been forced to change? She grabs her vibrating phone. "It's chaos here, Lydia, Chaos. I can't do this without you. Please come back to the city. Even if you help me finish this from the apartment, no one has to know. You'll be happy, I'll be happy."

Her last day in the apartment Rosa called begging her to fight for her job. Lydia was drawn to a picture of her family sitting beside the phone. They were all young, her father's hair black and full, his lithe frame healthy, her mother like china, beautiful and fragile, Sophie confidently gangly, Lydia hiding behind curtains of yellow hair, gripping her navy cotton dress with dandelions around the hem. Rosa crouched to her knees, pressed her forehead on the apartment floor.

"Lydia? You there."

That is when she knew she had to go home to move on.

"Don't go back, Lydia. It's not the same. That's not the home you mean, right?"

"What other home?"

"What the hell will you do there?"

"Think."

"Think?"

"I need time to think."

"Who can think in the country, it's too goddamn quiet."

"Rosa, please."

"My God, you spent your entire youth attempting to get out of the country. Don't do it Lydia, don't go back."

She lay on the floor, stared up at the ceiling, like she used to look at the sky from the bare floor of the woods.

"I'm going to recount my steps, figure out where I went wrong."

"Lydia, you did nothing wrong."

"I must have done something wrong. I missed a goddamn stitch somewhere. Look at me, I'm a mess."

"For Christ's sake, everyone is a mess. You're at the height of your career. You've got to fight through this."

She sat up, looked around.

"Charlie trashed the apartment, left me a goddamn note that said I reap what I sew. I reap what I sew, Rosa... sew, S.E.W."

I told the guests you'd help them sew the ceremonial robes, will you do that darling. I think it will be good for you to get right back on the horse.

Do, do, do, do, dododo do do...

Step right up folks and ride the magic carousel.

Would you do that darling I think it's time you get right back on the horse.

It's what you live for, Lydia.

Round and round and round and around we go...

It's time you get back right back on the horse...

Step right up folks and ride... and ride and ride and ride...

The horse, the horse, the horse...

Do, do, do, do, dododo do do dodo...

The things we live for change, the things we live for change, the things we live for change.

Howl like a wolf, purge your sorrows to the large-mouthed pure god.

"Hey Lydia, you there? Lydia?"

Lydia drops the phone and grips her face with her hands. "I'm here."

She feels sick, the nerves beneath her skin churning. She sits down on the bench by the Imperial bank and closes her eyes. *Don't be sick. Don't be sick.* She gulps back water. "Lydia? Lydia?" *Howl like the wolf*, she says, *howl like the wolf* and she does under her breath, as quietly as she can without drawing attention to herself. She is so sick of drawing attention to herself. What is she doing? And the staring and the staring. She focuses on the dry cleaners opposite her. A normal job, she's got a normal haircut now, short and exposing her face, something she was always afraid of, but here it is for everyone to see, the bare-faced Lydia, and she'll buy normal clothes. "Lydia, for Christ's sake where are you?" Her eyes pop open. "Where am I?" She takes a sip of water. People stare at her, always staring. *What? What?*

"Lydia, are you there? We have to talk. I need to talk to you."

Stop looking at me.

"Lydia?"

She stares at the yelping phone, lying on the path. A woman walks by and picks it up and takes it over to Lydia. "Is this yours?" she asks.

"Lydia for Christ's sake, where are you?"

The woman looks at the phone.

"You okay?" she asks.

Lydia doesn't know what to say.

"You lost?"

"Very."

"Oh." The woman places the screaming phone on the bench and walks away.

Lydia sees herself waiting with everything packed at her feet for Rosa to arrive. Lydia wandered over to Charlie's wet bar and poured a glass of Scotch. Her head pounded from the bitterness of the alcohol and the strain of crying. She refilled the mug. The thought of breaking the news to her mother who had been happily married for forty years made her ill. Failing was not something one did in their family. They had all been successful. Even Sophie, she married well, she married a rich man, had a pair of exotic twins she named after Greek islands, and ran a thriving bistro in the city called Cymbeline, which Rosa and Lydia decorated in flowing red velvet curtains, gold chandeliers and cherry wood tables and chairs with silver chalices for wine glasses.

She downed the Scotch and dialed.

The phone rang. Constance answered and Lydia choked. As soon as she heard her mother's voice she was taken over with the fear of admitting she failed at the three things her mother excelled at: career, marriage, and motherhood.

"Mom?"

"Lydia? What's wrong?" She said her voice sounded worn out, dejected. Lydia held the phone away. It amazed her how with one word her mother described exactly how she felt. She panicked, unable to tell her mother the truth. She made it physical, said her chest was tight, breathing had become laboured. "Oh dear," said Constance, "you're exhausted, all those hours you've been putting in, take a deep breath."

"Mom?"

"Take a drink of water and count to ten." Then she added, "Backwards, count to ten backwards." Lydia thought about it for a moment. She told her mother she didn't have the hiccups, this was much worse than having the hiccups and she hoped she didn't mind but she was coming home for a little while. She waited for a pause, the silence that infers disappointment. Then her mother said, "Or is that drink the water backwards?" Lydia poured more Scotch and drank it backwards and said, "I caught Charlie with another woman, Mom."

Something didn't sound right. "Mom?"

Constance jumped to her feet when headlights shone through the bay window.

"Mom?"

Three women emerged from the red van, dressed in colourful robes tied with wide sashes, their hair swept up in buns on the top of their heads. Constance rubbed her eyes. Glanced at the time again, shook her head. Was she dreaming? A tall figure draped in emerald silk stepped in front of the house, bowed at the women and held out a long arm as Raiden approached them from the side of the house. "Mom? Are you there?"

"Lydia, I have to go, I think the emperor is coming to tea."

"What?" Lydia held the phone away from her ear. There was silence on the other end but not the heavy kind. "Mom, did you hear me? My marriage is over. Everything's crumbled to pieces. I'm coming home."

Constance listened to her daughter's voice, as she continued to watch the women, taken in by their elaborate attire and their soft powdery skin, black-lined eyes. Constance sat on the slipper chair. It was hot, humid, her head spun. The silhouette in a long emerald robe, head down, turned toward the house.

Lydia stared at the phone, "The emperor?" The bottle of Scotch shone in front of her. She looked around at the dishevelled room, at the ripped and torn trunk hose, pictured Charlie in the arms of Imogen. She thought how much the sage damask curtains hung like the backs of weary monks. Beyond the window there was an unfamiliar hue. A white chalky substance coated the sky, not like clouds, planes or satellites. *Dust*, she swore it was dust. What a mess, she thought. She closed her eyes and counted to ten, backwards, then the house went black. There was applause, she swore she heard applause.

Constance hung up the phone. Raiden poked his head through the front door, "Constance? We're here."

"Coming, dear."

She glanced over at the mantelpiece, at the white rose and the maple box at its side. "She's coming home, Henry. She's finally coming home. Soon all your children will be back where they belong, wasn't that your dying wish?"

"LYDIA? LYDIA?" ROSA stomps her feet on the old stone floor, members of the cast roll their eyes. "How much longer do we need to wait for these alterations, we have rehearsal in one hour."

Charlie approaches Rosa, "What did she say?" Rosa stuffs the phone in her back pocket and storms off and up onto the fire escape to smoke *Hope* and think. Imogen watches from the hallway, dressed in mauve lined in gold, smirking.

Nails and Twine

AN OPAQUE HAZE hovers over Main Street. Pickup trucks lumber along, kicking up dust and miscellaneous debris. She didn't appreciate the buildings her grandparents raved about when she was young that now stand out to her, the 1800s architecture, Victorian, ornate mouldings. The instant her feet touch the sidewalk she had walked along every day of her youth she's seeing out of ten-year-old eyes and the buildings became nothing more than brick and mortar again. She remembers how it felt to be young there, on her way to and from school, holding her mother's hand as they headed into the grocery store on weekends. People beaming when they saw Constance, asking for autographs which Constance would blush at on cue, her eyes covered in thick black sunglasses, a scarf tied around her backcombed hair, muttering, *"Do not touch anyone's clothes, do you hear me?"*

Echoes of laughter emanate from the empty public school playground. The old English portable leans to one side. She hopes to see her father walking across the parking lot into the building he took so much pride working in; he said being a principal of that school enabled him to be the type of person he always wanted to be, a man who helped raise many children. Beside it the Japanese maple the school planted in Henry's honour has grown sturdier, radiant. Constance wished they'd never planted the tree there out in public, it's a constant reminder of things she would like to forget. Red tulips circle it. The cathedral spire looms in front of her. She imagines the Counselors in there and quickly looks the other way.

People move between and into the bank, the grocery store, the antique and drug stores, the cleaners and the hairdresser, the café and boutiques. None of the faces or gaits are recognizable, there's nothing in their demeanors that evidence these might be the grown-up children she'd gone to school with. No one looks familiar except Mr. Randal sitting on the front porch of his hardware store like he's done since before Lydia was born. He's shrunk with age which makes him appear less menacing. She doesn't want to talk to him but Constance needs nails and twine. *Nails and twine?* Lydia glances at the list again.

Mr. Randal stands up and brushes sawdust from his jeans. He stretches his hand toward Lydia, she grips the shopping list. She doesn't want him to feel the roughness of her hands. She really doesn't want to feel him. He quickly removes his fading baseball cap that says "John Deere" across the front and rubs his bare head like he meant to do that and not greet her with the respect he has for all the Templars. He says, "Heard you were back living with your mother. Good, that's good, Nice to see you, nice to see you."

"I'm not living with her," she says, "staying, just staying for a bit to help my mother with the bed and breakfast. I'll be returning in a couple of weeks or so," she adds. His eyes narrow and he smirks. *It's true,* she wants to say, but refuses to let him know that she cares what he thinks. The floorboards move when she walks inside.

"Are you good?" he asks.

She turns to face him, bites her tongue. On his crooked legs, he teeters in the doorway. He's been an acquaintance of Constance and Henry over the years. Not too close or too friendly. One of those staples in a person's life, a reliable person to know. He lives above his store and though Lydia has never been up there, she imagines it's dark and has a green wool carpet and mauve floral jacquard curtains, left over from when his mother was alive, and china cabinets full of his trophies, a reminder of how much potential he had but didn't do anything with. "What about you Mr. Randal? How are you?"

"Can't complain," he says.

One day, not today, she'll ask him why he never left town when he had the chance to fulfill one of the many football scholarships her parents said he was showered in. Constance thought it was a shame Mr. Randal never amounted to anything. He could have been an all-star, a pro, some kid's dad to be proud of. Constance detected the "potential" in people and did her best to encourage those with promise to be successful. "You only get one chance, girls. Don't flitter away your talents, because in this life it's not so much who you are, but what you do," *What a waste*, she'd say, *he or she could have really been something*. That stuck with Lydia. She was petrified of not amounting to anything *and now look at me*, she thinks. She sees her mother before her, hands on hips, waving her long pale finger, "That Mr. Randal is a perfect example of someone who could have done so much with his life but let it go. Learn from other people's mistakes girls, they're in our midst for a reason."

Don't go back she hears Rosa saying.

Sophie let diatribes of that nature go. She was successful at six, winning summer fair beauty pageants, and public speaking contests, and all the Brownie and 4H and Girl Guide badges, all of them, selling the most cookies, making the highest fire, setting up her tent quickest, clearing the most jumps with her own perfect push-button pony. The sisters convened in Sophie's room after one of those talks and Sophie stuck her finger down her throat and gagged. Her way of letting it go, purging the words. Pipit's voice floats in from the night she overheard her speaking to Little-Nan below her window, *Words have no power, Words have no power. They're just words*, Sophie always said. Things slid off Sophie. Lydia used to think she was reptilian, attractive, thick skinned, oblivious at times. Sophie was one of those women who followed the natural order of things without question. Lydia was petrified of convention, yet petrified of failing. "We've got to get out of this town, Sophie."

"I will, at least."

"Thanks."

"Oh for God's sake, let it go. Mom's just obsessed with the notion because she had to give up her dreams when she got pregnant."

"I thought we were her dreams. She didn't want us?"

"Why do you think she pushes us so hard to succeed?"

"I thought it was because she loved us so much."

Sophie draped her willowy arm over her sister, the arms they both got from their grandmother, and explained that when her parents met in the city, Constance was at the pinnacle of her acting career. When Henry got news that the estate was too much for his parents to handle and that job he'd always wanted — to be principal of the high school he'd attended — was open, he whisked his young wife off the stage and plunked her in the country, into the depth and layers of the Queen Anne. She arrived kicking and screaming, under the condition she'd give it a try for one month;

when she got pregnant there was no more driving into the city every day to continue living her dream. "It's okay," Constance said, one night when Lydia asked how hard it was to give up what she lived for, "the things we live for change."

LYDIA THROWS DOWN the nails she's rummaging through. *What on earth does she need all these nails for? She's not handy, she bakes, wonderfully, but this is absurd, absurd.*

"You need a hand, Ms. Templar?"

Ms. Templar. Ms. Templar. She keeps her back to Mr. Randal so he doesn't see the tears. "I'm fine," she says. "Thank you." And stuffs a handful of mismatched nails into a paper bag.

A woman walks in and snaps her gum. Lydia jumps. "Well, well, well, look who it is. Miss Lydia Templar, I never thought I'd see you back here in our humble little township."

Jane stares directly into her childhood friend's face the way people do when they knock on a door and no one answers right away. They put their hand up to the window and peer in. *God*, Lydia wonders, *do people take one look at me and wonder if there really is "anybody home?"*

"Returning wasn't part of the plan, Jane. I did buy a one-way ticket."

"Still 'funny,' I see. I heard you were in town. In fact, I've been at the house and not once did you come and say hello."

"I had no idea, I'm sorry." Constance didn't mention a word about Jane visiting. Lydia tries to walk past her to pay for her nails and Jane moves in front of her. Mr. Randal steps closer to Jane and asks if she's looking for anything in particular. Jane walks around him and follows Lydia to the counter.

"I like your hair, never thought you'd go pixie." Lydia sees red, lots and lots of red. Downs a mouthful of water from the bottle she's gripping. The Janes of the world wait like wolves for Lydias to fail. Grandma Templar planted that in Lydia's head years ago. "Just watch," she'd say, sitting on the rocking chair in her suite where Junko now stays, "watch the eyes light up when news hits Grandpa's firm is failing, just like when your mother left the stage. People were happy, happy that they were not special anymore. They'll think they're going to be ordinary now just like them and watch them pounce, pounce like wolves do on the weak or old."

"Grandma..."

"But they will never be ordinary, no matter what they do in life, they will never be like everybody else."

"Grandma," Lydia stood in front of the chair, leaned into her grandma's face, like into a shop window. Her eyes didn't move when she spoke; she rocked and rocked in the chair her husband built. It never creaked. Lydia turned around and tried to see what her grandma might be seeing. There was nothing there but some kind of thickness in the air.

"I'm so sorry that life's been rough on you," says Jane. "Is there anything we can do to help?"

She speaks slowly, enunciates her words and mouths each one as if Lydia is deaf or doesn't understand English. *We?*

"Life's rough on everyone though, right Jane? It's not what happens to you but how you deal with it." She rolls her inside eyes, the ones she doesn't let anyone else see.

"Well, girls, can I get you anything else?"

Don't worry, I'm not going to hit her. Mr. Randal's nervousness makes Lydia nervous. *How is she dealing with the roughness of life?* Her fingers run across her palms. She's no stranger to roughness. She's buying twine and nails, nails and twine, perfect for a hanging and nailing a coffin shut — Jane's. It's not Lydia's fault Jane messed up her future.

Jane steps in front of Lydia and pays for the WD40 she grabbed and a pack of Native Spirits she shoves into her purse as if she doesn't want Lydia to see that she smokes. She smoked when she was eight. Her lips press together accentuating the lines sprouting from them. "What's it like having those counsellors staying at your place." She makes quotation marks when she says counsellors like she did when she said "funny" and winks. *Don't go there, Jane.* "Not your ordinary counsellors, eh?" again her fingers affect quotations, flicking up and back down like she's President Nixon. "Your mom is the one who got them into the recreation program and we all know how the Templars get what they want around here ..." *Wolves*, whispers her Grandma and Lydia looks around to see if she is really there. "... and the cathedral hasn't had a wedding in it since when? Oh yes, since yours."

Lydia stares at her old friend, sees a hyena not a wolf; no, the wolf is more regal, clever, beautiful, nothing compares to the wolf. She wants to howl to the large-mouthed pure god, pray for it to shut Jane up. Rosa's voice joins the conversation of whispers in her head, "Don't go back, don't run back to the place you spent your entire life clawing your way out of." Lydia grabs her shirt, rubs it between her fingers, cotton offers little, she needs wool at that moment, alpaca.

Mr. Randal fiddles with receipts on the counter and clears his throat, hums. "It is hot, isn't it hot girls, for spring? Hot enough for a swim, remember when you used to swim in the Chase behind the Queen Anne on days like this?"

How did he know they swam in the Chase behind the house on days like this?

"I suppose they're good people all in all, just not your ordinary types?"

Lydia shrugs, "I don't know. I don't fraternize with the guests. And what is ordinary, Jane? I really do want to know."

You're ordinary, isn't that right and you can't stand that. Well maybe we can switch places, you and me.

"Don't you wonder where they came from?"

"What do you mean?"

"Well, we all know they're not from around here."

"They're counsellors from the city, here for a change and a wedding."

"Oh, is that what they told you?"

"What did they tell you?"

Jane laughs.

"Maybe I'll gather a few of the old gang and we can have tea."

Lydia wonders if she looks a lot older, more fragile than she realizes. "Maybe in a while," she says. They had been best friends, but she was never friends with Jane's friends. There was no old gang. If she wasn't with Jane, Lydia spent time alone. She attended a few of the kid's parties when she was young but that's because it is an average-sized town. Everyone was invited to everyone's birthday parties and if you rejected the invitation it caused too much trouble. Not going to the parties incurred rougher consequences than attending, especially being a Templar. "I hate being a Templar," she told Sophie one night, everyone wants something from you." Then she'd bury herself under some heavy fabric and not come out for hours. "I just want to be ordinary." Sophie scoffed and said, "We'll never be ordinary as long as Mom's around and you've never been ordinary period, reptile." *Tactile.* Jane was ordinary and she was good at it. Lydia envied that. She liked going to Jane's house. Her mother was quiet and mild-mannered and served things like hot dogs and macaroni and cheese. Jane got to wear anything she wanted and could speak out of turn at the table. She dated. Jane's mother wasn't a celebrity, her family wasn't "known." She didn't have to behave herself all the time to keep up the family name.

"Nice to see you, Lydia. See you around." Jane starts to leave, then stops. "In case you're wondering what I'm doing with my life, I am a milkmaid. I work for cows." She snaps her gum. Lydia catches a whiff of her polyester-blend blouse and her cheap drugstore makeup that Sophie always said smelled like wet dog. She's failed in Jane's eyes and that incenses her far more than how anyone else feels, even her mother.

Lydia calls her mother, she needs to hear her voice. She pretends she's calling to let her know she'll be home soon and as soon as she hears her voice she lashes out at her instead of Jane.

"How is it going, dear?"

"What do you need these nails for?"

"They're for Raiden and Kaito, so they have a few less things to do."

"Mom, they work across the street from here."

"They are so busy. It's the little things people need help with."

"You run a bed and breakfast, Mom. Bed and breakfasts don't throw dinner parties and supply nails and twine for the guests."

Lydia's attitude baffles Constance. She says that Raiden and Little-Nan have become dear friends since arriving here and with so few friends left she's happy to oblige. "Darling, one day you will experience what it's like when your circle gets smaller and smaller. You will understand how important it is to have caring people in your life."

One day? Lydia hears the clinking of china and shuffling. "What are you doing, Mom?"

"Having tea." The scuffling of a hand being placed over the receiver vibrates in her ear followed by muffled words as if she was trying to listen to someone speak while under water.

"Mom?"

"Have to go, pet, see you shortly."

Lydia places the items on the counter and pays. "It doesn't make sense," she says.

Mr. Randal packs the nails and twine into a paper bag, "It's for the stage they're building in there."

Across the road the cathedral looms self-consciously. She shakes her head. "I don't want to know," she says. He smiles back and reaches out his hand to shake hers and he slaps his other hand on top of it, "I heard you did really well for yourself in the city, were very successful, leaving here was good for you. Even if it didn't last, that's okay." *Thanks,* she thinks. "Nothing lasts forever, Lydia. You had a good ride." She looks at him closely, wonders if he's spending time with the Counselors, getting help. His sentiments don't match what she's always known of him, the moment, his words, touch her. If he had the nerve he might invite her up to his dark trophy-littered flat for a beer to talk about what it was like to get out of the town they grew up in and go after what one really wants in life. It must be an awful feeling to know it's too late to change your mind, too late to go back and do things differently. She grips his hand, "But it came at a price, Mr. Randal."

His eyes glaze over, almost as if she said what he's always wanted to hear from someone else to put all those years of regret behind him and enjoy the fact that he has his health and a thriving business in a precarious economy. He smiles and grips her hand tighter. It unsettles her further to know that her loss, her failure to reach the pinnacle of her dream, one month before the production opened, is making everyone else feel so much better.

"You helping Raiden prepare for that ceremony?"

She watches three crows land on the cathedral spire; she turns back to Mr. Randal and shakes her head. He raises his eyebrows.

"There's strange things going on in that old house of God," he says.

"Aren't there always strange things going on in the houses of God?"

SHUFFLING FEET SPEED down the opposite aisle, joined by singing, a melodic trickling like a little fountain. Silver hair glistens in the sunlight streaming through the windows Mr. Randal never cleans. Little-Nan's back is slightly rounded. Her hair piled on her tiny head in a shimmering bun. Through the space in the shelves, she peeks past the electric saws and drills. She bobs her head and smiles at Lydia. Lydia shoves herself against the cooler. The breathy lilac fabric of Little-Nan's attire is laden with minute pink flowers. The texture is fine, like it might disintegrate to the touch, or if she sneezes or sighs, poof. It draws Lydia down the aisle and over to the one she avoids the most, the one she is supposed to be helping. She says hello and attempts to say who she is in case Little-Nan doesn't recognize her outside of the house, "I know who you are, dear," she says. Though she keeps her delicately lined and grey eyes down. "Is that linen?" Lydia asks, then tries to pull her hair across her face, thinking most people would begin a conversation with How are you? Or even, Hello. "And handmade lace? Is that handmade lace? It's incredibly intricate, like a spider's web."

"It is wide-weave lace over gummed silk."

Lydia bites her tongue, annoyed that she said didn't know. "Gummed silk?"

"I was feeling particularly experimental the morning I made this one." She giggles but not like a school girl, like someone who's truly tickled by what they said, by what they mean. The intricacy of the lace mesmerizes Lydia. She's worked with many different laces, this is different. Her fingers want desperately to touch it, to hold it to her nose, run it across her cheeks. The silks she worked with were mostly treated. The designs called for heartier versions. They were rougher with them and used sewing machines. Lydia wants to know what it was about that particular morning that drove Little-Nan to create such a delicate yet complex garment but she bites her tongue, tries to quell her curiosity by shoving her hands into the bin of screws. She regains control of herself. Little-Nan shuffles past with hands full of twine. Mr. Randal places the twine in a bag and Little-Nan turns and heads back down the aisle to say goodbye to Lydia. "I'm sorry," says Lydia.

"Sorry?" says Little-Nan.

"I don't know how to word it. I don't have the words." She looks down. Keeps her hand immersed in the screws.

Little-Nan reaches over and gently removes it from the bin. Her palm is soft but not without its divots and scales. "Dear, words have no power. We will see you when we see you." She speeds up the aisle, out the door, across the street and into the cathedral. Lydia follows her out and stands on the front porch of the crumbling hardware store. *Why is she buying twine if I am buying twine?* From behind her she hears, "Yep, strange things going on in that old house of God."

The Program

TWO WOMEN WHISPER to each other and stare. Lydia tries to detect a familiar pair of eyes, lips, walk, or smile. All those years amongst other children and she doesn't recognize anyone she may have gone to school with. She could arrange an evening with the women of her graduating year, a reunion of sorts, just the women, hold it at the cathedral and talk. Find out what they've been up to, are doing with their lives, and if they're happy. If not happy, content, okay with things. Are they wives, mothers, career women, peasants, milkmaids, mistresses, nuns, wolves, goddesses?

In the grocery store, two women stop to say hello and ask how she is. Lydia's almost excited. They're from Sophie's circle of friends and anxious to hear about her sister, especially her beautiful twins. *Really, the girls?* The women are interested in hearing about the normal things Sophie is doing like being a mother, things they can relate to, and what her husband does, they really want to know what her husband does.

"He's an actuary," says Lydia and they look at each other confused. "Oh," says Lydia, "an actuary deals with the financial impact of risk and uncertainty. At least that's what the dictionary told me." They laugh and Lydia's not sure why. She frowns. What must it be like spending your life dealing with risk and uncertainty and getting paid for it when most people spend every day of their life dealing with risk and uncertainty and financial uncertainty and don't make a goddamn cent from it.

"You okay?" Lydia.

"I'm fine, thank you," she follows their eyes and realizes she's caressing a pear and she throws it back into the bin. "Too hard," she says and the women appear uncomfortable.

They don't ask about Sophie's successful restaurant or the celebrity chef who runs its kitchen. "Have you heard of it?" asks Lydia, "it's well known, it's called Cymbeline, named after an obscure play our mother acted in."

"Oh," they say. The don't ask about the famous theatre Lydia worked at, the one the local paper wrote about when she was hired, or the costumes she created or the well-known thespian she was married to, things she would be desperate to know if she were in their shoes. They ask if Lydia has kids. Then one of them takes a half-step back and says, "You can still have kids though, right? You're not too old yet, are you? How old are you now?"

It was tempting to say, as old as she was when she left, *we don't age in the city. You don't age when you don't have kids* but she changes the subject and says Sophie's restaurant is one of the top ten in the city. They don't react. *Wolves.*

"Yes, Grandma, I know."

"What did you say?"

"We miss our grandma."

"Oh, yes, quite the exceptional woman."

"Like a man," the shorter one says.

"Like a man?"

"Yes," they say and nod in agreement. "I hope my daughter grows up to be a woman like that. Strong and doing things normal women wouldn't do, like architecture and designing homes."

"Women do that," says Lydia.

"Is your Maisy inclined that way," asks the other.

"No, but it's still early."

"Of course."

The kids, the kids, the kids. Lydia attempts to leave, and is sidetracked by pineapples. "Look how expensive pineapples have become," she says and picks one up and studies every inch of it. "Such a complex fruit, wouldn't you say?" They grip their shopping carts. "An amazing texture, feel it." She shoves the pineapple toward them. The women recoil. "Amazing texture, inside and out. Makes one feel a little like, risky, touch it." The women exchange glances and agree their kids love pineapples, then hesitate. Lydia misses Rosa. She'd understand.

The women talk to each other like she's not there and it makes Lydia look down at her feet to make sure she really is there. Had she stayed in the country, not moved to the city to pursue her dreams would she be like these women, shopping in poorly manufactured pastel outfits, planning what to feed the kids they seem to spend every moment obsessing over, happily? They aren't beautiful, but they're robust, skin smooth, bodies curved, the whites of their eyes white, a youthful white like young teeth and that's attractive. They're not harried or haggard. The women inch their shopping carts forward.

"Well, good luck to you," one says, the other one whispers, "It's a good thing she doesn't have kids." They push their carts off, chatting away with the energy gossip has and turn around every couple of steps to look Lydia up and down. She can't remember their names. She disappears down the sugar and spice aisle and stops, places her hands on her knees to catch her breath. *What is Rosa doing?* She pictures her on the fire escape smoking *Hope*, keeping it between her lips as she does and picking at her dried out cuticles with her free and aching hand, the Shiraz at her side, looking harried and haggard and in the city that's attractive.

A man walks past and stops. He stretches his arm up to grab grape jelly. He's a few inches shy of reaching it. Lydia notices and reaches it for him. He thanks her, then turns fully around. "I knew your father." She almost drops to her knees. "I worked for him. Albert, my name's Albert," he offers his hand and Lydia shakes it, notices how smooth his palms are, *peau de soie*. "I taught English at his school, at, you know." Lydia grips the jar. "I'm sorry about his passing. He was a great man." Albert sighs and pushes the wings of hair that frame his face behind his small ears. "Still is, I mean. You know, out there." He looks up at the Valu-Mart ceiling. She wishes she had something to lean on, to grab, not a shelf full of mostly glass jars. Albert sucks in his stomach, straightens himself like a cadet seconds before the sergeant checks his boots. "He'd be happy you're back. He said he always thought you belonged here and I understood. He meant it in a good way. He loved it here. This is your land." He removes the jar of jelly from her grip, thanks her, and carries on. *He is really gone, not just hiding somewhere in the Queen Anne because he wants to be alone, like he often did. You have to accept this, Lydia. Not yet, not yet. Our land. It's not our land. What does he mean?*

Lydia rushes up the aisle and looks around for Albert, she wants to thank him, to ask him if her father said anything else about her. Albert's nowhere to be seen.

She'll venture around town on a daily basis to pick up supplies for her mom, for the guest house. After seeing those women, getting a feel for their lot in life, Albert, it is essential she retrace her steps in the town she spent half her life in. She'll find the missing link, the stitch she may have missed along the way. Henry believed she belonged here. She finds that hard to believe, she thought he always wanted her to get out, to make a name for herself, be famous like her mother, like his mother and father, like Sophie is now. She doesn't want to be famous and she never did, she knows it doesn't make a damn bit of difference at the end of the day. She'll find a different path she could have gone down. The answer may not lie on a shelf in the sugar and spice aisle, or anywhere in the Valu-Mart, or Sophie's old friends, but the clues do.

She steps outside with her full grocery bags and glances back at the cathedral, at the large mahogany doors with the wrought-iron crosses on the front. Kaito walks out of the woods, across the road and through the mahogany doors. She thinks of going after him, she wants to know what it's like to revere a wolf, an animal, something that actually exists. She needs something to believe in and the large-mouthed pure god is the closest thing to tangible, perceptible by touch. Hélène Grimaud can vouch for that, she lives with wolves, they kiss her, love her. Perceptible by touch, like the ghost of Bach must be as it flows through her fingers. Tomorrow Lydia will wait by the bridge for Kaito to come out and chase away spirits.

"You look thirsty."

She takes a moment to think what thirsty looks like and pictures a bug-eyed gazelle tripping across a desert. She'll see herself that way from now on. Raiden smiles and says how hot it is; he's thirsty and would like to buy her a drink. They got off on the wrong foot, what better way to make amends. He points to the grocery bags, "Then I'll give you a lift back to the house."

"I'm fine," she says. "But thank you. I want to walk, I'm looking for something."

"I understand. Then let me at least alleviate you of the heaviness in your hands."

"What?"

"The grocery bags," he says. "But first, let me buy you a drink." The Carriage House pub faces them, a place she knows well but not from being in it. "You look like you could use one."

"The gazelle," she says. He thinks for a moment then doesn't say what he thinks.

"It would be pleasant to escape from the planning and executing of a ceremony that rarely brings out the good in people," he adds with a slight nod of his head. His loose hair falls over his face, in the way Lydia's used to and she wishes she could grab it off his head and run away with it, a new set of long locks, the complete opposite of hers, long and black opposed to long and yellow, not quite yellow. "Makes you wonder why anyone does it," she says.

"What?" he asks.

"Marriage."

"Ah, yes, marriage."

HE REACHES INTO the silver box around his neck. The monkey head smirks. She doesn't trust monkeys. He removes a cigarette from its silver tin.

"*Hope?*" she says.

"You know *Hope* when you see it. Lucky girl."

She pulls her shorn hair as far down over her forehead as she can, hoping to cover what she imagines is a flush face. "I don't think I do."

"Come on," he says, "let me buy you that drink. Do you drink?"

"Do you?"

Pipit exits the woods and crosses the road to the cathedral. Kaito exits the cathedral and stops when he sees Lydia and Raiden; he watches Raiden laugh. Raiden hasn't laughed in months. Lydia glances to her right. Kaito disappears into the woods. She wants to give Raiden the grocery bags and run after him, to howl with him, to have a chance to sift through the leaving spirits like old clothes before they're given away. Instead she agrees to have the drink.

Stretching his neck out as far as it can go across the damn front porch of his crumbling hardware store, Mr. Randal sniffs around. *It's none of your business.* She wants to like Mr. Randal. Constance told the girls Mr. Randal fell off his bike on purpose and wrecked his knee so that he couldn't play football anymore. He refused to leave his mother, like his father. Now the only family he has consists of nails, screws and power tools, and he can't even maintain his own place.

THE PUB'S FULL. The beer taps glisten. The walls are caked in framed drunks laughing. The bartender greets Raiden with a regular's handshake and asks how he's doing. He inquires about how the wedding plans are coming along and winks. Lydia never imagined Raiden frequented a place like this or that he even drinks. She likes the sound of clinking glasses, even the slurred diatribes of people worse off than her. The bartender says hello. He points and squints his eyes, "Lydia? Hey, good to see you. I heard you were back in town." He notices a blankness in her eyes and says, "Jim, it's Jimmy Reese, your dad's vice-principal's son, I was his son..." His cheeks turn red. "I am his son. He's the principal now. Shit, I'm sorry." There's nothing familiar in his face, in his mismatched teeth. "God, that was so confusing, sorry, I..."

"It's okay."

"I didn't recognize you with short hair."

"Oh," she says.

"What can I get you? It's on the house."

"Pint of Blue, I guess, what the hell."

"Yes, Blue," repeats Raiden, "the colour of hopelessness, the colour of melancholy." He chuckles like he's said something funny. The crisp bubbling liquid fills the glasses and she regrets not ordering the one with red in the name.

They sit at the back by one of the few windows. Raiden wraps his long fingers around the glass, sips his beer. Deep blue streams flow through his elongated fingers, delicate wrists. She asks about the house, when he bought it and how he likes it. It's a simple house, two bedrooms, living room with a fireplace, kitchen. No basement. A cabin really and that's what he loves about it. The location is ideal, beneath the pines, the river at his side, the isolation he likes. At this point in his life, he feels drawn to nature. Lydia drinks her beer quickly and drifts off as he speaks. Rosa will be struggling to complete the final alterations. It's the little things that are the hardest to perfect. Rosa isn't known for paying attention to the minutia, that was Lydia's job and if she doesn't get those things exact it will throw off the entire personality of the garment, the buttons, the lace or velvet trim, tassels, ribbons.

"... that the body has become dismembered." says Raiden.

"Wait, what?" she says. "Can you repeat that, I didn't hear what you said?"

"I read about and connected with the elements of dismemberment on many levels and felt I, too, wanted to ward off evil that way, to be able to express my whole self in my work, our whole selves, including my team."

"What does that have to do with the house?"

"The house?"

She attempts to piece together what he's saying without asking him to repeat himself and prove she wasn't listening. He keeps talking, "Many of us are trying to escape the claws and fangs of the dharma cave, the false truths one's raised with — conditioning, false expectations." He speaks without pause. Lydia's head spins. *What the hell is he talking about?* He spent a lot of time searching for where he belonged, he says. "For a home. For my home. Family."

She finishes her beer. She doesn't have to catch Jimmy's eye. He hasn't stopped watching her. She signals for him to bring her another, something she learned from Rosa, the swivelling finger she does in her sleep. His eyes light up and he nods too much and he's at the table in an instant.

"So you're good?" he says and places the beer in front of her.

"No."

"Oh..."

Raiden keeps his eyes down and Jimmy spins then leaves.

Raiden explains that his program is designed to ensure young people have the guidance to overcome obstacles, to find their way in the world and to have faith in themselves to go forward, to work toward possessing the key to unlock the barriers that prevent them from going forward, from past loss of any kind, faith, self-esteem, family, home, friends, pets, he laughs, anything and to never stop searching for happiness, for what makes them happy, not what they think they have to do, to follow their own path and to never stop striving. Raiden's philosophy echoed her father's.

"There is not only one enlightenment to be had," he says and swallows a mouthful of beer. "I call it the Dragon Staff Certificate program."

"The what?"

"My program, the Dragon Staff Certificate program."

She can't help but roll her eyes and she says sorry and looks around the bar, hoping that no one can hear what he's saying, but the old man in the corner is hooked on them.

"In the late 1600s there was a Zen master named Hakuin whom my grandfather told me about years ago. My grandfather followed his teachings because he said Hakuin was different from the others at the time. He helped ordinary people, the layman, reach satori."

"Satori?" she says.

"The ultimate enlightenment," he says.

It never dawned on Lydia that the ordinary had any chance of experiencing enlightenment, let alone the ultimate one. *What was enlightenment after all? A metaphorical light bulb dangling in front of one's eyes, the bulb on a miner's hat.*

Raiden keeps his eyes on the barely touched drink in front of him and says that when Hakuin's students had completed his tests, his koans, and he says, "defied the claws and fangs of the dharma cave" then they were on their way to possessing the key to the barriers that lead beyond..." He stops and looks up at Lydia who's running her hands across the napkin, "Let me put it in layman's terms, when the student sees into the true nature of self, the darkness is illuminated. We help our students work through their issues and reach a point where they are able to cope and move on, when they strive for and attain true happiness, see into the true nature of themselves..." *Is this laymen terms?* She gulps her beer. "...when they pass the koans, the tests, they are given their earned Dragon Staff Certificates. A bookmark-like object with Hakuin's drawing of a wooden priest's walking stick with the head of a dragon symbolizing the student's achievement of enlightenment; wrapped around the stick is a *hossu*, the ceremonial whisk of a Zen master; below it a smaller branch with the inscription of the recipient's name and the place and date where it was awarded, and the certification that he or she had truly passed Hakuin's two koans."

His lips move as his face transforms into what she imagines is a large-mouthed pure god. She closes her eyes. Raiden keeps still. So does everything else.

"Koans?" she says, "as in ice cream?"

"Does ice cream make you happy?"

"I like sherbet better."

"The sound of one hand and put a stop to all sounds on two sugar cones please."

"What kind of test is that?"

Raiden sips his beer, eyes brighter than they've been in months.

The mission of Raiden's program is to ensure that ordinary people have the guidance to overcome obstacles, find strength within themselves to strive for happiness and fulfillment, to possess the key to the barriers that lead beyond. He leans across the table, "One should not stop striving for enlightenment," he says, "and enlightenment and enlightenment and enlightenment."

The more he spoke, the dizzier she felt.

"Can children really reach enlightenment?"

He leans back in his chair, back straight as a board, eyes still, no smile. "I assure you that everyone who comes to us leaves on a better road than the one they came in on."

He calls his program the Dragon Staff Certificate program because he found that when the kids had something to work for, something tangible, that they could hold in the palm of their hands, hang on their walls, put in their cabinets, like a trophy, he found they stuck with the program and they kept striving for happiness and fulfillment after the program.

"By telling my students there is something to work toward, an object, something they can hold onto, grip onto, work toward like a medal, they stop doubting the possibilities of achieving what, to many, seems unattainable."

Lydia scoffs.

"The program can help you."

"Oh, I don't think so. I'm not much of a believer in that kind of thing."

"What kind of thing is that?"

"Those . . . " she waves her finger in the air, but not like Rosa's "another round" signal, as she attempts to express what she means without insulting him. " . . . kind of spiritual self-help type things."

He laughs and sips his beer.

"And I don't want to move on. I just got here. I'm tired."

She excuses herself. Raiden places his hand on her arm. "I apologize, I should know better than to discuss a dream in front of a simpleton."

"What did you say?"

"Don't take it personally, it is part of an ancient proverb I think of often."

"I don't like your proverbs. They're mean."

"Mean?" He smiles and finally drinks his beer like the other men in the bar, long hauls and lip-licking afterwards, large-mouthed laymen, striving for enlightenment at the bottom of a glass. "I need to go. I really need to go."

Raiden stands up and nods his head once, "Please," he says, "I am truly sorry."

She sits down but she has no idea why. Because she doesn't want to go outside? Doesn't want to remind herself she isn't where she used to be.

"My grandfather used to say it in his sleep:
'One should not discuss a dream
In front of a simpleton
Why has Bodhidharma no beard?
What an absurd question.'"

"And?"

"That is it." He claps his hands.

It is absurd. Lydia imagines the sword killing the man.

"Do you believe in *Oguchi no Magami*?" she asks.

Raiden raises his eyebrows. *Kaito.* "You've met my assistant."

His tone's changed.

"Briefly."

"Not that briefly, long enough to learn of legends, of gods."

Lydia's hands, hands like voles, blinded by daylight, Raiden observes, scurry across the surface of things searching for nutrients, so hungry, erratic, seeking, seeking the surface of things, the table, the napkin, the glass, finally rest like two goslings curled up in the cashmere cardigan she wears despite the heat. "*Oguchi no Magami* is a great thing to believe in," he says, "but getting too close is inadvisable. Even a god can be dangerous." He laughs. "But for now, tell me about your costumes."

The goslings wake and turn to fists and thump on the tabletop.

She leans in and whispers, "I am here to try and salvage myself, to get a grip, to move on. I am, and I'm sorry I snapped at you, at your crazy philosophies, your Dragon Staff Certificates. I think it's wonderful that you are so charitable and kind to those in need, children, lost youth. I wish I was young and could benefit from such a thing, I really do ... but I'm not and I am not a simpleton, far from it. I may not feel things like you do, or believe in what you do, but I have my own beliefs and ... "

"Age has nothing to do with it."

"Pardon?"

She raises her arm and swivels her finger. Jimmy nods and Lydia points to Raiden and back at herself and mouths, TWO. He nods again. Raiden keeps his eyes lowered. *Is he thinking? Scheming? Sleeping? Does he turn off and on when she looks away, a robot, programmed to transmit and respond only when she is facing him, to save energy, batteries?*

"Where do you come from?"

"The same place you come from."

"The city?"

He waits, eyes drop, then raise and squint. "Sure. Yes. The city."

"Why do people come here?" she says. "Just because the country has a healthier environment, less pollution and noise? Why the hell come here? It's no less frightening or threatening. The business of the city, the chaos, the variety of things to do, the wealth of job opportunities keeps one occupied so they can avoid the challenges that the country forces you to face, like really thinking about what matters in life. Maybe the country is the dharma cave and we're all falling prey to its claws and fangs. Maybe that's what's wrong with poor Junko, she's stuck in the claws and fangs of the dharma cave. That is why she does not want to get married. Marriage is one of the claws and fangs of the dharma cave, conditioning, expectation."

He raises his hand, and claps once. *Don't turn off*, she thinks, *stay with me*. "The country is frightening. It's frightening."

Jimmy places the beer on the table. He's quiet. Raiden smiles and Jimmy leaves. "Wait," says Lydia. Raiden shifts in his seat, takes a long drink of his cold beer. He's warm, tired, but not yet ready to get back to work. He wants to see the voles rest again, to transform into goslings. Jimmy pulls a chair up to the table, turns it around and sits, resting his arms on its back. "What's up?"

"If someone said to you they can help you escape the claws and fangs of a dharma cave, and give you this thing after with a head of a dragon on it, what would you say? Honestly."

He looks at Raiden. Raiden watches him.

"You don't know?" he asks Lydia.

"What? Know what?"

"That's part of Raiden's program. He teaches that here. Me and Gordo, my bar-back, we're in the program. Yeah, we're a month in now." He nods. "It's really helping. Sometimes you go through stuff you think you'll never get over, you know, and the Chase tempts all of us at one point or another."

Lydia wants him to stop talking, to shut up. "But you know everyone experiences loss, everyone. You move on..."

Someone calls him from the bar. Jimmy puts the chair back in the exact spot it came from and brushes his hand over Lydia's shoulder when he leaves. She remembers him now. Raiden's eyes gleam. Remembers Jimmy's brother, Syd, sunken blue eyes, a sandy mop of hair. He rode his bike into the river one night. The bike surfaced.

Raiden raises his beer. "The question was absurd," he says.

LYDIA GAZES THROUGH her beer, blue the colour of melancholy. "I don't get it Raiden, and I don't know what ordinary person would."

He points to her hands rubbing against each other. "You are not ordinary, Lydia."

The old man who looks like he's been drinking in the same spot his entire adult life raises his beer to Raiden. It seems as if everyone's watching Raiden as he continues, "When you understand, you belong to the family. When you do not understand, you are a stranger."

Not ordinary? She hears her mother's voice, "We think she might be blind." The doctors: "She's not blind." *Not blind but not ordinary.* She slugs on her beer "I'm sorry, but you are the stranger. We are strangers. And I think it best you stay away from my family."

Raiden exhales and closes his eyes. She's sorry, she really is, but isn't ready to tell him. *When you understand, you belong to the family. When you do not understand, you are a stranger. The sword that kills the man, is the sword that saves the man. Those who think one's insight exceeds others, has no eyes.* She's been reciting each one of the proverbs at night before sleep, on her walks in the woods, one after the other, hoping to break through the riddles and discover what it all means. But words have no power, Little-Nan says, so where does that leave the riddles of the masters?

"I left this town to try and fulfill my dreams. My husband cheated on me. I'm dying inside. I lost my job because of it, my career. Lost my job, the only thing that ever mattered to me. *The sword that kills the man, is the sword that saves the man?* Well it better not save Charlie after all this."

The jukebox plays, "Magic Carpet Ride." She grips the wooden chair. Her fingers feel nothing. "I understand and I don't understand. So where does that leave me?"

"In a strange family."

The old man shakes his head. The bartender touches his heart. The ceiling fan blows a napkin across her feet. In bold red letters, HAPPY HOUR. She stares at Raiden, at his shining black hair and eyes, eyes that she sees now have a glint of red in them, like the napkin, like the flames of a dragon, like the red silk she saw swaying in the woods. He lowers his head and says he'll take her home. On her way out the old man touches her arm and says, "Well, did you fulfill your dreams?"

The air is as heavy as a double-weaved Gosard. The man waits for her answer. Raiden looks at her — everyone looks at her, even Marilyn Monroe from a signed poster above the jukebox. "Yeah," she says, "all of them, but they didn't end the way I dreamt they would."

The door sighs when she opens it. Sunlight blinds her. Behind her in the dark, the old man mumbles, "Dreams don't end, dear, they dissipate."

She wants to call Imogen and ask her how she'd feel if the shoe were on the other foot, if she'd have killed herself yet. When she gets to that scene in the play does she decide it might be best to take it to another level for the hurt she's caused? If she's figured out that dreams are best left to when one sleeps? Lydia gazes back at the closed windowless wooden door of the pub, imagines that if she were to pull it open again, there'd be nothing behind it.

The Picnic

THREE MUGS REST on a tartan blanket that Pipit brought from the B&B. She'd always wanted to picnic with parasols by the river, sipping sparkling wine and giggling. The light of the sun cascades upon her making everything sparkle like angel dust, and a slight breeze kept too much heat and insects at bay. She giggles because that was what 1920s flappers did at picnics and that afternoon she wanted to be a flapper, sipping champagne by the river beneath her parasol. Her floral headscarf tied tightly over her eyes and her Mary Janes a little too big for her minute feet, the white dress she found along with the shoes in the unlocked armoire at the back of her room. The outfit bound together, the hat, the shoes, the glitzy pearls, the white dress with the drop waist and fringes and feathers around the collar and cuffs, a velvet ribbon, with the label Daisy dangling from it.

"I made that."

Pipit jumps and spills her champagne over the hem of the dress. Horrified, she tries to wipe it quickly with a damp napkin.

"Don't worry, it won't stain. May I?"

"Please." Pipit moves over and Lydia sits down next to her and they both stare out over the water, the weeping willow gently fanning them in the breeze.

"I wanted to be someone else for a day. I'm sorry I should have asked permission to wear these clothes."

Lydia had watched Pipit from her window, come and go across the backyard, disappearing into the woods, holding up her long robes as she ran. Always running, in a hurry. *She works so hard,* and had no idea at what but it was clear she was busy, and tired, and harried, even out here in the country. Weddings are stressful.

"I understand," says Lydia. "It's part of why I loved what I did. I made this for my mom years ago, when I'd first joined the theatre. I was practicing, always practicing and when she was upset with me, which I always thought she was, I'd make something she could put on and become someone else." Pipit pours two glasses of champagne and hands one to Lydia.

"She always wished she could have played Daisy. She never got that part so Rosa helped me and I created it for her, so she could be Daisy any time she wanted."

"I wish I could have helped my mother play the role she wanted to play. In a way it is what she is about to do. Be the wife of the man she loved, finally."

Lydia turns to Pipit. She looks away. "You are lucky to have grown up here. This is a sacred place, beneath the pines, by the river. A holy place."

She turns her pale-yellow parasol to hide her face from the sun.

"I see why Raiden wants to stay after the ceremony. We've travelled so much searching for this place."

"Raiden scares me."

"He's only keeping things in order," says Pipit. "He is very good at what he does."

"Helping people reach enlightenment?"

"It is so much more than that; he helps people to let go of what it is that prevents them from leading happy lives, or deaths."

Lydia laughs, "Or deaths?"

Pipit sips her drink, "Not everyone can reach enlightenment and very few women do."

"That's unfair."

Pipit laughs, peeks out from under the parasol and says: "Women have earned the reputation of holding grudges more than men and one cannot achieve enlightenment if they hold a grudge."

Lydia frowns and glances at the sky, thinks about the spirits Kaito chases away, the forgiving ones.

"Part of Raiden's teaching is to let everything go, so one can move on. Or else you'll remain on earth as a ghost," she said.

"A ghost?" Lydia pictured her mother. How frail she had become, not the woman she used to know. Her heart was broken, pining away for Henry, and Lydia has no idea how to help her.

"Female ghosts have long black hair, wear white kimonos and have no feet," says Pipit.

"It's so strange," Lydia said. "Out of the blue one night my mother said, I don't think the emperor has feet."

"Maybe your mother's emperor was a bitter woman in his last life!"

They laugh, but Lydia's not sure it is funny.

"If you don't let go Lydia, you will never rest."

I have feet. My hair is not black, nor as long as a bitter dead woman's ghost. I came here to rest, not to move on. She sips her drink and gazes into the river.

Mask of the Dead

"MOM?"

The house is quiet. Lydia places the groceries on the kitchen counter. Two teacups sit side by side, one with a drop of tea in it, the other empty and clean. Two plates, two napkins.

"Mom?"

Footsteps clomp above her. She walks down the long hall toward the stairs. She doesn't look at the photos hanging on the wall, or the shadows on the wall, she ignores the buzzing in her pocket her phone makes and the gnawing at her palms for the upholstery lurking in every room she passes. Her jaw is sore from pressing it together, helping to suppress urges and instincts.

"Mom?"

The banister is warm. It has always been warm as if the hundreds of times it's been clutched keeps it eternally heated, or maybe it's just the banister itself, which her grandfather said came from one of the greatest living, breathing beings out there — trees.

Moaning echoes down the empty hall. Lydia thinks it's the house, its melancholic heart. It envelops her with a greater grip than it ever has, more hollow, like the exterior of an unstuffed chocolate egg.

"Mom," she says, quiet enough not to be heard. *Does a mother decide to stop being a mother when they reach a certain age? Or does motherhood simply run its course and end?*

Sconces hang between the doors of each room, emitting a yellow light meant to act like candlelight. The dark-wood walls close in on her. Each of the mahogany doors look like people standing on guard. Faint scents of another time leak from the hardwood floors, the cracks in the walls that Henry would patch up but seemed to return with every new breath the house takes. Lydia tiptoes toward her mother's room. The moaning coming from there is accompanied by little squeals and murmurs. Lydia presses her ear against the door; she knocks lightly, afraid to frighten her. "Mom," she whispers. When she pokes her head through the crack in the door, Constance is visibly dreaming. Her small mouth open, lips moving. Her lithe arm glides up and down and her feet twitch beneath the covers. The bed appears larger. She realizes why. Her mother looks painfully fragile lying alone in it, deep in a dream, her subconscious trying desperately to tell one of them something.

"Mom, are you okay?" Constance's arm shoots up and Lydia jumps back. Constance sits up and stares at her. "Lydia? What are you doing?" Outside, the tinkling of the *biwa* carries through the woods and howling, she thinks she hears howling. "I wanted to see if you were alright?"

"I'm fine. I'm sleeping." Constance looks at the time. "Why don't you see if I'm alright when I'm awake?"

"You were moaning in your sleep."

"Nonsense."

Her eyes gaze back at her daughter. Lydia says, "Mom, I thought I did everything right. I worked hard, I . . . "

"You can't question what you did."

"But how can I not?"

"Because it doesn't make any difference. It's done. It won't change anything."

"Don't you ever question things you've done?"

"What does that mean?"

"I don't know, in general. Now Dad is gone..."

"How dare you?"

"I didn't mean..."

"Goodnight, Lydia."

"Mom, it's not night."

"You need to rest. People go through this every day. You'll get over it. We all get over the men in our lives."

"What?" says Lydia.

"Goodnight, we both need a good night's sleep."

She wanders back to her room, stops at Sophie's old room and peers in. Everything remains as it was from when she'd lived there, impeccable, like a museum: pictures, books, figurines, clothes. Seeing the clothes is the strangest thing, hanging limply in the closet like they did on the girls. A door closes, and then another. She sits up, listens. Junko stands on the other side of Lydia's bedroom door. Raises her hand. Lowers it. Feels for Lydia's energy, "Is she or isn't she home?" She slides down the wall, grasps her knees with her long wiry arms. She hums but thinks the humming might vibrate through the walls. Without realizing that might be what she wants, like a cat that whines outside a stranger's door for food. For the food, of course, one hundred percent for food, but something in the creature wants the attention from the stranger, to hear their soothing voice, to be made a fuss of, but not to come inside for good, not to become theirs. Junko is hungry, starving, in need of attention from a stranger, a stranger because she is a blank slate with a stranger, new.

Lydia turns off the light and closes the door to Sophie's room. She touches her hands, thinks about venturing up into the turret, *why not, just to look around*, then she freezes, tries not to breathe, not to move in the slightest way. One moves most when trying not to, like silence not being devoid of sound, stillness is not without movement, the body sways, the heart pumps, temples vibrate, nerves leap beneath skin, lips and eyes twitch. The pumping, the leaping, the swaying, the twitching, the thrumming grows the more you try to be still. The body vibrates. Blood swooshes, white rapids and all the stillness create the loudest noise; silence is not without sound. It's not quiet. Silence is a particular sound. It is a thing. Lydia grabs her head and whispers, "Stop, stop, stop." She doesn't want this thing to see her.

Junko rocks forward, backward, her hums not quite hums, like a bird's singing is not really song-like but snippets of notes unfinished. Her head is large in the position she's in. It dwarfs her, legs cut in half, curled over them the large head, spherical through the nest of black hair, each strand standing out on its own, separate wires attached to the engine beneath the hood of an old car.

"Little pearl, you caught me."

Lydia grips the door frame, glances toward her mother's door. *Mom? Mom?* Wills her cries to reach her mother's ears. Junko unfolds herself, rises to her feet, the taller and thinner, the more hauntingly radiant she gets, draped in white cotton, uncreased and whisper-white. Through the slit in her motionless face, she bares her teeth. She opens Lydia's bedroom door. The top of her hair touches the top of the doorframe. Lydia doesn't want to take her eyes off her to look down at her feet. *Does this creature have feet?*

"You are feeling better these days, hmm?"

Through the mask her voice is low and gravelly, like that of an old man.

"Better?"

"Different?"

"Different?"

"A circle will not release us. Are you willing to take yourself round and round and round and round? To be a dog chasing its tail. Did you know a dog chases its tail when stressed? Yes, it is not a game, it is not for fun. The chasing of the tail is trouble."

How do you know that? Lydia wants to ask.

The door into the guest quarters stands wide open, inside the hall, a glimmer of flame, candlelight.

"Chew tighter on that frame," says Junko, "than on your cheeks. The chewing I can see your teeth have on them through the twitching. Yum Yum. You will be sick with dizziness and no further ahead from where you started. I have time. I am used to dizziness now. Fine."

"What? Stop, please."

"You're dizzy? Dizzy, dizzy, dizzy, dizzy."

"Stop."

Junko nods. She holds her arms out to the sides. Palms up. "Stop, stop," she says mimicking Lydia, a high-pitched, voice. Her head turns to the left, then to the right. Lydia wonders about the thick façade on her face, through the slit for a mouth she watches teeth disappear.

"Why are you doing this to me?"

The head moves sideways.

"The mask? Why the mask?"

"Hmm, yes, why the mask? Good start. Better."

"Better?"

"Different?"

"You said..."

"Why the mask?"

She nods and retreats down the hall through the guest quarter's door.

"Why the mask, good question, little one. And an eternal one, no?"

She curtsies and closes the door, a click of the lock and a flurry of high-pitched questioning from Pipit follows, the words indecipherable, the tone audible, like silence.

LYDIA RUSHES INTO her room, shuts the door, considers shoving her dresser across it and turns the night table light on. She gasps. Her clowns are in her bed, their heads on her pillow, grimacing at her. "Jesus," she says and stares at the wall she knows Junko is on the other side of, runs her hand over it. She can't sleep here anymore. A knock at her door startles her.

"Lydia, I'm sorry to bother you, it's Pipit."

Lydia waits, unsure if Junko is playing a trick with her voice.

"May I come in?"

"Okay."

Pipit pokes her head into the room. She waves at Lydia, steps in and closes the door.

"I apologize. Junko is not quite herself."

"Perhaps she is more herself than you realize."

Pipit holds her hand up to her mouth. "She is going through a lot."

"It's hard for me to sympathize."

"We are doing all we can."

"Why?"

"Pardon?"

"Why are you making her do something she doesn't want to do? She's clearly miserable."

Pipit backs away and opens the bedroom door. She looks over at Lydia's bed, then back at Lydia. "I'm sorry to have bothered you."

"I'm sorry, what did I say?"

"She is making us do something we don't want to do."

Pipit closes the door behind her.

"God," Lydia leaps to her feet and runs after Pipit. The hallway's dark, the door closes to the bed and breakfast. Everything's quiet. Too quiet to risk knocking. Quiet, but not silent.

A Stop to All Sounds

THE MORNING AIR is cool for the first time in weeks, the sun slices through clouds, warming sections of Raiden and Kaito's walk. Scents of fresh cut grass and pine remind Raiden of spring mornings as a child walking to school. The surroundings quiet enough to hear birds and the occasional voice or cough, the murmur of early commuters' cars, a wrench, or some type of tool, dropping onto concrete, a barking dog, frogs. He loved those mornings, when not everyone had risen and specific sounds were audible, and smells decipherable, and the sense of freedom he felt amidst them. He slows his gait so he can watch Kaito without being obvious. Kaito is the age that Raiden was when things changed, he wants to see if Kaito might be reaching a similar phase. Is he looking down instead of up in wonderment at the tall pines, the woodpeckers as large as crows, the lilac sky inching through cracks in the treetops, is he daydreaming, with a slight glide to his step, are his shoulders straight or hunching over, is he picking up his feet or dragging them?

Kaito stops. He doesn't turn around. Raiden's not sure if he should keep walking past him, or also stop. He laughs to himself.

Clever boy, he thinks. *You are not me and in that I feel you are on a completely different path than I was at your age.*

"Touché," says Raiden.

"Be careful what you teach, master, it is you who gave me eyes in the back of my head."

They walk the rest of the way in silence.

RAIDEN PLACES NAILS and a hammer onto the counter and rings the small bell. Mr. Randal comes from upstairs. "You trust leaving your shop alone like this?"

"I don't trust anything. I have a camera. I was watching you."

Raiden laughs, but it's unsettling to know he was being watched.

"More nails?"

"A few more, yes."

Raiden hesitates asking the questions he needs answers to. Knowing cameras are in place to watch people, he's unsure of the conclusions Mr. Randal will jump to. Now Raiden senses he's like those who gossip, especially the older they get. He'd lived in villages where gossip ran rampant, the bored and nosy, sniffing around everyone's business like rats. Mr. Randal doesn't strike Raiden as rat-like though, his nose rises into the air more like an astute dog catching a scent.

"Did you know Henry Templar well?"

"Yes, everyone did."

"I mean, *really* know him?"

"Oh," Mr. Randal touches his chin and thinks for a minute. "Well, I don't know. I suppose I always thought I did. Such a good man, the kind you take the word of."

Kaito pokes his head into the store and asks Raiden if he's ready. The class is about to start, the boys are waiting. He nods, takes his bag of nails and hammer and leaves.

Jane pops her head in and asks Mr. Randal if he needs any milk. He thanks her and says he's fine, then goes after her and asks if she has a minute. She stops for him. "What does your boy say about that lot?"

She shrugs. "He likes them. He likes them better than me."

"Well, that's good then."

"No, it's not."

Mr. Randal apologizes, says he didn't mean it like that.

"All he says is every one of them has sacrificed something to do what it is they feel driven to do."

"What does that mean?"

"I don't know. I haven't had a chance to find out. You know teenagers, it's like pulling teeth."

There was something familiar about Raiden and Mr. Randal won't rest until he figures it out. Nails. *Who buys nails like that, a few here and there?*

LYDIA BOLTS UPRIGHT and gasps. A figure looms at the foot of the bed, from the wide arms of a long white veil, bent black fingernails claw the darkness, the face pearl white, scarlet lines jutting out from the corners of the eyes. The ruby mouth widens, screaming without sound. Lydia grabs the sheets, holds them to her chin. The figure moves closer to the bed, towers over as if on stilts. The mouth closes and stretches across the still pale palette and giggles.

"What do you want?" asks Lydia.

"It is about time someone answered you. That's what you want isn't it, for someone to give you answers?"

She tries to speak again but can't.

"Were you happy?" it asks.

Its breath is warm. Its hoarse voice rattles her bones. Lydia stares at the blankets, stares at the tips of her fingers, at her hands. Those rough hands. To stop a nightmare, stare at your hands. When she looks up to attempt an answer, it is gone. The silver birch branches wave and scratch against the window. The sky's brightening. She slams her head back down on the pillow. She's sweating, cold, out of answers. *Happy?* She has no clue where to go from here, not even back to sleep where the demons are.

The door flies open. Lydia jumps. Constance storms into the room, past the bed, and stops at the window. She throws open the puddle of voile and knotted draperies, grabs the sheets from over Lydia and says, "That's it! I'm not going to watch you throw away your talent, all your experience. That boy kept you in repertory theatre when you could have been designing costumes for Broadway, the movies, the queen's wardrobe. Your father would be horrified to see you lying around like this, feeling sorry for yourself. Templars don't wallow they..."

"Work?"

"They survive!"

Constance grips the back of the pale blue slipper chair.

What is she talking about? Repertory theatre?

"And there's no time like the present to mend a broken heart."

Constance sits on the edge of the bed and points to the window. "It's time to get back on that horse."

Lydia's voice storms up from her gut, "What horse?" She pictures a thundering black steed approaching her in the woods, then the gold and decorated carousel, and the white pony with the overgrown hooves from her childhood. She grabs her head.

Constance puts her hands on her daughter's feet and says, "Raiden and Little-Nan are expecting you at ten o'clock this morning at the cathedral, Lydia. It's all arranged."

"You didn't check with me."

"This is my house."

"Mom."

Constance demands she shower, does something with her choppy hair and applies a bit of mascara and lipstick to her wan face, something she hasn't done since leaving the city. "I want to see you downstairs in twenty minutes." Constance rummages through the closet. Onto the bed she throws a pair of unworn dark blue jeans and a floral blouse that Lydia has never seen before. She grabs it, runs her hands across the natural fibres, no synthetics, smells the purity.

"It's time to move on," says Constance. "You're not getting any younger, you know."

Then she turns around and holds her daughter's chin in her cool hand. "Do this for me, Lydia. I need to get on with my life too, and to be honest, you're bringing me down." Her tiny grey eyes water. She throws Lydia's painter's dungarees, which she always wore at the theatre, into the laundry chute and slams its door. "Do not wallow in the past, Lydia. Take it from me."

Constance storms around the room tidying, mumbling about when they were girls she wanted nothing more than for them to be happy and no matter what kind of mother she tries to be she couldn't prevent the damage the wrong man can do. "I tried to warn you." *Did she?* Lydia had no recollection of her mother sitting her down and talking her out of marriage. In fact one of the reasons she got married was Sophie said it's what every mother wants for their daughters, a man to take them off their hands, and give them grandchildren to fill them again. She got married because she thought it was the right thing to do. She realized Sophie spent way too much time with their great-grandmother. Unlike their grandmother, she rallied for the claws and fangs of the dharma cave.

"I did all I could to dissuade you but you don't listen, Lydia. You do not listen and now I have a chance to make things right for you and it sure as hell is not going to be allowing you to live in the bed you grew up in. I'm doing this for you, for your father."

"For Dad?"

Constance hadn't held her in her arms like she needed her to or asked about what happened. She hadn't stroked her head and said, "It's okay, all men are a risk, especially actors." She didn't ask for the details. She always used to say, *come on then, tell me all about the day and don't leave out the details. I want to know everything.* There was so little to tell then. Now she's forcing Lydia to do something she doesn't want to do, which is out of character. *When in life does a child get to do exactly what they want without worrying about what their mother thinks? Like sleeping all day or even failing?*

When you become a mother, she imagines Sophie saying from a shining family photo on the wall.

Lydia fades into the white sheets, embarrassed, she feels too huge for the bed. She wants to escape her mother's frantic fussing and intolerance of her taking time to rest, to convalesce. It never occurred to her that just because she grew up in that house, she had no right to come back and call it home.

Constance pauses and walks toward the window. "You were

always a bit like a squirrel, Lydia Templar, industrious, extremely industrious, busy, busy, busy, but you forget. Forget the important things."

A squirrel, like a squirrel because she forgets the important things? Lydia peeks out from under the sheet, "Like where I buried a chestnut, Mom? I don't understand."

"What are you doing?" asks Pipit.
"Sshh," Junko giggles. "The waif is getting a talking to."
Pipit tiptoes to the wall and presses her ear against it.

"I hang onto everything, Mom. I don't forget." Constance watches the rising and falling of the white sheet, the point of her daughter's nose, the large round forehead Henry knew was the sign of a clever girl. *Clever girls don't bury themselves in the beds they grew up in.*

Lydia escapes the bed and reaches for the clothes. The breeze brushes the muslin sheers across her shoulder. The mirror catches their reflections, mother and daughter. They used to be the same height. Constance has lost inches. She is getting closer to the earth compared to when she used to reach for the sky. They are thin, faces pale, drawn and locked in the same expression, bewilderment. Lydia reaches out her hand. "I haven't forgotten what's important, Mom." Constance shoves it away and says, "The one time I needed you, the one time I needed you, you forgot I was alone. You never came home to me when I needed you." Lydia's mouth drops open. *My God, that's it.* Constance scurries out of the room and down the creaking stairs.

"You were never home, never here when I needed you — work,

work, work," she hears Charlie say. *From where? Charlie?* "Those damn fabrics; you love a goddamn terry cloth robe more than me." Lydia punches the duvet; it heaves. Rosa glares at her through polished glass. "Go to hell," Lydia says. "You're not that friggin' attentive either, pal."

Pipit covers her mouth and Junko laughs to herself, happy. "She is upset, good. Maybe it is about time someone else pried open her eyes. One cannot look inside forever."

Pipit rolls her eyes, *practice what you preach, oh wise one.* "Enough," she says. "She will sense you there, eavesdropping."

"Perhaps it is your nosy ear she will sense."

"Junko, please."

"Hmph, worry, worry, worry, all that worry will draw a map on your face leading you to death in a hurry."

"Death in a hurry, is that not what you want?"

Junko stands up and towers over Pipit, their eyes meet, challenging each other equally.

Pipit backs away and busies herself. She fluffs the down duvet and runs her hand over the cover, takes a moment to look around the room that she never sees lit up. It is covered in the mirrors Junko brought from the city, a thousand beds and vanities and slipper chairs, and flames stretch for leagues and leagues through them. "I cannot bear what is happening to you," Pipit says.

Junko waves her away. "Do not worry, *Makoto no Hana*, I have lived for this."

Pipit tries not to cry, attempts to remain professional. She studied hard to be able to handle patients like Junko. When she left the hospital to work with Raiden she knew what she was taking on. Everyone said she was a fool for leaving her position, but she needed more; she needed to return to what she loved. When she first saw Junko in the hospital waiting room, her hair dishevelled and static, eyes fixed on a faraway goal, Pipit's heart swelled, and she bowed without thinking.

She leaves Junko alone to calm down, and get herself ready for the day. Junko locks the bedroom door behind her. She removes the blue robe hanging in front of her and drapes it over her frail body, just like Pipit dresses her. Imagine all those years she dressed Pipit and now she is dressed by her own child. "Where have my claws gone. Wagtail. What do I have except for death? This little Pipit has control over my actions, this little Pipit." Junko chuckles.

"I heard that," says Pipit and reaches into her pocket to ensure she has the key that Constance has given her.

"My own mother used to wrap my kimono differently!" yells Junko through the door. Pipit rolls her eyes and runs downstairs, her hand picking gold dust off the banister.

LYDIA RUBS HER hair with the towel, and pulls on the jeans, one leg and then the other, slowly, like a schoolgirl reluctant to go to school; the cotton blouse is light and fresh against her cleansed and fragrant skin. A new sensation, or maybe one she'd felt a long time ago but had forgotten. She checks the mascara her mother bought for her and left on the vanity; despite herself she adds a small line of green shadow on her eyelids to pick up the green in the blouse matching the leaves of the red roses and realizes it matches the colour of her eyes. Eyes she hadn't looked at this closely in years. Eyes usually hidden by hair. She was always looking into other people's eyes, in mirrors, backwards eyes. Her lips grow with the strokes of red she applies to them to match the roses. Her face smiles at her, which makes her shyly wave at it.

She spins around when she hears a tapping on the wall. It grows louder, becomes a knock. She walks toward the sound and stares at the wall. Three more knocks and, "Lydia?" Lydia grabs her head. "No," she says. "Stop."

"You must listen to your mother."

Eyes press painfully together, "I know, I know, please stop, leave me alone."

Lydia runs her hand down the striped wallpaper, its texture like stucco, pink and pale blue. She presses her palm against it, "What do you want from me?"

Junko presses her hand against her red wall, striped with gold, its texture velvet. "I want to know what it's like on the other side." Her whisper carries through the wall, Lydia jumps back.

JUNKO WAITS, THEN walks over to the vanity, stares at her pale face, and head, a perfect full moon. The results of treatment when an aching side came back terminal. She reaches for a bottle filled with thick gold liquid and it oozes onto her hand, she oils her face; from a small white tub she applies a thin layer of wax. She rubs her hand on a white towel. Lydia waits for the wall to speak again; it's quiet, but not a quiet she trusts. She runs a comb through her hair and realizes it's grown enough to grab into a small ponytail, which is a relief. She grabs her cashmere cardigan and rushes downstairs.

Junko takes a deep breath and applies her thick white-base makeup, made of rice powder, "Oshiroi," she whispers. "Oshiroi." To sound like her mother when she asked her years ago what she was applying to her already beautiful face, *Oshiroi*. She covers her face in it with broad strokes, one side, then the other, the eyelids, the chin, neck and down the back of her neck as far as she can reach. She lines her eyes in black, extending the edges out across her temples, and a thick red to her lips. She grabs the black wig from the Styrofoam head it rests on. She pulls it over her hairless head. From a standing hanger in the corner she removes an aquamarine robe lined in coral, the bottom embroidered with flowing vines, down its side a walking stick with the head of a dragon.

Pipit knocks on the door. "Ah, little one, your timing is perfect." Junko lets her in and Pipit begins to wrap the robe around her, gathering and gathering material until it is fit perfectly to Junko's frame. She ties the sash around her waist, the *obi*, she presses her ear to the wall. Stillness. Good, she thinks. We shall see you soon.

Lydia's ankles crack leaping down the stairs hoping to catch the one person a daughter should never let down. The voices were right, *listen to your mother, listen to your mother, she knows best*. Constance stands in front of the fireplace, her thin hands caress the wooden box on the mantelpiece. The sun pinches through the pleated jacquard weave curtains, and Lydia throws them open as she passes. "Mom?" Constance swats the air. She whispers something Lydia can't hear, then her head spins toward the window. "Look, look there he is, over there, over there, by the fish pond. Lydia, do you see that?"

Lydia rushes over and peers out the bay window almost afraid of what she'll see. There is nothing there.

"Look, look, there he is, the emperor."

The Japanese maple weaves in the wind. Its shadow dances against the white living room wall. There's no sign of anyone outside, inside on the walls are the faces in the shadows screaming without sound.

"Mom, what exactly do you see?"

She looks away from the window and deep into Lydia's eyes, but Lydia doesn't think it's her eyes she sees. Constance rubs her head, looks down at her feet. "Oh, Lydia." She hums, fingers flitter on the air like playing piano keys.

Constance plunks down on the floral chair. "Mom. I'm here, I'm ready. It's okay. I am here for you now." Lydia grabs her hand and Constance weeps. "Please, Mom, it's okay. Everything's going to be okay." But she has no idea what she means.

"Oh, Lydia, I'm so tired. I'm losing it."

"We're all losing it, Mom. It's what we do."

Constance grips onto her daughter. Lydia holds her in a way she hasn't held anyone and she never imagined a mother could feel so small, all viscose and bones. She vibrates with tears. The drone of the still house and sobbing drown out the swallows, the buzz of the neighbouring tractor. There was a time when Henry would have walked into the room and saved the day with a clap of his hands and a deep laugh, taken them both in his arms, singing something low and melodic, *I've got you deep in the heart of me* ... or *I've been working on the railroad all my live-long days, I've been working on the railroad* ... until they all laughed and felt like adversity was a myth, something that would never happen to their family. Lydia wants to scratch out the thunder of absence, her mother's tears, air, the sound of space, the constant, heavy murmur loss creates. "You were not there for me when I needed you, Lydia. My own girls. I was all alone in this unforgiving house. Everyone left me. My family, I had no family."

In the mirror, Lydia sees herself and despite the touch of colour on her face, and the fresh floral blouse, she looks grey and twitchy and vacant — a squirrel. From the top of the stairs Junko peers down on mother and daughter. She watches their arms drape around each other and wonders how that feels to be held by a daughter like that. *I am here to say goodbye to things I love, to move on. That girl does not know how lucky she is. If there is any role I have left to play in this life, I want to know what it is like to be you.*

LYDIA GRIPS HER mother close to her. *How does one mother a mother?* She peeks at the shadows watching from the wall, always watching on the wall. She pictures the figure at the end of her bed, the dream that breathed, that scratchy voice she swore was there in front of her, "Were you happy?" She pictures Raiden draped over his beer, talking about defiance and keys to barriers that lead to beyond and dragon staff certificates. She wants to howl, howl like a large-mouthed pure god.

"Mom, were you happy?"

"What?" She manages a slight laugh through her tears. "What kind of question is that?"

Lydia thinks of Raiden's riddles. "An absurd one?"

"Once," she says. "I was happy once."

If Raiden's words are true and enlightenment is like the search for happiness, then one should be happy more than once. "Mom, you can be happy again."

"No, dear, you can. I'm just waiting to join him now. I'm trying to keep busy until then."

Constance cries into Lydia's arms, like a heartbroken child. She pictures Charlie in costume, pontificating in a man-made town.

One who thinks one's insight exceeds others has no eyes.
The sword that kills the man is the sword that saves the man.
If you understand, you belong to the family...

She holds her mother out from her so she can look into her watered-down eyes. She shakes her slightly, a bit like a rag doll and says she has to go if she's going to be at the cathedral by ten. Constance smiles and buries her head into her daughter's arms.

"JUNKO," PIPIT WHISPERS as loudly as she can. She waves her back into the guest quarters. She hisses at Pipit as she passes. The door closes, locks.

"What do you think you are doing? I've told you time and time..."

"Do not speak to your mother like that."

The Boy in the Woods

LYDIA FACES THE two signs at the end of the lawn, glances back and up at the guest-room windows, the curtains remain shut. She looks over her other shoulder at the fish pond, just in case the emperor has returned, is fishing. Lydia stopped naming the fish. Once named she became too attached to them and when they died she mourned. "Who mourns fish?" asked Sophie. When she stopped naming them they lived longer, now the nameless fish are huge and outliving the rest of the family. Her phone has been quiet for two days. She's not sure if she's relieved or nervous. She steps onto the path leading to town; the trees watch, always watching, they watched her and Sophie for years. *What do the trees know? What do they say about Sophie and me?* She places her palm on the cool, curved bough of an elm. *It would have been lovely to walk a child through the woods. To watch a child run free, laughing, giggling through the trees, playing hide and seek, running, just running.* She stares up beyond the pines at the open sky, no clouds, the sun finding its own paths through the trees, lacing the canopy with ribbons of yellow.

"Hey, watch it!"

Lydia jumps and gasps. "My God, who are you?"

The boy gathers sticks and shoves them under his arm, he stands up and stares at Lydia. "You broke one, you stepped right on it."

"I'm sorry, I had no idea..."

"Watch where you're going next time."

She looks at his downturned mouth and scowls. "Excuse me, do you talk to all grown-ups that way?"

"These are not ordinary sticks."

"Okay."

He walks toward the river, and Lydia wonders why he's going that way. He stops and turns around and walks back a few steps; he says, "My mom waited and waited for you and you never came back. She missed you." The boy runs, his white T-shirt catching the light once.

Lydia bounds between the trees, "Wait," she says, but the brush is thick around the riverbank and he's gone, disappeared into the green tangle.

She crosses the bridge, stares at the little white house. It's quiet, still. She walks on.

IT TAKES TWO hands to open the iron-clad door. The stone walls retain the cool of winter. Come autumn it will have warmed up inside. Lydia whispers, "Hello." She says it louder; the word echoes back. She hasn't stepped into the cathedral since her wedding, since her father's funeral. The large sculpture of Jesus was removed years ago. The silhouette remains on the wall where the paint's preserved beneath it. Candles line the diameter of the main room, protruding from the ends of pews. She walks to the closest pew and lets the silence fill her. She pictures the smiling faces of those who attended her wedding, pinks and lilacs, greens and blues of the ladies' dresses, the neatly coiffed men, ties and suits, crisp white shirts. Sophie asked the guests to spread out so it wouldn't seem so sparse. Compared to Sophie's wedding, those invited to Lydia's barely filled three pews. She couldn't imagine making vows in front of people she didn't really know and trust, like family and Rosa, and Desmond because she trusted Desmond at the time. The saints, the Virgin Mary, wise men had left the building long before Lydia said "I do"; she didn't trust them either. In retrospect she wishes they'd been there. Henry said God was still there, he never leaves, and Henry had an in with him then and Lydia had yet to discover why. On hot summer nights, Henry visited the cathedral; he'd unlock the doors and lock them behind him, bring a flashlight and light candles, then he'd drop to his knees on the cold concrete floor and pray. Lydia looks at the spot where Henry knelt, still warm and alive with candlelight. A few nights he fell asleep there and Lydia wishes she could have asked him if he met God on those nights, or an angel, or some spirit looming in the candlelit dark. He'd tell tales of hearing things, like Lydia swears she hears in the Queen Anne.

The baroque arches lurk above her, lined in gold. The stained-glass windows decorate the aisles with ribbons of red, green, blue, yellow. In the city, many churches have been made into impressive condos, townhomes, but no matter how much one renovates, the rooms remain curved, pushing out toward the sky, God finds a way in, too-long hallways resonant with hymns. No matter what's stripped from the walls, a church can never be anything but.

Raiden walks across the room at the side of the pulpit that used to be the bishop's. Two wooden panels under his arms and a hammer dangling from his index finger. The hammer falls to the floor. He kneels to pick it up, remains kneeling and looks up. Lydia looks away; it feels wrong to spy on him. She supposes all weddings can be troubling, exhausting, especially when one has a new business they're trying to get off the ground in a tight-knit town. She wonders if his confidence is a shield then, an act.

The kaleidoscopic light streaming through the windows lines his black locks. Streams of colour surround him. He stretches his arms in front of him, glides his hands under the wide sleeves of his blue tunic, drops his head, then raises it. He lifts the hammer and walks toward the unfinished stage Mr. Randal mentioned. Lydia clears her throat.

Raiden turns toward her, and though he doesn't smile, seems pleased to see her. "You have arrived."

He motions for Lydia to follow him and leads her downstairs and along a narrow hallway. He doesn't say anything. They stop at the open door at the end of the hall. She feels sick. She pulls at her hair from the scalp to its ends. Sunlight streams through the basement windows of a small stone room. Seven black wigs rest on the heads of faceless mannequins. A teal robe embroidered with coral poppies and long vines hangs on a cross-like hanger. Lydia reaches out to touch it, but pulls her hand back and shoves it in her pocket.

Raiden organizes baskets and bolts of opulent silks. "Little-Nan is on her way." His hair falls over his shoulders, cloaking his face. "We are so grateful for your help, Lydia. I know this isn't easy for you."

"No, it isn't." She has to stop speaking her thoughts out loud. Don't let anyone know how you really feel, her grandmother used to say. They'll pounce. She watches the side of Raiden's face, wonders if his grandfather built the same cautionary walls in him.

He's good at not letting Lydia know how he feels. She picks

up leftover pieces of silk from one of the baskets and rubs it on her cheek. "I never understood why grandmother said I shouldn't be honest."

He turns to listen.

"Keep your thoughts inside, don't let anyone know how you really feel."

His eyes drop down. "And I did it you know, I did for years, but the funny thing is it was easy because I didn't know what I was feeling." She throws the silk back in the basket. Raiden disappears behind a black velvet curtain and returns with two wooden chairs. He places them in front of the sewing table where he set her Singer down. "Please, have a seat," he says and he smiles and adds, "make yourself at home." His voice matches the breeze flowing through the room. She sits down and wonders what he means; she braces herself for another one of his frightening verses. Raiden sits down across from her and strokes the silver box strung around his neck. The monkey head smirks. He holds the small silver tin away from his chest, the monkey head dangles. "This is an *inro*," he says. "Men's robes don't have pockets so the *inro* hangs from an *obi*, the sash that secures the robe, to store things." She wonders if he ever doesn't notice her noticing things. He caresses the mean-looking monkey head, "This is the *netsuke*, the miniature sculpture acts as a toggle that balances the weight of the *inro*. This was my grandfather's."

He never mentions his father, just his grandfather. "It was nice of him to give it to you." She doesn't know how to ask about his father. She's afraid of the response, *the question is absurd, if you do not understand, you are in a strange family*. It seems he is in a strange family. She imagines running upstairs, down the aisle and out the cumbersome wrought-iron doors that always amazed her were not made for entering with ease. "Are you alright, Lydia?" She nods and says, "No."

"So the wedding will be here?"

He shrugs. "I prefer to refer to it as a ceremony."

"Sorry."

"I would like it to be outside beneath the pines, by the river, your grandfather's bridge, the altar. Traditionally, that is the perfect setting, in nature."

"So why not there, the bridge is half yours now anyway..."

He laughs softly, "I have a superstitious wedding party; the bride fears rain."

She seems like she fears more than rain.

KAITO HAS BEEN busy painting pine trees onto wooden backdrops, he says. It is good for him. He looks out the window, and says Little-Nan is later than he expected. He apologizes and motions toward the door, like he wants more than anything to leave. "We're building the perfect setting inside. The students are helping. It is a good task for them. To help them focus, have a purpose, and see results of their efforts."

He pries open the window. Warm air drifts in. Cars murmur past, high heels clomp by, unfamiliar voices, and a few coughs stream into the room from outside. For a moment, Lydia thinks Rosa bounds through the door, past Raiden, plopping shopping bags and lattes onto the table, pulling out reams of cloth and ribbons she discovered on the way. Lydia stands up and walks around. Or is she getting up to walk away from the image of Rosa?

To her left, the teal robe hangs like a headless empress. She wonders if her mother has seen Little-Nan or Junko in an elegant garment like this and if that is her emperor. The man Constance sees but Lydia has yet to lay eyes on. Maybe she sees the emperor like Lydia sees Rosa, because she wants to. No one has mentioned the groom and that's wonderful, the less people she knows — especially a groom — the better, and if it's an emperor, all the best to them; you'd think an emperor could have hired a seamstress to make his fiancé's wedding robes. The less she knows about all of this the more detached she'll remain. Isn't that what they teach spies? Then if caught and asked what they know, they're not lying when they say, "nothing."

There's no clock in the room but Lydia hears ticking.

Ticking, the internal clock.

Should I have had children? Can I still have them now?

You're so selfish, Lydia. Mom and Dad need grandchildren.

Sophie?

Lydia, we should talk about kids.

Charlie?

Do do do dododo do do.

Step right up folks and ride the...

It's a good thing she never had kids.

You can still have kids though, right?

Walk it off, Lydia. Screw the pills and doctors, walk it off, walk it off.

I'm never picking up a needle and thread again.

This is what you lived for.

The things we live for change.

Do do do dodo...

What do you want, Lydia? You had everything.

Get back on the horse, get back on the horse.
Constance?
Yes, Jane.
I'm losing him.
Daniel?
"Stop!"
Raiden turns around.

"I have to go." Lydia grips her shirt, wrings it in her fists, "It's too painful. I cannot pick up a needle and thread again. I can't."

"The sword that..."

"Please..."

"We are both here because of broken hearts, Lydia."

She holds her breath. She doesn't want to know, to get personal, to divulge secrets or learn his. *Don't open up to me*, she pleads, wills him, with her eyes, not to be personal.

LITTLE-NAN ENTERS the room. Lydia lets out a sigh, her shoulders drop.

"You came," she says and takes Lydia's hands in hers. *Didn't she know I was coming?*

"This is exciting," she says and scuttles around the room, humming and unrolling bolts of silk along the long wooden tables. Her silver hair glistens in the sunlight every time she passes the window. She reveals the many samples of antique and handwoven silks she has on hand, then brings out the lace and the multicoloured threads. Little-Nan notices how much attention they receive. Lydia's eyes dart from one to the other; she's on her feet in an instant and running her hands over every one, touching, smelling. Obstinacy, pure will, are not easy to crack but the adoration Little-Nan spots in her new assistant's eyes gives her faith her strategy might work. She has the one thing Lydia cannot resist.

"Have you ever created kimonos in your work?" she asks.

Raiden slips out of the room.

Lydia shakes her head, "Sixteenth century Shakespearean costumes and a lot of curtains mainly, heavy and elaborate, the antithesis of the kimono."

"In more ways than you realize," she says. "This has come at a good time then, the stage in your life when you must lighten things."

Her fingertips go numb. On the table, needles wait to be thread. She has to get out. She shoves her hands into her pockets. If she was going to turn her life around, move on, she thought it would be with a new vocation, gardening, waiting on tables, data entry, running the bed and breakfast. Not sewing. For her mother, her father, she'd help Little-Nan complete the wedding robes because that matters to her mother. She refuses to get involved with them. It will be purely mechanical, thread the needle, follow the seam, in and out, in and out, no thoughts, visions, no feelings.

Eat when you eat, sleep when you sleep, she heard Raiden say to her mother one night when she overheard them speaking in the backyard. He was telling her not to worry, that the past is the past and one must believe each day is a new beginning. She's sad, and Lydia assumes she's caused the upset. *Sew when you sew.* She likes Little-Nan, there's something of her grandmother in her eyes, in her strong stance and wise words. She'd never met a woman like her grandmother, not until now. *What would Rosa say if she had any idea I was about to sew wedding dresses for real women?*

The True Blossom

CONSTANCE POLISHES THE glass of every photograph that lines the hall from the front to the back of the house. She stops at the picture of her on opening night of one of her productions and traces her fingers around her twenty-five-year-old face. She was asked to leave Junko in peace during the day; the girls would look after cleaning the place and laundering bed linens. Constance hoped she would be able to do the usual services she offered guests: bake, feed them breakfast, tidy and clean, wash the bed linens. It kept her busy, her mind off the large empty house; perhaps it was time to sell, to find something smaller, a place with less memories. She loved that photo of her more than any others, she was Blanche DuBois, she lived and breathed every morsel of that woman and loved it. *Sure, Stanley wasn't worth it, but in the end what man was?* Then she bit her lip, realizing that was not her speaking in her head, it was Blanche; she'd come back as she often did throughout the years, not like an old friend, more like an alter-ego. In the living room she walks past the mantelpiece without glancing at Henry, she turns on the stereo and presses START. Bach. *The Well-Tempered Clavier*, it was the last thing Henry listened to, he died to this music, it was part of his plan. She wouldn't dare change the disc. It hurt to hear it over and over again but sometimes it was the hurting Constance wanted to feel.

She pours herself a glass of sherry, walks upstairs, her indoor shoes clip-clopping. She places the crystal glass on her vanity and thumbs through the wardrobe, the back of it, where she keeps costumes she'd worn on stage — the red one, yes, that was it. She slid into it, it fits her loosely now; Blanche was curvier in her day. The shoes still fit, they're high, beige, strappy, she feels like a tramp in them. She picks up the wrinkled and yellowing program, flips it open:

> When the play begins, Blanche is already a fallen woman in society's eyes. Her family fortune and estate are gone, she lost her young husband years earlier, she is an aging belle who lives in a state of perpetual panic about her fading beauty. Her manner is dainty and frail, and she sports a wardrobe of showy but cheap evening clothes.

Constance closes the brochure, *I miss being someone else*, finishes dressing for her performance. Her feet take on a new role, she walks differently without thinking, a strut, and she struts up to the third floor, with her sherry and an empty cigarette holder, pretending to snap gum, enters the old ballroom that has not hosted a real ball since the early 1900s and she dances, she dances and she sings until she's dizzy. Dizzy from the spinning, the sherry, the past, age, and the unfamiliar pang of happiness. "You are allowed to be happy without him," she whispers. She leans against the wall. A tall figure appears in the middle of the room. Constance sees long black hair, frizzy, jetting out in all directions, then the red lips, black-lined eyes, projected through loose strands obscuring the figure's entire face. On her thin frame, a white robe, like a hospital gown. Junko holds out her hand. Constance stands perfectly still in her high-heeled shoes. The music fills the room, Junko takes her limp hand and they dance. One, two, three, one, two, three, without a word, in perfect harmony, until the music stops. Junko releases her arm from around Constance's thin waist, curtsies and says, "Thank you." She bows her head, turns and leaves the room.

"Good heavens," says Constance and presses her pounding chest.

THE SCHOOL BELL sounds. A few children run past the window, blowing in a gust of air. The hammering of the stage intensifies, the preparations for the ceremony are coming together, incorporating the students' help works for everyone, students and teachers alike. The students have a task, hammering *or is it stomping*, Lydia thinks, *Kaito's barefoot stomping*, connecting the feet to the ground. She doesn't look up and into the doorway for fear a variety of spirits are coming and going.

Constance ran drama classes out of the old cathedral. After school Lydia and Sophie would spend time there until their mother had finished teaching. They never joined in and Constance didn't force them. Lydia would watch to see how people acted, how her mother seemed to grow and speak differently in front of other children. Henry would join them when his work was done. He'd saunter over from across the road, and call his girls' names when he walked into the large main hall. His voice filled the entire place and Lydia could always tell he called with a smile. They were free. Always free within the parametres of large open places, the Queen Anne, the woods, the cathedral. She smells the regal robe on the hanger. Smells of the road she knows it has travelled on, spiced with death and frankincense, distance and sandalwood. A silk road. "I don't belong here," she whispers. "I need to get out." Maybe she'll take Constance back to the world she thrived in, give her a chance to do what her mother once loved before she had children, the Queen Anne and Henry. She looks at her hands, and begins pacing in the beam of yellow filtering into the room. *I don't belong here.*

Lydia worked up the courage to visit her father in hospital, wires streamed from his thinning chest, tubes from his nose. He pulled her closer to him and whispered, *get me out of here.* His eyes pleaded for her to do something. She searched the cold hospital ward for an escape route. Watched the squiggling lines of the monitor and imagined them going straight. "I can't," she said. "You need to be here." She'd never seen him look so angry. He didn't believe in hospitals, wanted out. He begged her like she was his last hope, his little girl, even she couldn't set him free.

His face reddened and he said through gritted teeth. "I don't belong here." He attempted to rip out his IV and his heart monitors until a hard-nosed nurse stormed in and told him off. No one told Henry off, they never had to. *Get me out of here, I don't belong here,* he mouthed to her, eyes screaming.

She grips pink silk, *peau de soie, get me out of here.* He was not prepared to die.

"I don't belong here."

"No, none of us belong here," Little-Nan says.

Lydia had no idea she'd spoken out loud.

"I don't understand. Then why are you here?"

"Nature calls us, Lydia. We are drawn back, often without our knowledge, to places we are meant to be. I do believe, at your age, I would have balked at the notion. Ran from it, which I did. I ran away from where I came, only to be drawn back over time."

"You were born here?"

"Not here," she laughs, "in the country."

The stone walls, the sewing machine on the desk, the faceless mannequins with their perfectly coiffed curls and buns, a different room and yet far too familiar. Little-Nan grasps a thread needle and plunges it into red silk with gold emblems emblazoned in it. She pulls a stool close to Lydia. "When you spend a little more time with Raiden he will tell you that realizing the impermanence of everything is a good step to moving past the things that have made you suffer, the losses we endure."

"He's mentioned that." Lydia turns her back on the looming kimono, the gleaming silk. "If everything is impermanent, then how does one explain marriage?"

Little-Nan sits Lydia down on a stool. She points to the sewing machine and shakes her head. "We sew by hand." *Always work with your hands, Lydia; Always work with your hands, son.* Their legacy won't die, but even great men's plans are changed by those who think they can do better. Of all the citizens in the community who revered Henry and his father, there were always people in their midst who were jealous of them, of the love and admiration others felt. When Henry died, those people moved in and swept the boardroom clean of Henry's people. Except for Constance, she was determined to keep her husband's work alive, his plans to improve the town, to help the community and its young thrive in a healthy, beautiful environment. They needed that program; she too believed it was important to keep tradition alive, even if it was a different approach, it had everyone's best interests at heart, to help those in need of happiness.

Lydia reaches behind Little-Nan to grab a silver thimble ringed with scratches. She puts it on her thumb and takes it off quickly, clenches it in her fist.

Little-Nan continues to sort and organize. "Yes," she says.

"Where have you been?" whispers Pipit.

Junko slides into her room and sits down at the vanity, she stares at herself in the mirror and sweeps a ball across her eyes, smearing black kohl across her white face — a rabid zebra.

"Are you mad? You must not leave these quarters. I looked everywhere for you."

She says, "I heard singing. When is the last time my ears have been filled with the warmth of music?"

"I would love to have music, you refuse."

"Nonsense."

"You must stay here, rest. You are not well and it is important you are in good health for the ceremony. Please, Raiden is counting on you. He needs you."

"I am tired. Let me go, just let me go." She waves Pipit away, her hands long, fingernails like talons, knuckles like a man's.

"You are a good girl, Pipit. I wish your father could have known you."

LYDIA'S FINGERS VIBRATE. She feels them reaching for the silk. Little-Nan removes the sewing machine from under the table. Lydia jumps toward it, "Where are you going with that?"

"You will feel better if it is out of sight," she said. "Too many memories."

"It's the memories I want to avoid by not sewing at all." She grabs her head, tries to silence the carnival music, the tinny repetition and images of long-nosed masks and thin legs leaping around in ballet slippers.

"Not remembering and not letting go are different, dear."

Little-Nan plunks two bolts of blue and red silk onto the table. It is soft, feels ancient yet full of life. Her eyes twinkle when she points to the indigo silk lined with swallows. "Kimono means 'thing to wear'," she says, "and every kimono tells a story." She runs her hand across the silk and looks up at Lydia.

She unwraps a bolt of green silk embroidered with red lanterns, sleeping farmers and abandoned carts. "These characters symbolize prosperity, longevity, and fortune."

Lydia slumps onto the stool and watches as Little-Nan unwinds two bolts of blue and red silk onto the table. Rosa's hemming gowns and fixing the little things, sewing lace around cuffs, velvet over buttons, ribbon onto headdresses. Little-Nan opens the black curtains. Rows of kimonos stare back at them. Lydia rises to her feet. "What on earth?" A black cloak embroidered with gold silk dominates the room. Little-Nan caresses it. "There are many different types of kimonos," she says. Many had been handed down in her family for generations. "This is a *furisode*, they are distinguishable by their long swinging sleeves." She thought of the day she arrived, the red silk swaying in the woods. "The embroidered symbols are the purse of inexhaustible riches and various treasures that represent prosperity, long life, and good fortune." She moves to the one beside it, points to the waterfalls flowing around it, "This was a common motif during the Edo period. The lions and peonies symbolize nobility." Lydia touches the raised flowers and ornate lions, wide-eyed and crouching, *ready to pounce,* she thinks, *like wolves*. There's something so real about them, a presence, Lydia wonders if when left alone in the evening they come to life and wander around the old cathedral, and outside, along the path that leads to the river. If they sway the wide sleeves between the trees like flags. She worked her whole life to be amidst treasures such as these. Little-Nan points to a white robe missing sleeves, its collar and lining. "This will be Junko's *shiromuku*," she says, the brides traditional wedding kimono. She explains that "Shiro" means white and "muku" pure. "It signifies the purity of the bride's intention to fit into her husband's family."

Constance listens from the hall at the bottom of the stairs, her tiny head heavy with perfectly set hair bends toward the lit room. "Typical," Lydia says to herself, "to have to fit into the husband's family." Kaito ambles into the hall, Constance places her finger over her mouth to shush him. He tiptoes beside and listens too. "It was believed," says Little-Nan, "the bride dressing in white meant she was open to be 'dyed' by the customs and ways of her husband's household." Lydia shakes her head. Little-Nan says, "I know, I know, tradition is both beautiful and constricting and yet there are many people who are not averse to these customs."

The blankness of Junko's wedding robe in comparison to the two beside it is ghostly. It's like the unjust element of the bird kingdom. The male is almost always more colourful than the female. "I hope that doesn't scare her away," says Constance.

Kaito says, "It is not the story of the *shiromuko* that will scare her away, it's the one who wears it. We've come to call her *kyojo*. It means mad woman. There was a time she was such a beautiful, vibrant woman, *Makoto no Hana*."

"I know," says Constance.

Constance turns her own wedding band. Sophie had asked her why she still wears it. The question made her go cold. "We're not divorced, dear." Sophie didn't understand. "I just want you to move on, Mom. You have to move on." She tiptoes closer to the room, peeks in to see what Lydia is doing. She wants to be assured Lydia can move on. Kaito catches the wistful twinkle in Constance's eye and clears his throat quietly.

"Yes, dear," whispers Constance.

"You are a very special person to do this for us, Mrs. Templar. I hope you know how much we appreciate everything you are sacrificing for us."

She places her hand on his shoulder, he drops his head like a knight. "This is not a sacrifice, this is fulfilling a wish. The sacrifice was many years ago."

Upstairs the ceiling thuds with hammering and thumping. Kaito touches Constance's shoulder. The hammering turns rhythmic, tribal. The occasional hum of young boys laughing and then a moment of stillness and then again stomping, rhythmic, tribal. Constance is reminded of the strange touch of Junko's arm around her waist, her breath soft by her face, and one, two, three, one, two, three, one, two, three as they waltzed around the hidden ballroom. Never in a million years did she think she would see her again. No one outside the family knows about the ballroom. The stairway is hidden on the other side of the house, in the family's wing. Constance thinks of Junko alone in the house. They should talk, they need to talk. It's not fair that Pipit is caught in the middle, the go-between. She tiptoes back up the stairs with Kaito in tow, "This is my last obligation," she tells him, thinking of Henry. "I'm tired and now with Lydia... children run down the hall laughing." She smiles, wishes one would stop and hold her like the mothers they should have had. They run past like she's not even there.

Lydia hears the sound of tires on gravel and takes a quick look out the window, then back at the door to the little stone room. The stomping ceases and the sounds of the cardinals and finches leak in through the window. Little-Nan attempts to draw Lydia back to the allure of the robes around her, of the titillating sensation of the silks. "You will learn a lot about yourself, Lydia. The very act of putting on the kimono joins it to human life and gives it form. The moment the wearer puts it on, they begin to feel fortunate."

"I don't want to depend on cloth anymore to make me feel or be fortunate." She gets up and walks around the rows of robes, standing there like chess pieces. "What could possibly be left to sew, it looks like you have plenty of kimonos here for ten ceremonies."

"Oh, these are not for the wedding," she says as she surgically slides green thread through the eye of a needle. "They are part of the program."

Charlie was a mannequin in her mind, like the cross-like hangers in front of her. She created him, gave him life, with every garment he adorned he became who he was supposed to be. Without his carefully created wardrobe, every fabric chosen to convey the moods and traits of his character, the way a brocade hung compared to linen, tweed opposed to nylon, wool over satin, velvet, silk sheets. She shakes her head. Yellow streams across the concrete floor, or she thinks it does for the moment anyway, every where yellow, bright, not misty or pollution-ridden — electric.

A few of the boys run into the room and startle Lydia. Little-Nan grabs them as if they were sweet dogs playing, seeking attention from an owner they love. They are not little, they are gangly, awkward, voices up and down like pitch pipes. Clothes loose, long shorts revealing their naturally bruised and knobby knees. The quiet one strolls through the rows of kimonos, running his hand across them. Lydia watches him, follows him into the silk crowd. *It's you, from the woods, with your special sticks.* He leans his cheek against the black kimono layered with golden cities and lion head motifs. "What do you feel?" asks Lydia. The boy's eyes turn toward her without the slightest movement from his gangly body — he had sensed her presence.

"Strength," he says, lifting his cheek from the kimono, and removing the robe from the hanger.

Lydia quickly looks behind her in case Little-Nan sees. "What are you doing?" He puts one arm into the wide sleeve then the other. Lydia steps in front of him. "You shouldn't do that. Put that back."

Behind them the boys are chatting. She hears the receptive inflections of Little-Nan's voice, listening and reacting with enthusiasm. The black robe hangs over the boy's body like the skin of a black bear, too huge, too noble, for his young bones. It buries him. "You're Jane's son."

"No, I am Teito. I am an emperor."

She laughs. "I don't think you're the emperor, kiddo, but it's something to work toward."

His face drops like the robe around him. Dark, black, heavy.

"Daniel?" Little-Nan calls, followed by the other boys. "Hey? Daniel? Hey, Daniel."

HE PRESSES HIS hands together in front of his chest and drops his small head, his long fringe falls over his face. *You were in Jane's stomach when I left. Now look at you. You're beautiful.*

"Okay, Teito, back to work. Don't let them know who you are, they'll try to pull you down. Leave your robe here and join the others as if you are one of them. It'll be our secret, how special you really are," says Lydia.

He shakes his hair away from his face and looks up at Lydia. "No, Miss Templar, my secret is far more special than you realize."

He runs off through the still silk crowd, stopping for a second to turn and wave to her, then he disappears. Little-Nan greets Daniel and asks where he was, then notices Lydia appear through the kimonos. Daniel looks at Little-Nan, as if to say, it's okay. Little-Nan pats him on the shoulder and ushers the boys out of the room. "On you go now to your next task," she says.

She closes the door and smiles at Lydia. He's a wonderful soul, she says. Lydia nods. "There's something unusual about him. I can't put my finger on it."

"We've got a great group, lovely children with so much promise."

"How do you help them?"

"My job is to teach them to work out their fears and sorrows, to overcome the obstacles in their lives by telling a story through the sewing of the kimonos." In the beginning of the student's journey the garments hung limply and squint upon the mannequins. By the time the students were done with Little-Nan and Raiden's teachings, the colours and symbols became more hopeful, the seams straighter. "We had many sad kimonos and *kosodes* and *fukasari* hanging in the recreation centre in the city and here they are just beginning their stories," says Little-Nan. "My grandmother helped me through a lot of trials this way. For years, like you, I created them for other people, politicians, socialites, made quite a name for myself. I was very successful at what I did, Lydia."

"What happened?"

"I walked away from it."

Lydia pulls the stool closer to Little-Nan. "It became false to me and lost the beauty of what I was taught. I no longer felt my self."

She went back to the village she was raised in by her grandmother and carried on the work she'd learned to help those in need. "It's how I got my name," she says. "Big-Nan was my grandmother, when she died, I carried on her work, until I was asked by Raiden to help." Lydia picked up a pin and began twirling it. "Raiden knew Junko's lover and promised him that if anything ever happened to him that he would look after Junko." Lydia feels a sharp pinch. She sees red, lots and lots of red. A sharp pain shoots through her eyes and the blood forming in a ball on her fingertip takes her back to her last afternoon in the theatre, the needle sticking in the eye of the red poppy, the prick that amounted to nothing.

"Is Raiden marrying Junko?"

Little-Nan stops and shuffles over to the white robe. She takes it off its hanger and lies it flat on the tabletop. She picks up a needle, threads it and starts sewing. "I must not talk about it." She shouldn't have spoken about it. *Shush, shush. What were you told? This is not the time.* "Please, Little-Nan, I want to know what's going on."

"Oh, dear, there is nothing 'going on.' It is all quite simple really. Junko has a wish we are helping her fulfill. Isn't it every woman's wish to be married to the one they love?"

Lydia thinks about it. "No," she says. "For some, the person they love is not marriage material."

Little-Nan puts down her needle and tilts her head toward Lydia, anticipation glinting in her kind eyes. Lydia imagines Little-Nan packing her things and walking away from her successful career. She touches the silk on her lap, looks around. A wave of softness washes over her. She listens to the birds outside, the breeze, the occasional footsteps above her. She tries to picture Rosa scurrying around the wardrobe room; the image is fuzzy.

"What do you want me to do?" asks Lydia. "I'm at your service."

"How wonderful!" Little-Nan picks up the needle she's thread with green and passes it to Lydia. Little-Nan watches Lydia eye the cloth in front of her. She must be very careful in what she is leading her to, the obstacles ahead are tricky. Little-Nan needs to strengthen Lydia first before opening the next set of doors. *Poor man*, thinks Lydia, as she wonders how Raiden can sacrifice himself for the love of someone else's life.

"Why does Junko stay inside all day?"

"She is very tired. She needs rest."

"I..."

"Come on, come on, no time for chit-chat. Now wipe your hands for me." She hands Lydia a damp cloth and then a dry one. "This is *tsumugi*, spun silk. Junko will have nothing less than the real thing; your hands must be dry and clean."

Lydia looks for a pattern, something to help her know what to do. She suddenly feels like she has never run thread through fabric. "Pattern?" laughs Little-Nan. "Traditionally kimonos were made from scraps of discarded fabrics. Funny to think now they hang in galleries and museums. No measurements, they are the same shape and standard size that can be worn by anyone, man or woman, regardless of weight or height. This gives the kimono versatility unlike western dress." She runs her graceful hands across her own beautiful garment. Little-Nan searches for thread in a large dark wicker basket. She produces a small red fan dusted with plum blossom and waves it in front of her delicate face, then opens the windows wider. The temperature continues to rise to unseasonable heights. Little-Nan taps the fan back together and places it on the table.

What seems like one of the mannequins moves and comes to life. Junko's thick black hair is piled on top of her head in three perfectly round bunches. Her face shimmers but doesn't move. The expressionless glaze, a wooden mask. Lydia fears the face hidden behind it. The slits for the eyes outlined in thick ebony, lids and lips a dusting of red. The mouth slightly parted. She stands still, barely breathing, bones hidden under a robe of pale yellow. She fills the doorway. Pipit stands off to her side, head lowered. Little-Nan raises her head and turns around. "Junko," she says and looks at the clock on the wall, "you're early."

"According to the nurse at my side I am days late."

Little-Nan whispers to Lydia, "Don't be alarmed, dear."

"We've met," she says and greets Junko with a soft hello and a bow like she's watched the counsellors do. She waits. Junko approaches her like an apparition. Thick black fingernails grip the mask and lower it. The real pale face is more smooth and porcelain-like than the hard-shelled façade. Her black-lined eyes and red lips stun Lydia, how can a face be so unreal?

With a giraffe-like gait and height, Junko peers down on her new seamstress. From a little pouch attached to her *obi*, she pulls a small black fan dotted with buttercups and fans herself. The cool air wafts against Lydia's skin. It feels wrong to breathe as if she might offend Junko or do something out of protocol.

"Lydia," she whispers. Though unmasked, her face remains devoid of expression. Pipit grips Junko's other face to her stomach, keeping her eyes forward. Her own attire, pale blue and plain, a dark blue sash with small white flowers wraps her small frame together.

"So we meet again," she walks in around Lydia eyeing her up and down. "You relented and entered our world," red lips and squinting black eyes approach and stop inches from Lydia's face. Cool breath hits her skin. She looks away. Little-Nan and Pipit exchange glances behind Junko's back. Junko tips up Lydia's chin with a long talon. *My God, let go of me.* She takes a step back, the talon falls.

"Lydia," Junko whispers. "*Makoto no Hana*, the true blossom."

She leans down, and her breathing, in and out, in and out, seeps through Lydia's skin.

"We are all heartbroken *Makoto no Hana*. We have many commonalities you and I, like sisters, kin, we are perhaps kindred spirits, no?"

Junko backs away, a tiptoe at a time, hands held out with the gracefulness of a ballerina. She turns and stops before Little-Nan who takes her fan and unties the floral patterned *obi* around her waist, releasing her *kosode*, removing it from Junko. Lydia tries to avert her eyes but can't. Junko raises her powdery arms higher and Pipit lifts the white robe from the mannequin and drapes it over her.

"Come," says Little-Nan, "we'll start the lesson now."

Lydia rushes over to Little-Nan's side. Pipit fans Junko. Little-Nan keeps the fabric grazing the ground as she pulls and folds the fabric up from the waist and over on itself. It begins to take shape. Lydia senses Junko's impatience. She doesn't seem like a woman who stands with her arms held in the air for long. Not unlike some of the actresses she's worked for in the past. "You are gifted I hear, *Makoto no Hana*. I am lucky to have you, I'm told by one who thinks very highly of you. You have caught the attention of an admirer."

Pipit prays she won't refer to her as the waif. The heat beneath Lydia's skin rises. Little-Nan moves quicker, pulling and folding the fabric tighter and closer to Junko's frame.

"Ouch," says Junko. She swats the side of Little-Nan's head. "Watch yourself."

Little-Nan apologizes and glances at Lydia who is incensed at Junko's actions. *To be so rude to such a sweet old woman.* Junko whispers to Pipit, her eyes on Little-Nan. Pipit nods and whispers to her aunt. They proceed to remove the white robe, unravelling and unravelling and unravelling, Little-Nan's face tightens. Her delicate hands form fists. Lydia avoids Junko's gaze, her large façade peering down on her. Little-Nan grabs the discarded kimono and places it on the mannequin. Pipit redresses Junko. The mask's raised over her immaculate face. Pipit straightens her *obi*, its silk like a salve against her palms. Without a word they leave.

Little-Nan slips into the chair by the window.

"We will never get this done if she does not cooperate."

"She hit you."

Little-Nan stands up and raises her arms into the air. "She is like a wild dog you cannot tame."

"A wolf?"

"A jackal."

Little-Nan seems too preoccupied to ask questions. For Raiden she seems to be making concessions. Everyone's making concessions for Raiden and for Junko. A woman whose heart has not healed from the death of her husband, Little-Nan told her, and Raiden is determined to relieve that burden from her. *If she does not let go, she will not possess the key to the barriers that lead beyond.*

Little-Nan points to the green thread and a needle by the four pieces of fabric she's laid out for Lydia. Her throat dries, nerves twitching. The sewing needle glistens against the emerald silk embroidered with plows and sparrows. Outside, footsteps march by.

Lydia wipes her hands on her jeans and wanders over to another piece of fabric, avoiding the needle that Little-Nan attempts to get into her hand. "I can't do this."

Her fingers touch red lanterns, sleeping farmers and abandoned carts. She strokes the silk to experience what prosperity, longevity, and fortune feel like. *I had been so close to finding out.*

Little-Nan grasps Lydia's hands, turns them back and forth.

"Good kimono-making hands?" she asks.

"A bit rough," Little-Nan says, "but they will soften over time."

She blames it on the era, the brocades, tapestries, the leather. She looks closer at her palms. "Long life?"

"I am not a fortune-teller, Lydia."

She envisions her kimono with wheelless carts stuck in swamps. No cherry blossoms, travelling minstrels, or falcons. Little-Nan points to the plow on the emerald silk and says it is a symbol for perseverance. "That one is for the wedding, Lydia, for marriage and for not giving up." She looks up at Lydia's pale face. "Farmers persevere. Oxen plow their patience."

Lydia places her palm onto the oxen. It seems far from romantic, far from beautiful enough for a wedding. A plow, a farmer's vehicle, pulled by an oxen. "I was hoping for something prettier," she says. "Like cherry blossoms or orchids, swans."

"Perseverance is not pretty, Lydia. Handsome, yes, but not pretty."

Peeking through the kimonos she spots hollow eyes and red lips.

She moves past Little-Nan to the back of the room. On a long, thin table, stone and wooden faces gaze back at her. Slits for eyes, some wide, some squinting. Red lips, black lips, wide, screaming, colourless mouths. Pale cheeks, red cheeks, pink cheeks. Straw hair; electrified, red, wiry, hair; black, stringy hair, bald oval skulls. Round, square, oblong façades gaze back like ghosts, with no curtains to close the steadfast openings that someone's eyes are meant to fill. Lydia raises her arms and waits for an explanation from Little-Nan but she has resumed sewing and is humming like a trickling fountain as if this was all perfectly normal. "What kind of wedding are we preparing for?" Lydia whispers. The stone faces that had never cracked a smile did not respond. A table of masks, an army of kimonos, she's puzzled by the amount of garments and wonders what on earth they need her help for. More and more she wonders if her mother has any idea who these people are. If anyone in town does.

"These masks distinguish the living from the dead," says Little-Nan.

Lydia imagines the needle between her thumb and index finger. She pokes her finger through the eye of a sneering woman's façade. "Why are they here?"

"It is a long story."

"One I can find in these?" Lydia says, pointing to the kimonos.

Little-Nan doesn't turn around. "If you can discover which one, you might be on your way to defying the claws and fangs of the dharma cave."

She shakes her head. *So many riddles. No wonder they are behind.*

Little-Nan hands Lydia the four cut pieces of the emerald silk with plows and sparrows. "I imagine someone of your experience will simply see the line and just sew." Lydia looks at the masks, the faces of the dead, at the headless kimonos standing like the figures of clad ghosts.

"I trust you will work with your instinct."

"No measurements?"

"No measurements. It is the wearer of the kimono that gives it life."

She pulls out an old stool from under a weathered wooden table and lies the silk across it. "There is no need to give up what once made you happy. You do not need to keep your curtains drawn. We are trying to convince Junko of the same things."

"Why?"

Little-Nan shakes her head. "We have all been disillusioned by the things we loved. That's why we are here."

Junko's breath lingers on her skin. The wan face of the guest house surprised Lydia when she arrived. It was hard to believe it was even occupied. It is unusual for all the curtains to remain drawn and very little light shining through them in the evenings. Whenever it's occupied with guests it comes to life, curtains and windows open like it was smiling, voices emanate through them, laughter, and the lingering smell of Constance's baking bring the place alive. In the off-season it sleeps. Each time she walks past the guest wing it appears heavier and darker and breathes deeply like it remains fast asleep — is empty. The needle between her fingers, its thin body a perfect fit between the grooves in her skin, pierces her insides. *Where are the costumes, Lydia? What have you been doing all this time? Where are you?* Recalling Charlie's smile, her body caves in, his eyes green in the stage lights, blue at home. She swallows a surge she can't describe. *Don't cry, not here, do not cry.* She focuses on the plow, the oxen. Wants to draw her eyelids closed.

Flashes of the theatre shoot before her eyes, snippets of Rosa's voice and actors' lines, and clomping shoes buzz in and out, the way sound does when searching the radio for a station. She sees red, lots and lots of red; the suffocating fabric, stabbed red poppies. Flashes of colour and Rosa, and Charlie. Little-Nan wipes her brow with a small flowered hanky. A slight tremor moves through her hand. A memory perhaps, an experience that never left. She tucks the hanky into her *obi* and glides out of the room.

The Theatre

IT WAS A SUFFOCATING fabric, an Asian-inspired, wool brocade salvaged from a dead woman's couch. The needle stuck in the eye of a red poppy, the machine clunked to a stop. It would not budge. Time was running out. Rosa glanced over at Lydia. Her body slumped over the Singer HD-110 Mechanical she loved like a pet. "Now what," she said. She'd given up attempting to sew the last hem by hand. The tips of her fingers raw and she still refused to use the thimble left to her by her grandmother. Rosa rushed around searching through Post-it notes hanging from sewing machines, wardrobes, BUY MORE MUSLIN, PIN CUSHIONS, SIXTY MORE PEACOCK FEATHERS BY FRIDAY. MEASUREMENTS FOR IMOGEN, ALTER BUSTIER BY TWO INCHES.

Lydia fixated on the gleaming needle broken and stuck in the seam of the inside left thigh of Charlie's trunk hose. The clock ticked, it ticked, it ticked. She left the needle where it lay. She peeked at Rosa who was searching for the exact measurements of the leading lady's bustier. "Christ, I swore they were here a minute ago. She says she can't breathe and I know I took those damn measurements accurately."

Lydia reached across her sewing table and grabbed her grandmother's antique pincushion. Rosa sneezed, dust floated everywhere in the cold stone room, tightened the scarf she always wore around her neck. Despite the heat outside, the old church stones held onto the cool of winters. Dress rehearsal was scheduled to begin at 3 PM. There were always last-minute alterations, costumes to be finished, but Lydia laboured over the final costume. For Charlie, she was determined to make a pair of trunk hose he'd never forget; her choice of fabric was key.

Lydia found the vintage brocade at an estate sale uptown. It had been stripped from a Victorian claw and ball foot settee and preserved in a cool room; metallic thread gleamed in a ray of light emanating from a half-lit chandelier dangling from fraying wire. "I wonder who the hell lived here?" said Rosa. Lydia grabbed Rosa's arm and stopped her. "There's more to this fabric than meets the eye." Rosa's eyes rolled. Her skepticism, those acrobatic eyes, Lydia was used to. She drew the ornate bundle to her chest, smelled it, ran it across her cheek. "Yes," she said, "yes, this has been preserved for a reason."

"You're crazy," said Rosa. "It weighs a ton. It's prickly." She grabbed it in her hands and tried to bend it with her fingers. "Not flexible enough, it should have stayed on the couch it came off. This is only worthy of someone's ass sitting on it."

Lydia grabbed it back. "Exactly."

Rosa pointed to the set of floral poly-cotton curtains being given away, not sold. "No," said Lydia. "No." She waved her long finger, the one with the ring on it. The gold band Charlie slid on that finger eight years ago almost to the day. It was thinner now, the skin a different shade of white. "The idea is to crush him beneath the weight of his sins," she said. "This is perfect, perfect, the fabric does not breathe. The one who wears it won't breathe in it."

"Lydia, get a grip, you're tired. There is nothing going on with Imogen, they're acting. It's their roles for Christ's sake."

"It is heavy and it is prickly. It will be like a suit of nibbling rats when I'm done with it."

The auctioneer rhymed off its amount, Rosa balked. "That's half of our entire budget. This is too antique, too authentic, we can't afford it."

Lydia raised her free hand. The auctioneer scanned the room. There were no other bidders. When the gavel slammed against the pedestal, Rosa dropped her head.

"Sold."

Lydia smiled. "Perfect."

Charlie had been staying out later than the scheduled rehearsals, arriving home with mint-disguised booze breath, eyes twinkling, flushed cheeks, too quick to answer, before she'd even asked, he was rehearsing at Mercutio's. Throughout their marriage he'd played the lover, the husband, the muse of a variety of stunning thespians. Lydia was used to watching him affect adoration toward other women but she'd never felt a distance in their union quite like this. "It's the nature of the play," said Rosa. "Everyone's getting caught up in the romance."

"Everyone?"

Lydia checked her watch, 2:45 AM. She pressed down on the sewing machine's foot pedal. It didn't budge. Cast members filled the room, scurried like mosquitoes. The frenetic buzzing, the sing-song exchanges, the guttural vocal chord stretching she was accustomed to, a background noise of a different timbre disrupted her concentration. Adolescent cooing, giggling — sounds that were not in the script. Desmond believed one must fully embody the role, must live the part on and off stage for the entire production. His practice was gruelling, often isolating, but he was one of the most sought-after directors, brought in from the oldest theatres that had closed down, so many accomplished designers, actors, technicians let go, making it harder and harder to find work in the field. Many buckled under Desmond's regiment. Charlie embraced it. The costumes needed to be as near completion as possible long before opening night. Costume forms the exterior life of the character, Desmond believed, but it infuses the inner life. Once an actor dons their costume the character comes to life. A belief Lydia more than appreciated. Desmond also believed outside of rehearsals and when in production nothing must leave the troupe's mouths that was not in keeping with the part. He provided notebooks and pencils to be used to communicate in the real world for practical everyday discourse.

The cooing crept beneath her skin, justified her suspicions. They were unrehearsed, spontaneous. The lines did not sing, lilt or march with the iambic pentameter of the script. No clever quips, music or wit in their words. One of them in particular had a familiar off-key ring to it. She knew it was Charlie, out of character.

A second needle stuck and snapped off in the eye of the poppy, Lydia gripped the sewing table. She saw red, lots and lots of red. From the corner of the theatre's small stone wardrobe room, Lydia caught Charlie embracing his leading lady out of the context of the play. Her heart stopped. She counted the seconds, one to sixty, then it started up again with a beat unlike before — five stresses, ten syllables; unstressed, stressed, unstressed, stressed, unstressed. She fell into a strange kind of blank verse.

The actors followed Lydia's gaze. Masks covered shocked powdered faces adorned with red lips and black-lined eyes that gazed at Charlie's real wife through peacock feathers. Pencils scribbled. Pages flipped. Trained expressive eyes and speechless gaping mouths spoke volumes.

Rosa stopped buttoning Lady Capulet's bustier. She turned to her friend who had removed the trunk hose from the sewing machine and methodically completed the seam by hand in a catatonic trance. "Lydia, it isn't how it seems."

"I told you there was something going on." She gripped the costume and glared at the lingering cast. "What the hell are you staring at?" Understudies curtsied, bowed, and backed away.

She'd approached Charlie. He turned his back and marched away, scribbling into his notepad, dismissing her accusations as jealousy, madness, it was all in her mind. Her gut screamed back — *it's true, your suspicions are true*. Add up the signs, the distance, the late nights, the shortness of temper, quiet dinners, if they even ate together. *Shut up*, she'd say to the nagging voices. *Shut up*. When a wife suspects her husband's up to something she makes a choice to lose them or ignore the doubts and the fears altogether. She had a job to do and nothing was going to get in her way. She dealt with her suspicions the only way she knew how. Rosa measured every one of the actors and cut the patterns to fit. Lydia chose the fabrics to reflect each character's traits and to convey emotion, mood, and action of each scene. Lydia had been staying later than Rosa. "You go home and rest," she'd say, "I'm going to keep going." More fear and paranoia crept into her as she eyed the measurements, reconsidered the type of fabric, its weight, texture, and altered them according to how she felt that day and who she felt was in on the deception. Rosa never double-checked her friend's pieces of cloth that were handed back to her to sew together and never rechecked the measurements that she always jotted down in pencil; easy for Lydia to erase and shrink.

Cast members questioned the obscure and vibrant choice of fabrics and motifs, sixteenth century-inspired brocades with hanging men and gasping hounds. Lady Montague and Capulet, Juliet's nurse, complained of the tightness of their gowns, the weight and edginess of their headdresses, scribbling and scribbling into those little notepads:

My chest hurts. I cannot breathe with ease.

Though stunning, our headdresses are lethally sharp at the peak and could hurt someone if they fall.

They are straining our necks and heads.

Lydia slammed her fist on the sewing table, "The ladies dost protest too much! Far, far too much, ladies!" They nodded their heavy heads and withdrew from her presence. The demonic masks with severe black slits for eyes and gnarled, bent and elongated noses even Desmond found sinister. He argued that he failed to see the gothic side of Shakespeare's most romantic play. As a master of his craft, a Parisienne, it shocked Lydia that he failed to see the gothic side of anything. No one ventured into the room of masks. Rosa couldn't understand where she must have gone wrong, her measurements were always accurate. Is she tired, less efficient than before?

THE MORE LYDIA'S suspicions and insecurities ate away at her the more she devised clever ways to weave it into her work. She became obsessed with mistresses and wives and courtesans of the time. She researched French, Spanish, and Italian influences to create vibrant unctuous gowns reminiscent of Henry the II's mistress Diane de Poitiers, and his wife Catherine de' Medici of Florence's jade velvet gown lined in gold she'd found in one of her many costume books. At the time, fashion was dictated by European courts and Lydia found comfort in that. Justice will be served.

Rosa and her laboured over perfecting cone-shaped farthingales and wheel-shaped French farthingales to wring the little neck of every actress who had been friendly with Juliet. They were stiff and high-cupping, and chafed their chins. For the insufferable extras that became chummier and chummier with Juliet over time, Venetian courtesan costumes to be worn with chopines, high-soled boxy shoes popular in Venice in the late 1500s. From the front they resembled cruise ships or ocean liners head-on. They were at least six inches high and virtually impossible for modern young ladies to walk in. Lydia scoured the city and eventually bought six pairs from another theatre company that was closing down. That will teach them to side with the enemy, she thought, as she tightened and tightened bodices and waistlines and the troupe scribbled complaints of blisters and rashes and back aches in bold capital letters in their little leather notepads.

The men's costumes, though not nearly as ornate, were equally as rich in colour and texture. Lydia rose to the challenge of creating paned doublets with narrow skirts and round, puffed and paned trunk hose, sashes and stoles, long robes and sleeved cloaks in fabrics even horses would find heavy in peach and lilac and periwinkle blue, colours a horse would not see but to humans were glaring and off-putting. With the distance broadening in her marriage, everything inside Lydia had been turning grey and shapeless so she delved into more vibrant and less sombre colours of previous performances, something the men took issue with, even the most effeminate of the troupe. "What on earth would Shakespeare think," scribbled Tybalt. Lydia's confidence in Shakespeare's acceptance of her choices never faltered. According to Oscar Wilde he was completely indifferent to costume.

With each stitch and completed seam, the garments transformed before them into layered sculptures that brought even the dullest humans in the cast to life and the guilty excruciating discomfort.

Lydia completed the last stitch, knotted the thread and bit the remaining length with her teeth. The broken needle gleamed in the poppy. In the seat of the ornate puffed and paned trunk hose she placed a longer fabric needle, another in the leather cod piece and littered the expanse of the inner thigh and derrière until the pincushion was empty.

"What are you doing?" whispered Rosa. "Desmond will kill you."

"Quiet."

Charlie appeared at her side. She handed him the barbed attire. He bowed and avoided eye contact. Desmond forbade Lydia to fraternize with the cast outside of her realm of things and Charlie knew this. He had even gone so far as to suggest that for the time being Charlie and her live apart. "In the name of your art," he said, "in the name of your art." But she refused. *How ridiculous*, she thought. *How far can a director take things?* She said she understood the boundaries, but would not sacrifice real life outside of work. "Nonsense," he said. "Life is in the work, the work is life," he said in English first and then he repeated it in French with flowing hand gestures. She was amazed at how beautiful nonsense sounded in a foreign language and the gutting letdown seconds after one says it in English and realizes it's not nonsense at all, it's true.

Charlie was safe, he knew it, safe in his role. He glanced over his shoulder at his blushing leading lady whose mulberry sateen gown Rosa attempted to zip up while she complained about the drab, drab colour then gasped and slapped her hand over her mouth.

"You've gained weight," said Rosa.

Imogen stomped her foot, pounded her strangled stomach at the accusation. She hadn't gained weight. The minute thespian survived on soybeans and watermelon to maintain her lithe frame. Rosa even balked at the hideous choice of fabric and failed to notice that Lydia reduced the measurements in order to cause severe discomfort. Charlie removed his jeans, and slipped into his trunk hose. He too gasped, slapped his hand over his mouth and reached for his pencil. Lydia snatched it from his hand. "Too late," she said, "everyone's heard the truth from you." She flipped through the sparse pages in search of proclamations of real love. Desmond grabbed the notepad from Lydia and ushered Charlie and Imogen to the dress rehearsal. "*Très rapidement*," he repeated and repeated and repeated as they marched down the old church hall, up the cold stone stairs to the stage that once elevated choirboys and priests.

"It's three o' clock," whispered Rosa. Lydia gazed down at the empty pincushion.

She leapt to her feet and grabbed Rosa. They fled to the wings. From behind the aubergine velvet curtains Lydia had sewn in the off-season, they watched the dress rehearsal. With every overacted gesture, Charlie winced. Lydia willed him to plunk his ass on the edge of the ornate fountain that decorated the centre of a man-made Verona. From the sheer weight of the fabric she witnessed him, pricked and torn, drown in sweat under the blazing lights.

"Lydia, you're crazy!" whispered Rosa.

"He deserves it."

"*Qu'est-ce que c'est?*" said Desmond from the blackened house. "What is it that it is?" Charlie buckled over, balanced himself against Tybalt. Desmond rose to his feet, threw his steno pad on the floor and stomped on it. "What is it that it is? Wardrobe!"

Rosa grabbed Lydia's thinning arm, "You'll never get away with this," and dragged her back to the sewing room. "You've got to get a grip. You're exhausted, seeing things." Rosa was convinced Lydia had been working too hard, was getting caught up in the illusory world of theatre, the mimetic magic of the drama, unable to differentiate from reality and fantasy. It was a risk working long hours in a half-lit room, day in and day out dealing with a bygone era while the real world changed around them, one of the many occupational hazards of the theatre. She hadn't been the same since the loss of her father, strained, detached, more driven than ever to get her work done. What she didn't know was that she was trying to make it matter, to make sense of creating things for people who do not really exist. All the time and effort put into an illusion. The more she delved into the fabric, the costumes, the further she hoped to dig into the significance of it all, hoping that beneath the next layer there would be a meaning to it all. No one expects a parent to live forever, but seeing Henry breathless before he was too old to want to hang on took the feeling out of her hands and into herself for the first time. She didn't need to do this anymore. Rosa reached into the drawer of her sewing table and pulled out a bottle of Diazepam, handed one to Lydia. "Do not jeopardize this opportunity. You're tired, things are not as they seem."

"I caught them red-handed."

Rosa placed the French wheeled farthingale she'd been hand-sewing into Lydia's arms. "Look at your masterpieces. Keep focused."

"I'm done. I can't watch him carry on with another woman like this?'"

"It's their job."

"It's a prostitute's job to sleep with a married man."

"Take the pill. Take two pills, here."

"I can't do this anymore. I can't. I'm tired. I'm empty."

Rosa begged her to calm down. She had to separate her personal life from the job. "You've worked too hard to walk away from everything you've ever wanted."

Charlie limped backstage for a costume change. He glared at the woman he wed. Glared at her like a brother does a sister. Lydia proclaimed innocence and hoped with the removal of the needles he'd deflate like an antiquated balloon. He didn't, not figuratively or literally. Free of the sweltering costume, the man Lydia married seethed and ran into the arms of the woman he'd leave her for.

Arm in arm, they pranced away like centaurs, unreal, not human. Lydia's dry hands ached. She rubbed and rubbed them but couldn't relieve them of the coarseness of the suffocating fabric. She grabbed Rosa's shoulders. "I have to listen to their testimonies of love every single day on that goddamn stage and now I know they mean it. If they don't kill themselves for real, I will kill them. I will shrink and shrink and shrink their attire until flowing gowns and pantaloons suck every last breath out of them."

The intern gasped and shoved her pinking shears into a drawer. Rosa raised her tiny rough hands into the thick air. "Lydia, please, what you're feeling is natural, you'll get through this."

"This is natural? Look around you..." Court jesters dressed as harlequins exchanged still glances with maidens in pointy-nosed masks, crinoline tutus, red ringlet wigs, and pink-sequined ballet slippers. "...None of this is natural."

"You're tired, stressed. There's a lot of pressure on you right now."

Imogen pitter-pattered past wardrobe. She held her stomach.

Rosa slammed the door. "It's all an act, Lydia. Do not let it ruin your life. This is what we've worked for. We created them, look, they're beautiful."

Lydia glanced at the headless costumes that she swore could perform on their own. Then walked toward the barred basement window and opened it wide. She tried to feel the sun, hear voices, connect with the unadorned faces of businessmen, teachers, lawyers, ad executives, models, mothers, real people. She wanted to hear their breath, listen to their unscripted conversations, to touch their maskless faces.

One of the set designers approached and hugged her like a son would his mother.

"It's okay," he said. "Deceit, heartbreak, it's a traumatic experience. But it will change your life for the better. You'll achieve great things because of this."

Lydia pulled away from him. He was small, his eyes dewy from youth. Then he said, "Look at Jay Gatsby..." His arms flew up in the air. "Mark Zuckerberg."

"Mark Zuckerberg?" said Rosa.

Gatsby? thought Rosa.

"Unrequited love," he said. "Those men achieved great things because of unrequited love." He spoke with a bravado of the men they dressed. "Just think, there'd be no Facebook if Zuckerberg's girlfriend hadn't dumped his ass."

"What?" said Lydia.

Rosa threw down the flowing veil she'd been attempting to steam. "Mark Zuckerberg?"

"Gatsby?" said Lydia.

"Mark Zuckerberg," Rosa repeated and shoved him out of the room.

Lydia gathered her things. Rosa lifted headdresses, gowns, and masks they'd spent months creating. "Look," she said, "look, you'll miss this. This is who you are."

"A costume? I'll never pick up a needle and thread again."

"I don't believe you."

"I've been betrayed."

"You live for this, for the fabrics. Think of the fabrics."

Lydia stared at the forlorn brocade she'd dragged home from the estate sale, at its wilting poppies. "The things we live for change." She thrust her hands into her tattered painter's dungarees; pockets full of pins and fabric needles, scraps of lace and a thimble she kept handy but never used. The contents plunged into the waste bin. She hung onto the swatch of red velvet her grandmother had given her.

Lydia had persevered to get to this point, struggled to work her way up. She and Charlie lived in a tiny one-bedroom apartment, scrimped and scrimped for the love of their craft. As soon as the production opened and her costumes were recognized, doors would open.

A screeching "Cut!" came from the theatre. Rosa widened her eyes and mouthed, *Hide*. Lydia stood unfazed and barely breathing beside her. She twiddled her second-hand wedding band and thought, *Charlie will suffer, worse than the role he embodies, worse than Desmond himself, a man of ill-health and never devoid of pain.* Desmond stormed up behind Lydia and, like he'd done many times before, warned her that her personal issues were hampering the production and it had to stop. "Did you see what is happening out there, *bêtises. Arrête tes bêtises*. Stop your nonsense. This is scandalous. *Scandeleux*."

"This is between Charlie and me. It's nobody else's business."

"You are making it everybody's business. It has to stop."

Lydia ignored his previous warnings. She was not the one in the wrong and she'd continue to place fabric pins in Charlie's trunk hose, his beige suede low boots and Imogen's empire waist gowns. That was her realm of things.

The stage manager scuttled into the sewing room and asked for a phone. "Imogen is blue. She's passed out on stage." Desmond paced back and forth, his hands in fists. Rosa shot Lydia a look. She shrugged and said, "It wasn't that tight."

Desmond pulled Lydia aside, said he wanted to see her in his office in ten minutes. She wondered about the significance of ten minutes. Why not five, eight, fifteen? Why not now? Rosa dragged her friend out to the fire escape where they always took their breaks, watching the city thrum beneath them. Rosa smoked. Lydia observed the monks coming and going from the temple across the road. It calmed her. She admired their long dark robes with the bright yellow sashes gleaming across their shoulders and tied at their waists holding their meditation mats to their bodies. They appeared to move on air. The juxtaposition of the monks and the everyday people fascinated her; coming and going on parallel planes like they were separated by translucent funnels. At night she often dreamt of them, of the life they must lead, peaceful, significant. "Eat when you Eat, Sleep when you Sleep", she read on the board outside the temple. She twiddled her ring, rubbed and picked at the calluses irritating her index fingers, her rough palms. She felt nothing like she imagined she should feel.

She went back inside and proceeded down the long stone hall. She pictured her mother's perfectly made-up face turn pale when she told her she didn't want to be an actress like she'd hoped. "You don't want to be an actress's seamstress, darling. There's no glamour in that. You belong in the spotlight."

"No, mom, I belong in the wings."

As she walked backstage, she suddenly had no clue where she belonged.

Desmond's office was half-lit and smoke-filled. His dyed-black hair hung over his left eye, silver sparkled at the temples. He drew on his lit cigarillo that smelled of whisky.

"Lydia, there is a reason to believe that Imogen hyperventilated from a too-tight bodice."

"She's gaining weight."

"You are wrong." He slammed his fist on the desk. Books, scripts, the flickering light lifted from the blow. Lydia gripped the canvas cushion at her side. The stage manager pressed herself harder against the wall. The witness. Desmond stood up and moved to the front of the desk. His tight black jeans emphasized his aging and arthritic physique.

"I am sorry to lose you, Lydia. You are one of the most innovative I have worked with. But I have no choice than to let you go."

"Let me go?"

"You are a risk to the production, to yourself."

"You're firing me?" The thought hadn't entered her mind. He needed her. She *was* the production. The clothes maketh the man. "My husband destroys our marriage and I lose my job?"

Desmond threw an envelope onto her lap. In flowing black letters her name graced the front, Lydia Templar. She should have been an actress with a name like that, the way it looked written out, even with a dollar-store calligraphy pen. She should have listened to her mother, the successful Broadway actress who wanted nothing more than one of her daughters to follow in her footsteps. She could have been Juliet, Desdemona, Lady Macbeth.

"Inside, you'll find a letter regarding the reason for your dismissal and a cheque for two weeks' pay."

"But those are my costumes. They're mine and Rosa's designs."

"We will credit you in the program."

"Credit me in the program?"

"You should have thought before you acted."

If only he'd said the last line in French. She didn't want to understand the words spewing from his mouth.

The cast lingered on the other side of the office door, taffeta swished, whispers, sniffles. She wondered if she sat there a little longer, Desmond might change his mind. If he went for a short walk, he'd realize the implications of losing her at this crucial stage. Opening night was a month away. They were angry, egos and hearts stomped on; with a few minutes of thought, a compromise could be reached. Compromise lurked in the wings. She listened for its breath, the sound of compromise, a heavy breather, like one of those people that sit next to you on subway trains breathing audibly, but you don't get up and move because you don't want to offend them; that is compromise. She compromised for Charlie when she said I do, when she moved in with him; he wanted someone to share the cost of living with, didn't like sleeping or eating alone; he loved her he said but he also loved Scotch and William Shakespeare and a small Italian restaurant called Maria's, and other women. She compromised when she ignored the goddamn mint-disguised booze breath. She compromised, lulled by the audible breathing. Maybe that was it, compromise always lurked in the wings, threatening to sit down next to you, breathing heavily, challenging your willpower and character. Next time she'll get up and move to another seat. She looked through Desmond, past the old stone wall of the once functional church, onto the sunny streets thrumming with real people.

DESMOND CLEARED HIS throat, mumbled a few French words. They were sharp and illegible. She had trusted Desmond. She felt someone finally understood her approach when he handed her the opportunity to follow her vision. The opportunity she'd worked for he snatched back. All it takes is one influential person to believe in you, her father said to her one night when she called in tears saying it's too hard to keep fighting for what she believed in. Desmond stomped to the door and opened it. "It is best now you leave."

She looked into each of the actor's learned expressions and actions. All she recognized were the question marks in their eyes reflecting what she imagined were the question marks in hers.

Lydia grasped the envelope in her teeth and packed up her Singer HD-110 Mechanical she'd saved and saved for, placed her favourite antique pin jar and hand-sewn lace into her late grandmother's velvet keepsake box. Her breathing quickened, chest tightened. Rosa touched her arm. "Leave it; I'll drive it over to you later."

"What's happening?" said Lydia.

Rosa dropped her head.

A pall cloaked the still church. The cold stone walls hung onto the cool of winter, it seeped into Lydia's bones. Rosa gripped her friend's arm. Opening night, one month away. She offered to talk to Desmond and negotiate with him to change his mind. "Anything it takes."

The curtains hung immobile from sixteen feet above her. Every pleat held perfectly. She was proud of those curtains. She ran her hand across the vintage velvet, salvaged from the same dead woman's estate as the brocade. A woman she now believed must have been an infidel's wife and wanted Lydia to discover the truth about her own husband. That fabric found her. Lydia drew the curtains. They moved like Belgian horses through water and vibrated when they met in the middle. "No, Rosa, don't. It's over."

Without turning around, Lydia left the theatre.

The Stitch

OUTSIDE LAUGHTER TRICKLES across the street and through the window. Hours have moved the sun overhead. School children. Recess. The black kimono with the purse of inexhaustible riches faces her. She imagines shoguns and samurai, imagines Charlie shoving a knife into his gut. *The sword that kills the man...*

Lydia is stooped on the stool, eyes fixed on the silk before her. *I have nothing left except this. Where do I go from here, I have nothing except this.* She runs her fingers over a plow, the emerald field it rests on. Her eyes gleam as she picks up the needle, a ball of breath moves up through her body. She sputters, surprised by the loudness, a small tear of relief almost forcing its way out of her eyes.

She weaves the needle in and out of thread, and spends the afternoon swimming in and out of cool, calm water.

SHE DOESN'T NOTICE Little-Nan enter. Little-Nan notices she's quieter, pensive. "It must have been very hard to walk away from something you love so much."

She startles Lydia. Lydia sets the needle down and breathes deeply. "Little-Nan, I didn't walk away from what I loved." Her tiny face stiffens. "I was fired."

...Is the sword that saves the man?

Lydia grips the emerald silk. "I acted," Lydia holds her hands out to her sides, shrugs, "unprofessionally?"

"No, no, no, don't be so hard on yourself," she rubs her hands together and smirks. "Even monkeys fall from trees."

"Pardon?"

"Even experts make mistakes, Lydia, we are human."

Little-Nan picks up the threaded needle and hands it to Lydia one more time. She relents, thrusts the needle into the silk as if into Charlie's heart. She thinks she hears Little-Nan say, "Sew, just sew," though her lips are still. The morning breeze dissipates and the basement room heats up exactly like the old sewing room her and Rosa spent hours in. Lydia grips the needle.

Little-Nan says, "How one wears the kimono reflects their inner nature, opposed to how your costumes disguise the real self. The kimono has the opposite effect of the costumes you sew for your actors in order to transform them into other people."

"What do you mean?"

"It is meaningless for the wearer of the kimono to imitate another person's physical presence. It is what's inside the wearer that gives the kimono its true form."

It is meaningless for the one who wears the kimono to imitate another person's physical presence. It is what's inside the wearer that gives the kimono its true form. Little-Nan's eyes follow her own needle in and out of white silk. She speaks and her words smile. She's minute yet fills the space she occupies with a presence that defies her frame, her bending skeleton. The completed kimonos hang around the room erect and knowingly. Storks glance in Lydia's direction. She pulls the dangling silk up and over her knee. Little-Nan approaches her and advises that the fabric needs to remain straight and flat. Lydia smoothes it across the table.

No measurements. The kimono's form is created by the person who wears it. Every kimono is unlike any other. "The simple form is so that it can be folded for storage and taken apart and resewn into the shape of the one piece it originally was." Lydia pauses. *Take me apart and sew me back into my original shape, into good shape, better shape than I am now.* She weaves the thread through the silk, feels the generosity in each measured stitch, the patient curl of the wrist, the tense care when looping the needle through fabric.

"I'm trying to find my old self. To get back to who I used to be..."

"You can't," says Little-Nan. "You are who you are at this moment."

"I can't do this."

"You're doing it."

Lydia's hands begin to vibrate, her mouth feels like... "Follow your breath," Little-Nan says. She doesn't look up this time. *There is no breath, there is no breath.*

A swallow rests on a plow. A cool wave of air blows into the room. Lydia worked her entire career to get to the point where she would be recognized, known in the industry, sanctioned to design her own work. Why do it otherwise, why bother? She hadn't worked so hard to be sewing kimonos in the basement of an old cathedral in a town she sewed her way out of — an unknown, a has-been, bottoming out at the pinnacle of her career. "I can't do this," she says and places the threaded needle onto the tabletop. Rosa's right, *one can't run away from things.* Little-Nan's determination is not about to elapse; she has far too many tricks up the wide sleeves of her *forsode*. "The West is a culture that does," she says. "The East is a culture that becomes. We can learn from each other."

"The West is a culture that does, Lydia. The East is a culture that becomes."

Lydia weaves green thread through silk. Exhaustion weights her eyes. *The West is a culture that does. The East is a culture that becomes.* Her head spins. *The West is a culture that does. The East is a culture that becomes.* The needle and thread weave up a seam, the sides come together. *The West is a culture that does. The East is a culture that becomes. It is what's inside the wearer that gives the kimono its true form.*

"Why not finish one more seam today. Then that side of things is done, no need to revisit it."

The plow embroidered into the emerald silk quivers beneath her hands like an engine attempting to start. *Or stop, for the day.* Her head pounds, the tiptaptiptaptiptap of cast members' shoes from the theatre pass back and forth and back and forth in her ears like they did passing back and forth and back forth from the wardrobe room to the stage and back. Little-Nan tells her to persevere, or was it the plow telling her to persevere, or Henry, or Constance — all she's been doing is persevering. She has never given up on anything. "You gave up on me. You gave up on me."

"Charlie?"

The silk slips across her fingertips, the needle glides through it, in and out and in and out like a dolphin through water. The sparrow guides her. The plow. Lydia breathes with the rhythm of the needle, in and out. *Even monkeys fall from trees. Even monkeys fall from trees.*

Upstairs, Kaito takes a break from piecing together the sparse stage. In the back room he practices his movements, stomps his feet on the cold concrete floor in unison to the drums playing softly in his head. Arms held out at his sides, knees slightly bent, feet stomping. His movements fluid, hypnotic. Arms, feet, head, move in one succinct flow.

Pipit rests on the couch in the guest quarters flipping through fashion magazines, gazing out the window at the flittering birds, the flowers. "Maybe I'm too young to see the good in you," she says. "I am trying, God knows I am trying."

Junko paces in a dark room, candles flickering, rehearsing and rehearsing her self-written vows, words she never imagined saying. Pipit looks out the window, craving light, watches Constance pour tea into two cups, chatting to an empty Edwardian wicker chair.

Raiden looms over the riverbed, throwing petals into the thick green liquid, inhaling and exhaling his stick of *Hope*.

Little-Nan rests her needle on red silk and walks toward the regal black kimono with its purse of inexhaustible riches and says, "Those who make the beauty of the kimono their own must first make their character and spirit a thing of beauty." She stands in the doorway as if she is about to leave. "Kimono is not a costume, *Makoto no Hana*, it is a way of life."

Across the room Lydia looks deep into the heart of the purse of inexhaustible riches and plunges the threaded needle into the silk. She did and didn't want to understand. *When you understand, you belong to the family. When you do not understand, you are a stranger.* At some point in our lives we all are strangers. Her head throbs with indecipherable riddles. She gets up, presses her hands together in front of her chest like she's watched the Counselors do since she arrived. She moves her arms in a circle in front of her, links her fingers and bows, wants to howl like the wolf, to seek solace in *Oguchi no Magami*, have it stalk and eat all those that have forsaken her and her family.

Little-Nan places her long delicate hand over her mouth and giggles. She says Lydia's bow is too deep. A deep bow is reserved for the elderly. Though she is mature, she is not yet elderly. "But I appreciate the gesture. Maybe one day Raiden will teach you the order of bowing."

"One thing at a time, Little-Nan, please."

Little-Nan suggests they break until tomorrow. She doesn't want to push things, load too much into Lydia's hands or head. She feels an affinity with Lydia, recognizes her young self in her. It is hard to know what to tell her and what not to. Raiden has a plan and they are instructed to follow his directions.

Lydia runs her hands across the plow. *Perseverance is not pretty, it is handsome. We don't belong here. You cannot search for who you once were. Everything is impermanent. Even marriage? The sword that kills the man, is the sword that saves the man. Persevere.*

Lydia crams her eyes shut tight to stop the tears, inhales a deep breath, counts to ten backwards, ten, nine, eight... she swears the long embroidered grass sways. There is no room for fear or pain or paranoia to be sewn into the field of plows and sparrows. She neatly folds the fabric and places it into a drawer. She grabs the shopping bags. Tonight she'll make Constance a nice meal and ask if they can go for a walk around the grounds and talk the talk she has had no idea how to initiate before.

"Even monkeys fall from trees," she whispers as she folds the fabric.

"Yes, dear, even monkeys fall from trees."

Black Ice

AN OPAQUE HAZE hovers over Main Street. Cars lumbered along, kicking up dust and miscellaneous debris. The instant Lydia's feet touched the sidewalk they shrunk to the size of a schoolgirl's. Children's laughter echoed from the empty playground of the school Henry ran like an extension of his family. She pictured herself standing on the edge of the soccer pitch like she used to do, wearing the navy dress with the dandelions around the hem, gazing up at the cathedral. She marvelled at the structure she knew had been built by her grandfather, the cathedral with the same surname as her, like an uncle. Her shrunken feet are clad in the clogs she wanted because the colour was like clouds against a blue sky. They were vinyl, made to look like leather. She was too young for leather. A horn honked. Countless times she drove by this very spot in the backseat of Henry's dark green Pontiac Parisienne. She loved that car as much as the clogs but not for the colour. The Parisienne appears through a cloud of dirt a passing pickup churns up. She thinks of the specific night her father was late arriving home. He'd gone to the city that day which was unusual because Henry rarely went back to the city. Constance slammed the front door when he left, ran upstairs, slammed the bedroom door and howled like a baby. "Like a baby," said Sophie.

The day changed into a cold night so much earlier than usual. Snowing, windy, icy on the roads; the radio Constance had on kept repeating at higher-than-normal volume. The same radio station that began every morning with, *it's fifteen degrees and cloudy in Jamestown*. Lydia was determined to go to Jamestown one day to see if it was always cloudy there, always fifteen degrees. Something heavy cloaked the hallway, upstairs, the kitchen. The house seemed half-lit except for the rooms where the snow brightened the space in a strange white light, colder and clearer than artificial light. Sophie wasn't allowed to play her stereo. They had to go to bed early. Whenever something was up, they were sent to bed early.

Constance spent half the evening slamming things and sighing. All night the phone didn't ring but Constance acted like she was waiting for something greater than a ring. Lydia had no idea what she was waiting for and then it rang. She jumped up and ran to the top of the stairs. Sophie was already there. They peered through the banister. Constance stared at the ringing phone, her hair in a beehive, lips red and shining, a black crocheted pantsuit clinging to her like a spider web. It always amazed her daughters how she dressed up for dinner like someone who was actually going out for dinner. She stared at the ringing phone, her hands on her cheeks. Then she picked it up and the house and everything in it held its breath. Sophie put her arm around Lydia; Lydia never forgot that. Constance gasped. Her free fist hit the wall. She bent over, dropped her forehead onto the counter. "Go," Lydia said to Sophie and she looked at her like she had no idea how to comfort a mother. Lydia shoved past Sophie and ran to her mother. She remembered looking up into her mother's red eyes and saying "Is it the Parisienne?" Constance didn't react right away, then she grabbed her daughter, held her tight, kissed her, and laughed, laughed as tears spilled down her made-up cheeks.

Henry arrived home in a police car from another town. He told the girls the car hit black ice. Black ice, Lydia had never seen black ice. "No one's seen black ice, that's the thing about it," said Sophie. "It's like the ghost of ice, demon ice." Henry was okay, a little shaken. He walloped his head against the window and hurt his shoulder. "Possibly whiplash," he said, "but the car's totalled." Lydia had no idea what that meant. Constance said it meant his neck will be sore and Lydia said, "No, what does totalled mean?" Constance placed her hand over her mouth and Henry said, "It means obliterated," which lost Lydia further. Constance kneeled down to her level and softly said, "The Parisienne didn't make it. It was killed in the accident." Lydia squeezed her eyes into slits like she'd watched angry people do on television and looked at her dad that way until his eyes grew watery. Standing in the cloudy street in front of the godforsaken cathedral, she's ashamed she blamed a father she didn't have anymore for killing her favourite car.

After the funeral she asked Sophie if she remembered the day Dad totalled the car on his way home from the city. Sophie went quiet. Then she said, "Why? Don't ever bring that up again."

"Why can't I bring it up? Because Dad's dead? Because for weeks after the accident Mom and Dad fought and whispered, *what are we going to do, what are we going to do?* And I heard Grandma say, "If you keep things inside, son, they eat away at you like cancer."

"Shut up, Lydia."

"And it's weird because Mom and Dad never fought before that and what is weirder, little sister, is that I'm oldest. Funny how it isn't me who knows the truth."

"That's not funny, it's because you're out of it. You don't care."

"What? What happened that night on the demon ice?"

"Black ice, he said black ice."

"There was no ice was there? That's why you can't see black ice, because it isn't there. It's alibi ice."

"You heard them say that."

Lydia hadn't thought about that for ages. She looks at the cathedral and wonders if it's trying to tell her something. This is what's she's been hoping for. "Please," she says to the spire, the only thing looming in the sky that feels holy. "Where did I go wrong?"

If it could speak, the spire would say, "You didn't go wrong, not you. One day you will know a lot more than you believe in."

Mr. Randal teeters onto the front porch of his hardware store. "You doing alright, Lydia?" She waves and nods and turns back to look at the school she spent every day of her youth in. Except for weekends and holidays of course, the occasional sick day, summer break, but that's a lot of days to be in one routine, one building when you're young, year in and year out, switching rooms and teachers as one grows and she barely remembers anyone she spent those days with. She remembers Jane and the occasional quiet kid who was always alone at recess and lunchtime. She glances back at Mr. Randal, *Thank you for asking. Are you?*

A tall man in a blue suit walks into the school. His stature and gait familiar. It could be Henry on his way to work or the son he never had, all grown up and following in his footsteps. *Albert.* She thinks of running after him. The school bell rings and changes her mind. She crosses the road and walks toward the swing set by the side of the cathedral where Sunday school kids used to play before the bishop left town. The swing whines when she sits on it. Her weight makes it float not whisk. The occasional pickup truck drives by but no more visions of the past emerge through the dust and the drivers almost always wave or call out to a passerby. *Hey, Bro, beautiful day. Jimbo, have a good one. Morning, Randal.*

Jane walks around the side of the building, a cigarette burning between her unpainted lips. She stops like a child found somewhere she's not supposed to be. Her eyes are red, puffy.

"Good morning, Jane."

"Morning."

"You doing okay?"

"Am I doing okay?"

Jane drops her cigarette and with her worn-out sneaker buries it in the sand. She sits on the other swing. The old friends sway back and forth saying nothing. Jane stretches her legs out, leans back and pumps herself higher and higher. Her breathing lumbers through the air. Each time she goes further back the swing set hiccups off the ground. Lydia sits still pressing her heels into the sand. She wants Jane to stop. She turns to say something and Jane releases the chains. She sails off the swing, and lands on her feet at the edge of the playground. She dusts off her hands, looks over her shoulder, winks and walks away.

"Wait," Lydia runs after her. Jane gets into her red Toyota. Lydia grabs the door before Jane closes it.

"Why won't you talk to me?"

Jane stares at the steering wheel.

"Why?"

"I don't owe you anything Lydia, not an explanation, not an apology, nothing."

"Why are you so angry? What was I supposed to do, give up

my dreams because you messed up yours?" Lydia turns and heads back across the playground. Jane thrusts the door open and gets out. Lydia hears heavy breathing behind her first, more feverish than compromise, then a presence, something dark, heavy, then a thud on her back. She lurches forward.

Lydia faces the gravel, the swing sways above her head. "You left me when I needed you most," Jane says. Lydia turns around to look up at Jane. Her face is amber, eyes pooling, her tears drop onto Lydia's cheeks. "You kept going, without a care in the world about me. You left without me, and you never looked back, not once, not a phone call, not a card. Nothing."

Lydia stares at the cathedral doors, up at the spire, *help me*, she thinks. Mr. Randal's face peers down into hers. "You alright, girls? I feared it would come to this."

"You were my best friend. We grew up together, Lydia. I was so scared. I had nobody. My life was over and you walked away and lived yours."

"Your life was over? You know nothing about a life being over."

"I know nothing about a life being over?"

"What was I supposed to do, marry you? Stay here and raise your baby? I didn't get you pregnant." She grasps the swing and pulls herself up. "At least you have a goddamn child. He's a good kid, Jane. What the hell do I have? Nothing. That must make you happy."

"Yeah, he was a great kid, Lydia, *was* a great kid."

The Dharma Cave

BAROQUE ARCHES LURK above her, lined in gold. Sun pushes its way through the stained-glass windows: red, green, yellow glimmer down the aisle from above what was once the pulpit. On the wall the silhouette of where a statue of Jesus used to hang. She walks into the confessional, sits down and is greeted by red velvet, she doesn't reach for it, her hands are still. There is nothing to confess. She gets up and leaves, when she does, a voice says, "Go in peace."

Two wooden panels and a hammer are wedged between Kaito's chin and his chest. The hammer falls to the floor with a bang. He kneels to pick it up. He remains kneeling. He shakes his head and looks up toward the kaleidoscopic light dazzling against the faded walls. Streams of colour surround him. He rounds his arms in front of him, links his fingers together and drops his head.

He lifts his head and sits down on the half-built ceremonial stage, he places the hammer beside him. Lydia enters the nave and brushes playground dust off her jeans. Her feet are still schoolgirl small, she's never felt so small, minuscule. Light streams in front of her like a yellow road she desperately wants to step onto and follow. The shadow that stretches across it makes her take a step back. Raiden stands in the doorway. "You are braver than you think," he whispers.

"Pardon?"

Two boys maybe twelve, fourteen, run down the hall. She wonders where they came from. They stop like they have brakes and with an enthusiasm devoid in modern youth. Their flawless faces are eclipsed by teeth and sparkling eyes. *Do teenage boys ever smile like that? They're beautiful* she thinks, *shining*. It makes her forget meeting face-to-face with the gravel they step on daily. They jump up and down, each one trying to outdo the other in height, look at me, no, look at me. "We figured it out," they say, "We figured it out." They playfully shove each other and Raiden laughs, places his broad hands on their shoulders to still them; the boys attempt to catch breaths. "Okay, okay," laughs Raiden.

"The sound of one hand clapping," the fair-haired boy screeches and pulls a notepad from his jean pocket and thrusts it at Raiden; the other one jumps up and down clapping both his hands. The boys' eyes dart back and forth to Lydia, "Daniel," she says. He winks. It's nice they share a secret. Lydia averts her eyes and tries to smoothe down her hair.

"Ha ha," says Raiden, "clever wizards. I knew you would. Go back to the others and we will compare notes." Off the boys sprint, shoving each other out of the way to attempt to be the first one back to the room they came from.

"What did they say?"

"I set up tests for them based on old teachings, but I make them able to discover the meaning through clues."

"What is the meaning?"

"You'd have to take the test."

"What are the clues?"

He ignores her and she imagines he's saying *the question is absurd*.

"I've never seen teenage boys sparkle. Is that part of the test."

"It is the outcome."

Lydia pictures Jane, feels the thud of the hand against her skin, pictures her face, it does not sparkle like her son's.

"That boy..."

"Was Jane Elliot's."

"What did you say to me when you first came in?"

"I said, you are more brave than you realize. I saw your encounter this morning in the playground..."

"Oh, that. I probably deserved it, I guess, I don't really know anymore."

Raiden shakes his head. "No," he says, "you didn't deserve it. I'd say it is the nail that sticks out must be pounded down."

Lydia steps toward him.

"Lydia, how wonderful of you to join us." Little-Nan scuttles down the aisle and takes Lydia's hand, pulls her away from Raiden. Lydia mouths the words, *I don't understand.*

Raiden mouths, *Take the test.*

Little-Nan holds Lydia close to her and speaks to her like a grandma would. "Come, let me show you what we have on our palettes today. Many colours to work with, dear. A rainbow."

Kaito runs his hand through the stream of kaleidoscopic light. He lifts his right foot and places it down hard on the floor, then his left foot. He stomps three times, raises his arms, opens his mouth wide and howls without sound.

The vast main hall is still except for youthful laughter. In a small room at the end of the hall, Raiden rests against a stool; in a semi-circle on the floor, a group of boys sit cross-legged, facing him. Raiden holds up an ink drawing of a walking stick with the head of a dragon on it. All the boys' arms raise into the air and they cheer. *Was Jane Elliot's? He "was" a good kid, Lydia.* She heads downstairs.

She dusts off the old table, removes her fabric from the drawer and studies the seam she's completed. The plows, the sparrows remain where they were. She expects them to be elsewhere in the fabric, to have moved, or been moved, to have flown or driven away in the night. Behind the black curtain Little-Nan appears. Her smile spreads across her delicate face. She pries open the window. Warm air drifts in. Cars murmur past, high heel shoes clomp by, unfamiliar voices, and a few coughs. If the sounds were a bit louder, and multiplied, Lydia swears, the city might be beyond the dirty glass. It's a metallic thought, irritating like... her mind's blank. *What does it feel like?*

She reminds herself that it is the individual wearer that gives the kimono life, unlike her costumes that bring the character to life. *The West is a culture that does, the East is a culture that becomes.* No matter how hard she tries she will never be from the East, so how does one become part of a club, the club of the incomparables, all the people so unlike her, that she can never be a natural member of? Little-Nan hums as she puts away a sheet of the kimono instructions and folds two pieces of blue silk and places them in a drawer.

"Little-Nan?"

"We've acquired a few more clients. It's getting so busy."

Lydia meanders through the kimonos in the other room, runs her hands over the outline of the lions, the peony roses, tries to peek into the purse of inexhaustible riches.

"I was told that I will never understand what happened to my daughter, so not to try. 'Too many steps have been taken returning to the root and the source. Better to have been blind and deaf from the beginning.'"

"Your daughter?" Lydia asks.

"Junko." She flitters her fingers, moves her hands up and down like butterflies. She says, "like water streaming down painted glass, everything falls away over time, life becomes less colourful, far more transparent." Little-Nan had walked into Raiden's studio one night, he had a portrait of Junko he'd painted on glass. He said, "Witness impermanence," and took the portrait over to the sink and ran it under hot water. Like melting skin the acrylic paint peeled off the glass and slithered into the sink, until the glass was perfectly clear again. He took it back to its place on the wall and rehung it. He said, "Now I see right through her and into my own nature."

"What does that mean?"

"Nothing stays the same."

She walks over to the framed glass she'd wondered about. It isn't empty. It is full. Little-Nan turns to Lydia and pauses, places her hands in front of her chest. "Like water streaming down painted glass, everything else falls away, becomes clear. When you experience great loss, life becomes less about illusion and far more transparent."

Pipit enters the room and asks Little-Nan if she needs anything before she heads back to the house. She is cloaked in colour, her lilac eyelids, her peach lips, rosy cheeks, her apricot *yukato*, embroidered with clusters of daffodils. Lydia points to Pipit. "This is the philosophy of the kimono. The kimono is a way of life, love, beauty, courtesy, and harmony. These are the heart of the matter.

This is not an illusion. It is a way of life." Pipit nods her head and backs out of the room.

"Who hurt Junko so badly?"

"Better to have been blind and deaf from the beginning."

Lydia grips the table. She pictures her husband; why did he chose to tell her when he did, all that work, sleeplessness, did he want her to fail? *I could have ignored the signs, I could have ignored them. He wanted me to know. He wanted to be caught.*

I chose to be blind and deaf from the beginning. Blind, maybe I was blind after all. "I've been living in a made-up world ever since I left home. My head's been buried in illusions." Little-Nan's eyes light up. "Perhaps I'll discover the missing link, Little-Nan, something in my past I left behind that would have changed my life, changed the outcome of things. That the truth was there in the beginning."

"Perhaps, or you'll discover what is important now. Not the missing link but the new link."

The Little White House in the Woods

JANE DROPS OFF the milk and Constance apologizes, she usually always makes scones. This morning she was so tired she couldn't. She isn't sleeping well. Jane says it's fine, she has to get back anyway to take Daniel to the program.

"Is he alright?"

"Yes, oddly. He's great."

"Oh good."

"I'm ready to forgive Lydia."

Constance looks at Jane. "For what?"

"For abandoning me."

Constance walks toward the screen door and stares outside.

"Mrs. Templar?"

Jane picks up the empty milk bottles and slips out the front door. Constance will be sorry not to see Jane again, but she is so happy that she will be able to move on; she has the key to unlock the barriers that lead to beyond. She too needs to learn how to forgive.

HENRY REHEARSED HOW he would break the news all the way back through the woods, walking past the path to the house to the other side of the river, and back past the house until he saw the passing cars driving through town, he walked back and forth and back and forth until the sun was setting and a dim light came on in the little white house.

"Henry?"

There was no answer.

Candle flames flickered. On the wall, Constance watched the shadow she thought she knew. The head draped down, shoulders hunched. Shame is vivid. There was nothing Henry could say to change a thing. Would it have been better not to tell Constance?

She sat at the old kitchen table, wished she'd brought a shawl. It was cool in the way a house that has been empty for years is cool. The room had not changed, not in the candlelight. In the daylight, signs of age would be evident. She wanted the house to have a nice family inhabit it. It had only been home to transient workers; in the last few years to a young family with a small child who had been born in the house, one of her father-in-law's employees, a quiet man with a natural talent for carpentry.

CONSTANCE SIPS HER tea, places the photographs back in the box she keeps beneath her bed. She doesn't want to think about Henry anymore in that way. She wishes she could go back to when she knew nothing. Pipit calls from the corridor, "Mrs. Templar, it is time."

Constance runs her hand over Henry's side of the bed, wonders if that woman had ever slept in this bed. The thought hadn't crossed her mind until now and she can't sleep here tonight she tells herself. She'll ask Pipit why she thinks she was able to block it out all these years. The most obvious of thoughts. "Forgiveness," she whispers, "do not go back, do not hold a grudge, do not hold a grudge." *If you hold a grudge you will remain on earth as a ghost and there is no peace in that, you must let go*. Pipit greets Constance at the foot of the stairs, she holds out her small hand and Constance smiles and takes it. She suddenly feels her age, old, small, not quite sure what's ahead of her, far ahead of her.

"We'll walk to the other house then?"

"If you think it's best."

"Sometimes being back in the place of the memory will help you rid yourself of it."

Constance hesitates. She seems frail, not the lively soul she met a few weeks before, greeting them at the door, with a huge smile and open arms. Pipit never felt so welcome, so at home. She takes Constance's arm in hers. They walk across the lawn, past the fish pond and stop at the signs at the end of the yard. To Town pointing to the right, To the Owl pointing to the left. Pipit watches Constance as she runs her hand across the signs. From the window, through a sliver of a crack Junko watches as well. She wants to understand Constance; she is a hard woman to know. From her exterior she is a bright light, always on, a star. The interior's curtains are closed. She hides herself well behind the closed curtains perhaps her daughter made. Junko thinks those curtains were not always there, they are relatively new. She retreats behind hers, lighting candles, now that she is all alone with the Queen Anne.

The little red lanterns sway in the breeze. Constance thinks they make a slight sound like light rain on a tin roof. They make her smile and feel as if she is somewhere else and that is a welcome feeling. She hesitates on the step to the house. "No one is home," says Pipit. "Raiden knows this is where we are conducting our session today."

"I'm not sure I can do this."

"Take your time."

"He was a good man. He really was."

Kaito hears the front door open. "Shoot," he says and looks at the clock on the desk. He goes to blow out the candle then realizes the smell will float into the other room. He doesn't want Constance to know he is there and ruin Pipit's way. "Shoot," he says. "How could I forget to get out before they came?"

The air feels coated with some kind of grime and Constance doesn't want that to remain in the house for her or for anyone else. She had scrubbed and scrubbed the entire place, walls, floors, taps, cupboards, floors, the toilet over and over and over to get rid of any scent of that woman. She scrubbed away her trust, her love, her dreams, her memories, she scrubbed and she scrubbed and she scrubbed as Henry lay in bed counting down the days they had given him, living the bell lap. "I should never have told her," he repeated over and over and over to himself.

"Why did he tell me?" she says.

"There is an old proverb Raiden told me once, 'Too many steps have been taken returning to the root and the source. Better to have been blind and deaf from the beginning.'"

CONSTANCE SHRUGS AND sits down on the small beige couch. "And if he had not told you and she arrived with the child, you would be angrier, hurt, and you'd say, why didn't he tell me?"

She removes her shoes and curls her legs under her and she's not sure why her body decides to get so comfortable. Perhaps pretending she was someone else, *Was this what Junko did when she came here? Curl herself up on the couch like she was at home? Did Henry tell her this was his home? Did he say, "Please take your shoes off, make yourself at home?"*

"What did she know?" she asks Pipit.

"What did he tell you?"

"He told me he wasn't sure why he let it happen. There was nothing wrong with our marriage, or me, he loved me, the children..." She pauses, gets up and walks toward the record player, runs her hands across it, lifts the needle and places it on the edge of the record that never seems to not be there. The cello, then the harpsichord.

My mother said she stole him, then fled with his child, better to have been deaf and blind.

Pipit moves into the kitchen and fills the kettle, "I'm listening," she says.

Kaito moves closer to his door and slides down the wall as he listens to Constance's voice waver, her words occasionally sticking in her throat, cracking her sweet voice, making it sound wounded.

"It wasn't easy for him, he was clearly broken that night, the pain in his body making everything else worse. Imagine, keeping it all inside until the week before he dies. Is that cruel? Did he do it for us, for me, or himself, so he could leave lighter and leave me with the burden of his truth, like passing a rugby ball? Here, it's yours now, run with it, run it between the goal posts for me."

Pipit places the teacup on the table in front of the beige couch and guides Constance back to it. "Sit," she says. "Drink your tea."

"What has your mother told you?"

"That she will not rest until she is with the man she loves."

"That is all?"

"Raiden brought us here. He found you. Raiden knows he has to let her go, for us all to move on, to be a happy family."

PIPIT WATCHES CONSTANCE pace the room, her bare feet pointed like a ballerina's, like the ballerina she admired hanging in the lounge. She rises and falls onto the balls of her feet, her hands moving with each inflection and arms waving like wings. *A swan*, thinks Pipit, *she is swan-like, beautiful, even in her misery*. Her voice projects across the room, *she's on stage*, thinks Pipit, *this is her performance, her testimonial, Henry's testimonial being acted out by his beautiful talented wife that he lied to and deceived and yet she has opened her heart to the result of his deceit, to Henry's other family*. "You are like no one I have ever met," says Pipit. Kaito peers around the corner to watch his sister, her voice now cracking, wounded. Constance stops and looks into her eyes. They are green, like Henry's.

The Other Side

LYDIA'S FINGERS HURT. She flips over the fabric to check the straightness of the seam. The sparrow peers in the opposite direction. The plow, though stationary, appears worn out. "Don't get tired," she whispers to it, "not you, perseverance, not you. Do not disillusion me. Not like everything else." She ties the thread in a small knot. Little-Nan smiles. "I think you made the right decision coming home. Sometimes you need to completely remove yourself from what you know to discover what you have yet to realize. After all, the past and the present are one."

"Please, do not tell me that. What a frightening thought."

Little-Nan turns and smiles. "I feel the same being here. In the city I am searching amongst concrete for answers. When you remain in a familiar environment, you only see what you know. One must extricate themselves from the familiar to be presented with answers, if not answers at least windows in which to see prospects through." She laughs and waves her fingers outside, as if hoping to catch something, butterflies, fresh air, a stranger passing by. "I have discovered that since coming to help Raiden here, I can no longer hide in the familiar. I am being forced to see things differently."

"To see things differently or different things?"

She laughs.

"What do you see?" asks Lydia.

"An unlocked door, I'm afraid to watch another soul walk through."

Lydia thinks of her mother, unlike the squirrel she thinks she is, she will remember what's important. Perhaps she'll remember what she's forgotten, where the chestnuts are buried, which side of the tree her nemesis is on.

Constance sleeps more in the afternoons. Sits down to take short rests and wakes later with a stiff neck and dry mouth, wondering where the day went, angry at herself for not getting her work done, the vacuuming, dusting, laundry. She never napped and didn't like it when Sophie and Lydia used to. Napping wasted the waking hours. Lydia calls from the kitchen, then finds her mother asleep in the ornate slipper chair Lydia reupholstered in a thick floral tapestry. Lydia doesn't run her hands across it like she used to. For some reason it's not calling to her. "I don't need you," she says. "What?" Constance says. "Oh, dear, please don't say things like that. It hurts."

"Not you, Mom, I need you more than ever."

Constance reaches out her hand. "I must have been dreaming. All this sleeping. I don't know what's happening in dreams or out there in the real world."

The world isn't real anymore, Rosa's voice echoes through the room and the car appears, the open road, the drive to the country, Bach, Yo-Yo Ma, the cello, there's the veil of yellow, the dirty dawn, the film rewinding and she's right back where she used to belong, the past and present as one, and it feels like a dream, like it never happened and she's been here in the Queen Anne forever. On the glass-top coffee table, two cups and saucers. One with remnants of a half-drunk tea, the other empty and clean. The ballerina watches from the wall. *Did she have company?* Constance struggles to wake up. She stares at the wall, Lydia follows her gaze. The shadows sway, slow dancing, keeping time with the breeze. The lonely ones, the faces in the corner, screaming without sound. Maybe they are the shadows of women who held grudges, they are stuck here on earth with no feet, trying to get someone's attention on the living room wall, begging for the key to get them the hell out of here and over to the other side. A rabbit bolts across the grass.

"Lydia, please dear, get some sleep. Come on."

Lydia sighs and hesitates, holding her ground. Constance reaches out her hand and Lydia sits down on the floor at her mother's feet and lets her head drop onto her lap. Constance lowers her eyes and thinks of Henry, always smiling at Lydia's stubbornness.

"You know what dear? I'm sorry I made you do something against your will. Tomorrow morning I'll help pack your sewing things."

Lydia is restless and heavy. She turns to be closer to Constance, curls like a baby, limbs clumsy and flaccid. Constance sits quiet beside her, the sun dancing on her lashes, eyes now aglow.

WHEN THE PHONE rings, they both jump and look at each other, neither wanting to answer because it's not going to be who they pray it will be, calling to say he'll be late, or he hit black ice.

It rings and it rings. Lydia looms above it, runs her finger over the calendar. It's a Monday. She's lost track of time. It has no bearing here. Constance grabs the phone and strokes Lydia's back, so many things unsaid in each caress. "Mom, I was fired for hurting people with the thing I loved more anything. I sabotaged my own future, why?" Constance opens her mouth, then closes it again and shakes her head. She picks up the phone, Lydia counts the days she's been here, forgetting the exact date she came. Numbers elude her. They are the first things she forgets.

Constance's tone lowers, her voice slows and she pauses, it triggers fear. Lydia braces herself for bad news; Constance left the hospital to rush home and pick up fresh pajamas for Henry. "It is a good time to go," said the nurse, "he's resting, peaceful, doesn't seem to be anguished, be quick." In the time she left and arrived at the house, he breathed his last breath. Lydia was home for the weekend. In between productions, she had come to visit Henry. She arrived at the same time the phone rang. The familiar quiet, hesitant, low voice, *something's died*, she thinks, *finished, ended*, she feels it, whatever it is, dissipating like dreams. "Oh yes, she is here, yes. Getting there...just one moment, please."

Constance, pale-faced, hands the phone to her daughter as if it were a wet cat she just pulled from the stream. She covers the earpiece and mouths *Charlie*. Lydia's eyes shoot inward. She glances at the end of her nose. *The sword that kills the man, is the sword that saves the man.* She wanders to the front window. The pit of her stomach turbulent. The sensation beneath her skin sharp pricks, wider than fabric pins, more flat, switchblades. She walks past the ballerina, avoids the stare. She stops in front of the bay window and looks over at the closed library door, her bare toes grip the thick cream rug and a softness like warm wind rises through them. His voice is high, nervous, she thinks. He's talking and talking. The green grass, the sun-filled driveway, the pristine Japanese maple aren't helping to curb the feeling of grit in her throat, over her skin, mudslide, the warm wind rising up and up, *hurry, get to the top of me quick.* The milk van makes its way up the long driveway and parks. In public school she wrote a paper on fear. If she researched it she thought she could learn to determine when she was feeling it. The textbook said, "Fear is a valuable, valid emotion, a good one. It's good to feel fear. It prevents us from doing things we shouldn't, like leaping off cliffs, stepping in front of moving vehicles or getting into cars with strange men." *Getting into cars with strange men? And what about signing contracts with strange men? It neglected to mention marriage.*

"Lydia? For Christ's sake, are you there, are you listening to me? Have you ever listened to me? To my feelings, to what I have to say?"

Rising couplets, crescendo. She wonders why it astounds her that Bach had nine children. She listens to Charlie's voice, he is not a father, not the type. Bach was successful and had nine children he loved. He had his work and family. He was able to do both. Lydia wonders if she would have ever been able to do both. Constance lost one for the other, Henry had his work but not all the children he wanted. Symphonies or solos.

"Lydia, I've got to get back to work, please."

Her good fear, the one wreaking havoc on her stomach, the one numbing her left side, turning her sight fuzzy, drying her mouth, says *Don't answer. Do not conduct this conversation — it's like leaping in front of a train.* Constance wavers in the background, hands on her face, hearing Henry's confession over and over and she wants to protect Lydia, like the ballerina she can't. It's too late. She should have told them a long time ago; it might have changed the outcome of so many things.

"Lydia?"

"I'm here."

"Lydia. I'm trying to resolve things with you, so we can move on."

"So we can move on."

"God, I'm trying, I'm trying."

A hummingbird zips up to the Rose of Sharon. Every morsel of its tiny, lace-like wings keeping it airborne as it eats from the purple blossom.

"No, Charlie, you aren't even close to trying."

The tulips Henry nurtured like children bent over in the growing wind. She tries to count the days since she left; she is three weeks in. "In one month you'll feel like a new woman," Rosa said. There is no point in ever going back to the city. She'll open an alteration business. That's it. She'll alter things, hems, waists, repair zippers, school uniforms. Altering and repairing one's wardrobe, the extension and expression of one's self. She can picture it, the little bell rings when the door opens, she looks up from her sewing machine, pushes the glasses she'll start wearing up and onto her head, so she can see at a distance more clearly. *Good morning, what can I alter for you Charlie, your bad decisions, your inability to tell the truth, to not act, to pretend you are someone else and that someone else, the other role, has his own lover, another life, another family? When do you need it by, is one month okay?*

"Lydia, the lease. We have to talk about the lease."

"The lease? You called about the lease?"

"And the doctors. God, Lydia, they keep calling and calling. You've missed so many appointments."

"Appointments?"

"You shouldn't be there, Lydia. You shouldn't have gone home."

Constance whispers from behind, "Keep calm, try not to get upset." She sees her husband out there in the garden, healthy and waving, hears Pipit whispering through the muslin sheers, *too many steps have been taken returning to the root and the source. Better to have been blind and deaf from the beginning.*

The screaming faces on the wall drive Lydia on, give it to him, give it to him. *Get it out, purge yourself of the grudges, the resentment, let it out, Oguchi no Magami.* Through the banister, black fingernails claw the air, Junko's long thin legs dangle down from the second-floor landing, swinging back and forth. Pipit looms behind her attaching an invisible leash around her neck, ready to pull on it, if she suddenly lunges downstairs.

"Do you have any idea what I lost because of you? All you had to do was be honest with me. This is not part of the play, Charlie. I am a real person, our marriage was real."

"No, it wasn't." He goes silent. She swears she hears a whisper in the background, and imagines Imogen sitting beside him telling him what to say, putting words in his mouth like a script because that's all he knows. She pictures Rosa attempting to hang onto the apartment in the hope that she'll be back. Or perhaps she's fed up being there and wants to get back to her own home. Imagines Rosa and Charlie and Imogen having a pint in one of the little pubs by the theatre. Having a pint, a pitcher of Blue, the colour of hopelessness, the colour of melancholy. The three of them, contemplating how to tell Lydia it was time to give up on her home, to move on, they were all moving on. Charlie is right, the marriage wasn't real. A truer word hadn't been spoken. She hangs up. She walks into the hall and stops. "Next time," she says and stretches her neck as long as it can go to pierce Junko's eyes with hers, "mind your own business."

Constance sits on the patio sipping plum wine. Lydia appears with an empty glass and bottle of red wine. "It's okay," Lydia says and kisses her mother on the cheek which Constance wants her to repeat and repeat and repeat and repeat. Lydia opens the bottle and pours a glass of wine, sits in the Edwardian wicker chair and says, "The problem with life is we get way too involved in it."

Praying for Wolves

THE OWL HOOTS. She wants desperately to find it. The sky's a country black. The stillness, the motionless trees are like a theatre at night when everyone's gone home and the man-made setting waits in a state of suspension for the next rise of the curtain. Like Verona did when the theatre emptied and she lingered in its finely constructed streets wondering what it would be like to really be there. Not just in Verona but Verona in the sixteenth century. Apart from the clothes, she wonders if much has changed. People are the same. Love continues to tear everyone apart.

Lydia turns right without thinking — habit — and instantly feels the comfort of the woods, the trees' breath. The sun is long gone. The sky remains her favourite colour, navy blue, and the crescent moon sparkles, newly polished or maybe just happy. It hangs there smiling. A ghost of fog hovers at knee level. She's careful to walk like a wolf, as if on air, not to crack a twig and alert her whereabouts. She listens for them, for the howling, pictures the plow, sparrows, feels the softness of silk, *peau de soie*. The red lanterns glimmer in Raiden's backyard. There's movement, like shadows dancing slow, swaying like the trees. Lydia tiptoes across the bridge, not to make any noise. She kneels behind a hedge and watches. Kaito, Little-Nan and Pipit stand in a line, arms floating up, down, feet shimmying across the grass, lifting up, down, knees slightly bent, a drum sounds and a flute, two boys sit on lawn chairs playing the instruments like professionals, serious faces, erect posture. "Daniel," she says, softly. His flat hands connecting with the drum with precision, like he's been doing this his whole life, pounding drums. Raiden is nowhere to be seen, she looks around for him, figured he would be the conductor, orchestrating this ritual or whatever it was they were doing. She stands up and moves behind a cluster of trees where she can still see them but hopes they can't see her. The bridge adjusts itself behind her like it does, makes noises like the Queen Anne, stretching, yawning, sighing. She holds her arms out to the side, like the counsellors, knees bend, she stomps and almost falls over. The boy playing the flute looks in her direction. She removes her sneakers and presses her feet into the dirt. She waits to feel the connection to nature, to learn something about herself, her body, through her feet. She presses them harder and harder into the cool ground and waits, nothing happens. The drumming is soothing, a heartbeat.

She envies their rituals, the significance of a symbol, a gesture, a stomping bare foot. There was solace in their stomping feet, in the slow beat of the drum, the whistling flute. One day maybe she'd join them but they haven't asked. It seemed like the kind of ritual one had to be invited to, like acquiring one's Dragon Staff Certificate. You can't just purchase one on the internet like a degree or a child, a husband or Oxycodone. Enlightenment has to be earned. It supercedes technology.

A branch cracks behind her. She turns around, screams. It's out of her mouth before she realizes. A large figure stands at the other end of the bridge. Startling red hair, flames of it, raging in all directions and hanging down each side of the figure to its knees. From behind the hair she catches sight of a sharp pointed nose, bent, a sinister mouth, screaming eyes. Its attire wide and bright, robes over robes — gold, red, orange. Lydia spins back toward the lanterns, the backyard. Raiden orders everyone to stop. He was there. Where? In the wings? Behind her? Above her, in the trees, spying, listening? Was it him making noises like the owl, pretending to be it? He stomps his foot on the ground unlike the regular stomping, his hands form fists. Lydia has no clue whether to run forward through the figure, or back into the safety of Pipit and Little-Nan's company. Raiden approaches the trees and stops on the other side of them like he was looking into her eyes, beyond the dark curtain she swore hid her from his view. Raiden puts up his hand, "Lydia, is that you?" The silhouette at the end of the bridge has disappeared. The wind howls, the wind, not the wolves. She prays for wolves.

"Lydia?"

The red lanterns sway. Raiden opens his tin and produces a cigarette. Everyone has entered the house. "There is something you might want to keep in mind."

The tone of his voice reminds her of her grandfather's.

"Is this another one of those crazy proverbs? I'm just not sure I believe in them, Raiden."

"It isn't a matter of believing or not, Lydia, it just is."

"Okay, what is it?"

He turns to walk away. She comes out from behind the trees and backs onto the bridge where she feels safe. She apologizes. Raiden stands on the edge of the bridge and inhales his cigarette and exhales. *Smoke, smoke, there is hope in every inhalation, in every exhalation.* Raiden walks to the middle of the bridge and sits down on its edge; his long thin legs dangle down to the water. He says,

"When I first bought the house, your mother had kept to herself." He'd see her at times through the trees, walking back and forth in the yard talking. She seemed pained, perplexed. Lydia asks whom she was talking to. Raiden says that isn't the point. Lydia finds his tone abrupt and considers leaving until he presses his hands together and bows like he knew he had been too hard on her. The point, he says, is she is talking now and Lydia fails to hear. *She hasn't said a word in days.* Raiden worried about Constance. Lydia thinks it tricky that he manages to divert her attention away from the figure in the woods, to her mother. What on earth triggered a talk about her mother?

"Who was that figure at the end of the bridge?"

Raiden puffs on his cigarette.

"You didn't see it?" she says.

Raiden smokes and drags his long bare feet through the cool water. Lydia imagines Charlie and sees herself over her sewing machine, wrapped in fabrics, enveloped in the joy of what she did, always in another room, at home, at the theatre, speaking to his side of the bed when he didn't come after scheduled rehearsals, then speaking to him after he snuck into bed and passed out, reeking of mint-veiled beer. He got caught, he grabbed his things, he moved out. She'd been avoiding him. How long has she been avoiding everything?

"You're very quiet," says Raiden.

CONSTANCE HASN'T BEEN sleeping well. Her dreams becoming more frightening, dreams of being chased and no one coming to her rescue. Her limbs won't move, she can't get away. Lydia keeps asking Raiden if he's noticed a change in her mother. He advises that loneliness plays terrible tricks on the mind. "Just loneliness?"

"It's all relative, Lydia."

"She keeps asking if I've seen the emperor."

"Be supportive and allow her the illusions that please her."

Raiden blows smoke rings that hypnotize; eyes closed he repeats, "It is important to be supportive and allow her the illusions that please her."

"You said that."

He lowers his cigarette. "You are listening."

She doesn't believe he did that as a test. No, he repeated himself unknowingly. Maybe his batteries are running out. He's short-circuiting. From the stress of the ceremony. He is human after all.

Lydia says, "Did you allow your mother the illusions that pleased her?"

Raiden stiffens. There is so much he wants to say about illusions, mothers, fathers, illusions, family, illusions, illusions. Through the hot spring she watches the cool of his breath. Would he crack if she pushed him? His eyes show a curve of white beneath them like a wolf's way of saying back off — to say, Don't fuck with me.

"Did you know your father well?"

"Yes, he was my father, of course I did."

"Your husband?"

"My husband? What are you saying?"

"One who thinks one's insight exceeds others has no eyes."

He gets up, bows and makes his way across the bridge. He loses sight of his agenda, the reigns fallen from grip, thoughts freed: *don't think about the years you thought the father was dead long before he was dead. The girl on the bridge who grew up with him, the mother being groomed for departure into the waiting arms of a man she'll die for. Stick to the program. Tomorrow Kaito will complete the bridge with the boys, they will rehearse the music, the dance, the lines, dress rehearsal beneath the man-made pines and the oil-paint river, reveal the key that unlocks the barrier that leads to beyond. Who really moves on when she goes to him?* He glances at the water moving on beneath him, sees the face he doesn't want to.

RAIDEN LEAPS ONTO his feet and makes his way back over the bridge and says loudly, "Lightning flashes, sparks shower, in a blink of an eye, you have missed seeing."

She ducks and looks at the sky.

"What do you mean?"

He continues walking toward his house. "God," she says. *His proverbs are exhausting, exhausting.* If he would just tell her what he means, plain and simple, straight. Lydia pushes herself up onto her feet. "She'd tell me if there was something wrong, talk to me, not talk to herself in the backyard or to the souls you say are out there, like that one that was right here, right here I saw it, or the emperor or whoever she talks to."

Raiden stops. "The emperor?" he says.

"Why can't you tell me in layman's terms what you mean? I thought Hakuin was all for the layman reaching enlightenment? Isn't that what you told me? The layman, ordinary people, give it to me in black and white."

Raiden strolls back over the bridge, the smoke from his cigarette clouds around him. "The sooner you realize that nothing is black and white, you will begin to see."

"Christ, they are so confusing." She punches her thighs. *Riddles,*

riddles, riddles, riddles. The red lanterns sway in a breeze she can't feel. There is no breeze. The pines close in on her. She calls after Raiden as he climbs the steps to the white house and turns the doorknob. "My mother says she has tea with an emperor, sees him outside the bay window, wandering in the backyard. I thought it was you. I thought you were the emperor."

Without stopping or turning around he says, "No Lydia, I am not the emperor."

The Infidel

LYDIA GAZES AT the backyard, at the yards and yards of green grass, tulips, the blue sky hanging over it like a newly pressed sheet. She grabs a picture of her mother from the wall; she's young and laughing, Henry at her side. Maybe she should listen to Raiden and not assume she knows her mother best. This morning she gives him the benefit of the doubt, if only to ensure he stops haunting, looming over her like a conscience.

When she saw Pipit in the garden the other day, she asked about the emperor, and she waved her fan in front of her face as if she was batting away Lydia's words like flies. Lydia assumed Junko was marrying the emperor. Pipit said one day she would try to explain but until the wedding they were not at liberty to divulge another person's personal information.

Lydia sneaks into the cathedral early and pulls her kimono from the drawer; her hands glide over the silk and stop. The sensation is different now. There is another message coming through the silk that defies touch and texture. It is quiet, uncategorical, it clears her head. She stops when she senses something looming in the door. Kaito stands there with a package in his hand. She leaps up when she sees him. "Your mother asked me to bring this to you. It came this morning." It's from Rosa, she opens it and out drops pictures of the stage, the costumes, opening night, newspaper clippings and a tin of *Hope*. The carousel music sounds in her head. "Everything, okay?" asks Kaito.

"Did you know that when the architect Louis Kahn died, his son discovered his dad had other families?"

"What made you tell me that?"

"I don't know. Something in your eyes, the softness of your hands."

She grips the package, smells Rosa's signature perfume that she's never known the name of. She closes her eyes, sees herself on the steps of the theatre unable to move. She swore she heard the door lock behind her. The air outside hung heavily, a velour shawl. She stood across the street and looked at the old church that possessed the past ten years of her life. The fire escape was empty, no Rosa, no empty wine bottle or smoke from her always burning cigarette. She waited for someone to come and go. Her phone had dozens of missed Rosa calls but it wasn't that she needed to speak to her dear friend, she needed to be on the other side of that door working beside her. She gripped her stinging hands. She stood there for ages, no idea which direction to go, left, right, or straight out into the busy street. She made her way down the steps toward the road. She glanced up at the traffic lights and when she saw green, she blindly stepped out into oncoming traffic. Car horns honked, brakes screeched, drivers yelled. A gentle hand reached around her thin arm. It was like air lifted her back onto the sidewalk. She'd glanced at the wrong light. The man who had been watching her held her arm. Then he bowed, winked and walked into the temple.

When he disappeared behind the closing door, horns blasted, breaks squealed, like the video games Charlie spent hours playing in the off-season. She considered heading into the temple to look for the man who saved her, to thank him, to see if they'd allow her to enter the translucent tunnels she swears they are separated in.

She concentrated on each step and tried to figure out if she didn't guide them in the direction they always went, where they would lead her. They continued on the same path they'd traipsed for years, down the steps to the A-Train, into the dark tunnel, out of the dark tunnel, up into the light and boarded the waiting bus.

She gazed out the window. Noticed trendy bars, quaint cafés and restaurants that had never stood out before. Noted how young everyone seemed, busy meeting each other, heading into those little joints for happy hour she guessed. Dressed in second-hand styles she knew weren't from vintage stores, but expensive designer boutiques. Baggy, faded Levi's, scuffed leather jackets, motif T-shirts, plaid shirts, too small for their frames but that was how it was meant to be. Straggly hair, perfectly designed to look just woken. It amazed her how real people dressed. How much money they spent on cheap fabrics with designer labels, how much money they spent to look poor.

She glanced down at her own costume, one she felt she hadn't changed in a decade; her worn out denim dungarees, tattered 100% cotton Thin White Duke T-shirt, twill army jacket and her favourite Converse now faded to beige. She shoved strands of her dishevelled waist-length hair behind her ears, studied her chipped fingernails, the gold band.

A few men sat alone with shoulders hunched gazing at girls exiting the local high schools. Women that looked around Lydia's age spoke on cell phones or read books. An older woman counted her fingers or counted something on them, perhaps how much time she had left. Four young women in burqas sat in front of Lydia immersed in conversation, harbouring serious opinions on what they must have learned in school that day. One had a sharper voice than the rest, animated. Their conversation was merely rhythms and inflections at first. A few words stood out here and there, tones rose and fell determined by the young women's stance on the subject.

Another bar passed, Lydia hadn't noticed it during all the years she'd taken the same route twice a day. Outside of it a handsome man embraced a handsome woman. They glanced over their shoulders before entering. Were they having an affair? Suddenly all the happy couples raised suspicion. The happy ones, giddy, embracing outside of inconspicuous cafés and bars, all infidels? It never occurred to her that the rosy-cheeked, the energetic, the cleverly-dressed, the frequenters of hidden cafés and bars and quaint French restaurants buried in obsolete auto shops and warehouses were having affairs, the unfaithful, gleaming like the sun at its midday peak, the happy moon — yellow.

Then one of the girls with a high-pitched voice said, "It is the worst plot, meaningless, stupid, who would do that?"

"What?" said another.

"*Romeo and Juliet*, the worst plot."

Lydia paid closer attention. The girls nodded their covered heads in unison and agreed that its plot was useless, untrue, that no one, especially young people would kill themselves for love. Then another mentioned it was their parents that caused all the trouble. The girls agreed that a parent preventing the union was plausible. Something they seemed to relate to by the inflections in their voices and their nodding cloaked heads. "But seriously," the one with the high-pitched voice said, "they wouldn't kill themselves, come on. Why write that? What a stupid plot." Another one argued that they didn't mean to kill themselves. It was an accident.

"Even worse," said the one with the high-pitched voice. They paused and the quieter of the girls who'd been gazing out the window asked if anyone had finished reading *The Bell Jar* yet. Lydia was amazed that they taught that book in high school and these girls seemed unaware of Sylvia Plath's and Ted Hughes' stupid plot. She wanted to tell the girls the parallels between Hughes and Plath and Romeo and Juliet were remarkable. In time they'll realize the parallels are everywhere. When Lydia's stop came, she stared at the open door, then back at the bus driver. The girls stopped talking and watched Lydia as the bus waited, while everyone waited for her to get off.

"Are you alright, ma'am?" asked the bus driver.

Lydia turned toward the cloaked young women, studied their bhangee cotton attire and said, "I married Romeo, you know. And you are right, you are right, it is a useless plot. Why kill yourself for love, even by accident."

SHE STEPPED OFF the bus and stood by the bench in front of the three-storey brownstone her apartment was in. She gripped the swatch of red velvet in her pocket she always kept in reach and climbed the three flights of stairs and stood at the apartment door. Her knees buckled. The door creaked when she walked in. One of the many things Charlie promised to fix but didn't get around to. The wind blowing in from the balcony threw the rose-pattern sheers across the harvest table. Headless poppies from the stifling brocade trunk hose littered the dish-cluttered sink, hung off lamps, across the hardwood floor. Lydia held her breath. She called out for her husband. There was no answer. There was a void in the atmosphere. She was alone. She couldn't believe

Charlie snuck out of the theatre and did this to their home, like Lydia was the infidel, the one in the wrong. She rushed to their wardrobe, opened his empty drawers, gazed at his cleared-out desk. He snuck in, cleaned out his stuff and rushed off with no discussion as to how they would wrap things up, who would pay for what, what happened or why, as if she was the one in the wrong. Stuck to the Chantilly mirror she noticed a Post-it note, scribbled on it was: You humiliated me in front of my peers. You think of no one but yourself. You reap what you sew Lydia, you reap what you sew.

"What?"

She tore the note from the glass. Framed in ornate gold, her illegible expression faced her: thin lips, a purple hue, cracked. Small dry eyes, pupils fading, blending into dark brown, a colour she always hated. Sophie was blessed with the sea-green eyes of her father that turned blue in the summer. A colour she doesn't even appreciate and covers with blue contacts in winter. She thought of calling her sister, *some sister, what a sister,* and didn't call.

She placed the note on the table. *You reap what you sew, Lydia. You reap what you sew.* Thick amber liquid beckoned to her from the wet bar. Scotch gurgled into the dirty blue mug left next to it. She poured honey into it, water, a squeeze of lemon and placed the tonic she'd grown up with into the microwave for one minute. She returned the cushions to the couch, grabbed a torn piece of the fabric off the floor and rubbed it over her cheek, "I humiliated you in front of your peers?"

At the height of her paranoia, questioning her husband's indifference toward her, sitting on the couch just like now, heart thumping, she threatened to leave him. Charlie scoffed. He glided across the living room to his bar, poured himself a cognac and said in his affected English accent, "You'll never leave."

She stared at the wedding picture Constance had framed for her and sent by FedEx without bubble wrap, the side of the glass cracked. She tried to detect love in their eyes. They stood stiffly, smiling like siblings. She always wondered if she'd married too young, the right man, if marriage was something she wanted. She became accustomed to Charlie's company; their familiarity with each other was comforting. All the things they had in common allowed her to concentrate on what she loved to do. They lived and thrived in the same universe, and were companions within that realm. It made life easy. Charlie made it easy. He was a man within the dream, not the man of her dreams, she told Rosa, one afternoon on the fire escape as Rosa smoked and Lydia watched the monks and listened to the chiming bells emanating from the temple's courtyard. "I can see him but I can't feel him, Rosa. It's the way I've always been, so it's okay, you know."

"For you," said Rosa. "Wish I'd had your affliction when it comes to men. I can see 'em, but I can't feel 'em, perfect. To me they're like goddamn corduroy."

"Frustrating," they said in unison.

Glancing around her dishevelled home, Lydia felt an overwhelming sense of satisfaction knowing that night after night Charlie's role ends in death.

She couldn't afford to stay in the apartment alone without a job. The thought of banging on doors, attempting to get into another theatre was agonizing. Some things you cannot repeat. She'd have to start from scratch and at her age in a cut-throat city, there was no way starting from scratch was an option. Jobs like hers were scarce.

The economic crisis and changing times wreaked havoc on theatre. Every day she heard of more and more productions closing down, companies merging or dying altogether. The underground, more independent theatres had lost their grip on spaces and funding. The new audience demanded musicals and comedies, simple premises, light and literal. Riddles and metaphor were a thing of the past; out with Beckett, Pinter, Genet, Williams and, one day, Shakespeare. That was obvious to her when she sat in the theatre on the other side. She'd have no control of her work there, even as the designer. Desmond said she'd become the most difficult to work with. Lydia had vision and isn't that what they wanted; she fought for that, fought for them not to change her way of doing things. The only chance she'd have now was to work under someone as a cutter. Something she hadn't done since her early twenties. She'd paid her dues. The hot whisky warmed her insides and made her head spin. She stared at the ringing phone, then out the window beyond the sheers into the lowering sun. She'd never imagined doing anything else in her life. Her mother spoke of reinventing herself; but was her situation reinvention, now that she'd been forced to change? She grabbed the phone. "It's chaos here, Lydia. Chaos. I can't do this without you. Desmond is a fool, a fool."

"Desmond is the fool, what about Charlie, Imogen, the cast, all the people that knew and didn't say anything, what about you Rosa?"

She crouched to her knees, pressed her forehead on the hardwood floor.

Rosa's voice echoed and echoed, and she heard herself saying, "It was not my fault."

"Maybe it was your fault."

"My husband cheated and I got fired."

"You got fired because you tried to maim him with fabric pins, and suffocate his mistress. I warned you." Rosa inhaled a cigarette and gulped what Lydia imagined was thick red wine. She was never without her Diazepam and Australian Shiraz and *Hope*. The simple pleasures in life she cannot do without. She heard buses lumber by. Rosa was on the fire escape. "Never go back, Lydia. What you're feeling is natural, hang on. Have a drink, I'll be there soon. This is natural."

"Natural? Why do you keep saying that? I've been living in a goddamn made-up world ever since I left home. It's time to go back to where I came from and remind myself what the real world is like."

"There is no 'real world' anymore, Lydia, face it."

"Why are you being so mean?"

"Because I love you."

Lydia punched the overstuffed cushions at her side, she punched the couch. She glanced around at the dishevelled apartment, initially designed to look romantic with edge, velvet, lace, ruby chandeliers, mismatched kitchen table chairs all copied from a scene from *A Streetcar Named Desire* she'd seen as a child, sitting backstage watching, one of those scenes that never leaves one's mind, the hysterical woman, with the hysterical man, in a shady apartment and the hysterical woman wearing too much makeup and screeching at an audience is your mother.

She ran those weathered hands that would never pick up a needle and thread again over the soft wood of the old chairs her grandfather handcrafted. Before he died he told Lydia to swear she would always continue to sew by hand. She promised but knew it would be a promise she couldn't keep. "Always remember the importance of using your own hands," he'd said, "of feeling what you touch." She ran her hand over the framed poster of the Tennessee Williams play her mother had starred in when she met Henry. She thought of Stanley Kowalski, of the two sisters vying for the same man. "None of this is natural," she said.

"Lydia, are you okay? It's going to be okay," Rosa said, but she had no idea what she meant.

She missed her mother. She needed her strength. "You are no one without family," Constance liked to remind her daughters. She was right. She was always right. When Henry died she felt cut off from family. He was the bridge that kept them all together.

Lydia gazed into the off-centre mirror at her unkempt blonde hair that hung in tangles to her waist. The same hair she'd worn since childhood. Rosa sniffed and rambled on about not giving up and not going back and mothers. Her voice was a rise and fall in air, wordless breaths and tones, a yellow veil, like Bach. Lydia placed the phone on the coffee table and grabbed the fabric scissors from her bag. She turned her head upside down and twisted her waist length hair. She sawed the scissors through the mass of blonde and snipped. It sounded like teeth chomping into an apple. The hair fell onto the floor and lay there like an animal hit and lying dead on the side of a country road.

"Change is good," Lydia said to Rosa, "maybe I'll open a little shop and sell things." She picked up the hair. "All the things I can't bear to keep around." She gazed at the myriad of trinkets she collected over the years. Blue, green, mauve bottles with fabric flowers shoved in each, decorative frames filled with textiles, and photos of people she never knew. Strangers' families of bygone eras and places she dreamed about but had never been: 1900s Rome, 1920s Paris, 1930s London, 1940s Berlin. She drew inspiration from their shoes and hats and petticoats and jewels and facial expressions and body language and the stodgy and unkempt hair. The black and white existence captured in a photograph. She could smell the heaviness of their attire and sense the heaviness of their lives from their eyes or how they held their black and white hands. "Perhaps I'll discover the missing link," she said to Rosa. "Something in my past I left behind that would have changed the outcome of things." She downed the Scotch. "Maybe I'll meet some small-town man and have small-town children and bake." Rosa inhaled and gulped red wine and buses continued to lumber by in the background.

"Who's to say that's not a great life? I want to live a regular life, be a normal woman. What does normal feel like, Rosa? We don't even know."

"Jesus Christ, Lydia. You can't say things like that. It's useless."

It was useless, a useless plot. It didn't matter. Lydia rummaged through her bag while Rosa rattled on through the phone line. She stuffed her hair in her grandmother's old keepsake box. She had to separate herself from Shakespeare, from the beautifully constructed past that led to nothing. She'd learn to exist in the real world. No more costumes, masks, scripts. She held her breath so Rosa wouldn't detect she was crying.

Convinced that after spending a few weeks in a town where Rosa believed there were no hidden gems waiting to be discovered, nothing that hadn't been unturned and exhausted in childhood, that Lydia would not adjust to "regular life," she would be back — sewing machine, fabric needles, thimble and all.

Lydia places the unopened package on the table and removes the needle from where she left off.

The Curtain Call

THE DINING ROOM table is set with pretty floral place mats and crystal wine glasses. A vase of wisteria blossoms graces its centre. The open windows welcome the hot spring air and a floating yellow veil from the setting sun. Constance greets Lydia with a kiss on the cheek. She glows. She tells her about the day. How the ebb and flow of sewing each stitch by hand is like sailing. Soothing like sailing. Silk has a healing quality. The fabrics and their symbols tell stories. Peonies and lions represent nobility. Cranes symbolize longevity. Constance listens as she prepares a salad in the kitchen.

Pipit enters the room. "I'm sorry I'm late."

Little-Nan appears at the screen door holding flowers and a wine bottle. The bottle almost the same size as her.

Lydia glances at her mother like, *what are they doing here?* She's been looking forward to spending time alone with Constance. "Go and sit outside with the girls, dear." She pours them each a glass of plum wine she picked upon the emperor's recommendation. The women exchange glances. They love plum wine. They sit outside on the garden chairs with the sun hazily hanging off to the east. Morning doves coo. A hint of moisture looms in the air, the smell of rain. The girls comment on the country setting; they're becoming accustomed to the sounds of nature. The pines and the birds keep them company in a way they hadn't expected.

"My mother used to pray beneath the pines in a park at the back of our house," says Pipit.

"Pines are sacred to the immortal spirits, spirits that are not from this world," says Little-Nan and Pipit grabs her hand.

"She believes my father's spirit is drawn to the pines."

Pipit keeps her head down. Constance stops what she's doing and joins them outside. "I believe that too, dear." She places her hand on Pipit's shoulder and their eyes watch Lydia. She's sipping her wine with one hand and fondling the lace coaster with the other. "Grandma didn't believe in spirits."

"Grandma?" says Constance.

"Funny because..." she stops and looks up at the women waiting to hear the rest. "Because she loved trees, that's all."

"Are you feeling alright? You've had a long day."

"I'm fine." She drops the coaster and walks toward the kitchen for the canvas bag she knows her mother keeps in the pantry.

Pipit sips her wine. "Too many steps have been taken returning to the root and the source. Better to have been blind and deaf from the beginning," she says.

Little-Nan fans her face and says, "*Makoto no Hana*. You are lost in a reverie. You are an authentic daydreamer. It is a skill."

"It is?" Lydia stands in the doorway gripping canvas.

"It was her best subject in school," says Constance, and the women giggle.

"That's a lie," says Lydia but it was true. Her parents had been called in by her grade three teacher to discuss her lack of productivity in class. "*She spends more time speaking with the rabbit and gazing out the window*," said the teacher. They all laughed and Lydia couldn't fathom that her mother was talking about the same

Lydia. Pipit withdrew her fan from in front of her face and said, "You should get a rabbit. Perhaps that is the answer." The girls laugh. Constance stares at the sky, wipes her hands on her apron and returns to the kitchen.

"Do you think she sees the emperor up there?" whispers Lydia.

Little-Nan and Pipit lift fans in front of their faces.

When Constance met Henry she was intimidated and nothing intimidated her. He was tall and dark and said very little. "Like the pines?" says Pipit. Lydia nodded.

"Like the pines," Constance says from the kitchen. "He was quiet but he was such a good man. He looked after his family. Everything he did was for us." She touches Lydia's arm and surprises her, how her mother can move from one room to another like air. Pipit curls her lips together. *His thoughts were a mystery. His wrinkled brow proved that he was rarely without them. Grandma Templar told Constance that he'll never tell you what's on his mind so if you can live with that, he's yours. Why have thoughts if you can't share them?* thought Lydia.

"Mom," she says, "did it ever make you feel lonely?"

Constance says, "Yes."

JUNKO PARTS THE curtains just enough to quietly open the window; the fresh air stuns her. She steps back, wafts it away with her jagged nails and papery hands, like something that should be hanging from a ceiling not attached to limbs. She sees the edge of Pipit's pale blue robe and the white of her socks sticking out from her wooden toeless shoes. The back of Little-Nan's head is barely visible. Lydia returns to her chair and Junko backs away, "Bull's eye," she says. "There you are waif, the perfect daughter, smack dab in the middle of my lens. Oh, how your father loved you." She picks up the ceramic pony she retrieved from Lydia's empty room and begins to gaze into it, mumbling and mumbling, her wiry hair vibrating as she shakes her maskless head. The face she could not bare to exist without rests on a mannequin clothed in an aquamarine robe lined in gold, down its side a walking stick with the head of a dragon.

Lydia feels a heaviness she can't explain, the woods are darkening, the candles Constance lit flicker in the dining room, casting a gold hue across the gloaming room. Her eyes catch an aura of the same gold agitating like water in wind. Without moving her head, she looks up, the curtains to her grandmother's old suite are parted, the beautiful suite that has now become a mirrored prison to a woman she will never understand. Black vines rock back and forth through the golden light, then go still. The white orb beneath the vines moves up slower than the old freight-lift in her grandfather's warehouse in town. The white of Junko's eyes glow and do not move, her red lips stretch apart to gritting teeth, revealing her pink gums, like another door opening, the teeth separate, and her mouth stretches and keeps stretching. Lydia thinks she will swallow the window frame and then howl.

"My God," says Constance.

The chilling cry sends birds leaping off branches into the sky, screeching, warning all the rest and anything out there on the ground to take flight.

"Junko!" Pipit leaps to her feet, knocking the crystal glass onto the stone patio and breaking slowly in two. She trips and scrambles to her feet as the howl goes deeper and colder and for a second Lydia thinks there is an echo and not the same howl bouncing back as a response.

Little-Nan apologizes and follows Pipit upstairs.

Constance stands in the doorway clutching a blue gingham dishcloth, tears crawling down her cheeks.

Lydia watches the curtains get tugged shut and the sudden silence practically knocks her over, like a tight grip someone just had on her is released. "Lydia?" says Constance. "Lydia?"

The large-mouthed pure god. She turns and runs into the woods.

"Lydia?"

THE SUN'S REMOVED and the sky's changed into a blue silken shawl. The moon is lit like a bright curtainless house. Through the trees red lanterns flicker against the blackness of the woods. The tinkle of the *biwa* floats through Raiden's backyard. Lydia stands on the edge of the bridge. Her phone rings and she quickly silences it, the startling numbers singe her eyes, a begging for attention — bright, not an illuminating one, not like enlightenment. It's Charlie. She looks at the date on the phone; she hadn't thought of dates or days. She realizes she's been living without deadlines for the first time in ten years, not struggling to perfect hems and zippers, curtains, deadlines. It wasn't about the clothes for her, the sewing, she had to learn to sew so she could immerse herself in the source of those garments, how to utilize what one loves. Unfortunately, to justify her need to personify fabrics, they had to become someone. Roses and black-clad beauties gliding around with champagne appear to her on the bridge, and the woods fill with the buzz of false accolades, the green-room congratulations prior to the curtain opening and the production coming to life after months of preparation, of living the part on and off the stage as Desmond demanded. "You've worked so hard, this is your big break, you look beautiful, stunning, Rosa we couldn't have done this without you, look at us, Desmond you are a genius." And the one hand clapping, and standing ovation for the eccentric Frenchman they all cursed behind his decaying back, and turning to face each other with the break a leg, break a leg, break a leg, break a leg and Lydia running through them with scissors and pins and ribbon strong enough to strangle, screaming *Break a leg, break every one of your goddamn spineless legs!*

Opening night.

Charlie calls moments before the curtain rises. She slams the phone into the Chase. Hopes it meets the wrath of a woman who leapt in there to escape her lying spouse, who killed herself for love. Jane watches from the riverbank, dripping, but not cold, relieved, Daniel at her side.

SHE KNOCKS ON the door of the little white house and waits. The music continues. She knocks louder. She sits down on the steps and realizes it's not the *biwa* she hears; it's deeper, moodier, a heavy yellow veil, like a dirty dawn. She leaps up, tries the door handle, opens the door and she swears nine smoky silhouettes rush past her, giggling, and dissipate at the foot of the woods like dust. She counted them without thinking. She tries to turn back and run home, but the house pulls her in gently, as if to say, it's fine, they're gone, come in, please, make yourself at home, again. She spent years in this house playing by herself, pretending to be grown up, married with children, not nine, running her own company. A businesswoman, imagine, as a kid, six, maybe ten, she wanted to be in charge, run her own company. At first it was horses, race horses, she made lists and lists of names of horses, and she drove a Mercedes; she pretended she was twenty-five, and that was old to her, all grown up to her then. But something changed. Sophie grew up and had the children, two exactly the same, twins, and owns a business called Cymbeline and has driven a Mercedes since she was twenty-five, used to own one horse, a pony, white, that she freed one day in the woods. Henry was mortified.

The house smells lilac soft. A vase of purple flowers on the coffee table in the small living room. The music veils the unsettling quiet around her. The type of quiet one hears when people are hiding. Any minute she expects someone to jump out from a room or behind a door. One of the bedroom doors is ajar. A pale light streams out of the room into the hallway. A bang startles her. In the hallway there's no movement. There are footsteps, stomping. Lydia approaches the room. Even with the door ajar, not visible, it feels dark. She stops. "Raiden, is that you?" The door flies open. What looks like Junko stands before her in multi-coloured and layered robes: red, orange, purple, layers and layers, wider than any doorway. Hair long and red and fuzzy like she had backcombed it. The mask pointy-nosed, blue and orange, eyes screaming, mouth wide enough to show moist red tonsils, but skin cracks like old concrete. The lips black. The arms lifted. The fingernails as long as frozen worms. *The spirit from the woods.* The red wiry hair, the screaming mouth, the layers of fabrics, pointy nose. *That was you*, she wanted to say but dared not speak. Candles crowd the black room, hundreds of flames flap in the darkness. Hundreds of flames she realizes are reflections of only a few candles. The walls are lined in mirrors, mirrors everywhere. Hundreds of flapping orange teardrops, candle flames and infinite backs of what she thinks could be Junko, infinite backs of Junko amongst the flames, going up in flames.

Lydia backs away.

Kaito removes the screaming mask and the fiery red-hair wig, the wooden mask.

"Kaito! What are you doing?"

"Pretending?"

He didn't know what to say.

"What are you pretending to be?"

"A ghost."

"Why?"

"It's part of my training, for the ceremony."

He plunks himself down on a kitchen chair and runs his hands through his hair, his head droops, legs spread and his elbows dig into his knees.

"I'm sorry I scared you. I was..."

"Attempting not to chase away spirits, well you chased away a few."

He smoothes back his hair. "What did you say?"

She walks toward the old bookshelf her grandfather built that was never really level, an early attempt at carpentry, at woodwork. The old record player makes her step back, it was her father's. She lifts the cover of the record, worn over time, Johann Sebastian Bach. The cello crackles, the record turns with a lope.

"Where did you get this record player?"

"I don't know, it's Pipit's."

"Pipit's. It's not Pipit's. It's mine."

"Yours?"

"That was my father's."

Kaito stares at the open window. He's tired of the lies.

Lydia walks around the house. *Something's wrong. Something bad is happening.* She has the feeling she had when her father was dying, she knew in her palms he was leaving, slipping away and there was nothing she could do to stop it.

Lydia rushes out of the house. Kaito rushes to the doorway. Raiden stands beneath the red lanterns, hands pressed together in front of him. He turns toward Kaito.

Kaito walks toward him. He holds back his smile, not sure if the gleam of a smile is what Raiden needs, or the understanding of an expressionless face. He wishes he was still wearing the mask. He releases a slow breath and the *I know, I know* of the warm hand on Raiden's stiff shoulder.

"Will we stay?"

"Yes."

LYDIA RUSHES THROUGH the woods and around the porch and over to the front of the house. Constance is bent over the sink, humming.

"Mom,"

"Yes, dear. Are you alright?"

Lydia smoothes down her hair, yanks on it. "I'm fine, fine. Are you?"

"Yes, darling. I'm preparing the cake."

"The cake, now?" she looks at the clock.

"Yes, for the ceremony."

Lydia paces around the kitchen table. "Where is Pipit?"

Constance wipes her hands on her apron and pours a glass of

water and hands it to Lydia. "Well, I think she's either upstairs with Junko or at the cathedral, dear. What is wrong with you?"

She thinks of Raiden's words. That Constance is speaking and Lydia isn't listening. *What is she trying to tell me but isn't? What is everyone trying to tell me?*

The Dragon Staff Certificate

PIPIT SAT BY the fish pond, draping her fingers through the water. One afternoon she told Lydia she has dreams that she's beneath the water swimming with the fish, and she giggled. "I looked so happy being amongst them, being one of them." She flapped a little fan in front of her glimmering face. *Go, Lydia, slip into the pond, be happy.*

"She's lovely, isn't she," says Constance.

She is, the epitome of what every mother would want her daughter to be.

"Think of the beautiful children she'll have. The mother she'll make."

When the phone rings, they both jump. Constance answers the phone and Lydia slips into the library. She runs her fingers across the books lying on the desk, Kahn, Le Corbusier, and the King James Bible, laying open. She lifts it up. "It's your sister." And drops it.

"I don't want to talk to her."

Constance sighs and passes the phone to Lydia. She covers the earpiece and says, "You shouldn't be in here, dear. Your father's trying to work." Lydia grabs the phone, glances at the bible and goes into the lounge, stands beneath the ballerina. Hears the library door close.

"Hi."

"Hey, kiddo."

Lydia held the phone away.

They lived on opposite sides of the city but rarely visited each other. They hadn't spoken after a conversation about children. Now Henry was gone, Sophie felt it was a good time for Lydia to have children. Lydia was appalled. It was the wrong time in her life, in her career, to have children. "I work with actors," she told Sophie. "I'm surrounded by children." "Not for you, for Mom," Sophie said. "Think of Mom, she needs grandchildren, to help fill the house, her life. Not for you idiot, God." She went on and on, their legs dangling over the side of the bridge. "How can a woman be whole without a child?" she said. And Lydia hated her for saying that. "You're so selfish," she said, "you never think of anyone but yourself and that isn't fair to Mom."

"Hey, come on Lyddy. I'm sorry, okay? Water under the bridge?"

The faces weren't on the wall, clouds covered everything, blue and grey coated the backyard with the aura of a Bergman film she'd seen years ago of a wandering man in a cape, that's all she remembered, the cape, the man wandering, grey and white and something about seals. She stepped outside into the grey. Five night herons flew above her from the west, circled, landed in the tree, then flew in one more circle and glided east. Pipit looked over at Lydia and waved. "A good sign," she said, pointing to the sky and entered the bed and breakfast. She was too lovely to become a fish.

"I don't want to talk right now. How are the girls? How is Cymbeline?"

Sophie's voice was softer than normal. She said she was sorry to hear about what happened and was there anything she could do. Then she went on to tell Lydia she'd been thinking of her a lot lately. "I even think I miss you," she said, like the idea of missing her had never crossed her mind. She'd actually bought tickets to the play. She wanted to see the costumes she'd been reading so much about in the papers. *In the papers?* It was shocking to hear her say that she was actually taking an interest in Lydia's work. Not shocking that it took a newspaper critic to say she was good for her to take notice. Lydia wandered around the garden as Sophie spoke, imagining herself in a long black cape with the hood pulled far over her head to obscure her face. She felt like she imagined Junko must feel, draped in her aura of black, her face hidden in masks.

Sophie said, "Cymbeline is great, hon. People fall in love here, Lydia."

"Of course they do."

How could one not fall in love in the company of velvet, flowing draperies, antique mirrors and ornate chandeliers. Lydia created the room from a picture of Henry the VIII's bedroom she found in a costume book. She didn't tell Sophie that. It was better she didn't know the association. She suggested she call the restaurant Cymbeline after one of Shakespeare's more operatic plays. She wasn't sure at first, "I don't want any bad vibes associated with the place. Is it a happy play, then?" *Not one of the ones where everyone's lying to everyone else and the people who love each other aren't allowed to be together, then fake their death to deceive everyone and then the one they really love thinks they're really dead and everyone's sad and unhappy in the end.* Lydia thought about it and said, *no it's a happy story, a true story about a really great dad.*

Rosa and Lydia frequented the restaurant when it first opened. She felt proud of her sister and wanted to help make it a success. It was an old building with an exposed brick wall. In the summer, the large floor to ceiling windows opened to a small veranda-like patio. They'd sourced most of the furniture and reupholstered the chairs in vermillion velvet, treated the expansive front windows with an antique gilt cornice, box-pleat valance and puddle damask draperies in gold velvet. In a neighbourhood of fusion restaurants and minimalist bars its romantic ambience drew crowds instantly.

Lydia invested a lot in her project but Sophie rarely came to see her work. She said not to take it personally, it was location more than anything. If she worked on the other side of the city it would be different. "You know kids and all," she said. But Lydia didn't understand. There was transit, babysitters, car services, cabs. She had a live-in nanny. Children liked theatre.

"I'm here," she said. "In your hood, eating dinner. "Thank God Mom called and told me. I was on the way to the play. Why the hell didn't you tell me you finally left the fool? I would have something to celebrate."

In "her hood," that she was actually going to one of the productions, now, when Lydia is no longer there. Dismissing her work as useless one night after too many martinis on the patio of Cymbeline, she confessed that she thought her sister should be designing clothes for real people. She thought it would be wise for Lydia to hook up with a businessman to fund her own label and ditch the actor. "I know so many of them," she'd said. Lydia tried to explain to Sophie that her label wouldn't appeal to the average consumer. She imagined a little boutique and a woman pulling out one of her many dresses and asking, "What is this?"

The shop clerk would say, "Oh, that's the latest by the Lydia label. It's called the Lady Macbeth line and over there, the Montague family's entire wardrobe." The Venetian courtesan outfits and the chopines might have a chance. Unlike Sophie, she was not interested in retail fashion.

"Will you still go? Please." Lydia said.

"You want me to go?"

"Please, I want to know what you think of the costumes and the audience's reaction to them."

She said she didn't know what she'd say if she had to speak to Charlie. She was worried that he'd spot her in the audience. Lydia hoped that he would see her. It would be perfect. He hated her. She could be unnerving. Then she whispered something to someone and ordered a martini.

"Is Rupert with you?"

"Look, honey, I have to go. I'll call you. I'll let you know how it goes. You hang in there, okay? We'll talk."

"Okay, thanks."

"And Lyddy, do what the doctors say. They just want to help."

Lydia held the phone away and shook her head. *She has no clue,* thought Sophie. *No clue.*

Constance took the phone. Lydia wandered over to the window, the Japanese maple fluttered in the breeze.

"Lydia, please dear, get some sleep. Come on."

CONSTANCE AND LYDIA walk upstairs, hands gripping each other. It is cool in the house, breezy. Constance's fingers brush against Sophie's door. Lydia enters her room. Constance releases her hand. She watches the door to the bed and breakfast. *Did*

Henry love her more than me, or was it that we were different? Just different.

"Mom?"

"Yes, dear. I'm coming."

Lydia sighs and huffs into her pillow. Constance lowers her eyes and thinks of Henry, always smiling at Lydia's stubbornness.

"You know what dear? I'm going to stay here and make sure you sleep."

Lydia is exhausted, unsure what to feel. She turns to lie on her back, her movements muffled and strangely calm. Constance lay quiet beside her, eyes already closed, her face stealing the moon's light.

"Lydia?"

"Yes?"

"You know I will always be proud of you, no matter what you do. I have always been proud of *you*."

Her hand holds onto her daughter's, the grip loosens. Lydia pulls up the blankets, and wraps her arms around her mother. Junko's dying from a broken heart. She won't eat. She's surrounded in mirrors that Pipit told her were a way to look into the spirit world in search of her lover's soul, for her soul. She will not rest. They were all falling prey to the claws and fangs of the dharma cave. How on earth was Raiden going to solve that?

She slowly gets up, walks toward the window, opens the curtains, one of her favourite pairs, a jacquard weave, the design called Central Park, cream and white. Elegant, like she always pictured her mother. She slides down the edge of the bed and holds her knees to her chest. She stares at the moon. Wolves howl. When the ceremony is over she'll take her mother to the national park, commune with *Oguchi no Magami*. She refuses to let her mother slip away from a broken heart, from loneliness. She refuses to let her family become extinct.

Her breathing lightens. It doesn't sound so strained. Lydia whispers her name to make sure she's safely sleeping and slips downstairs. It's not that late, the moon's lit and everything's coated in a sheen of blue. The colour of hopelessness. The colour of melancholy. Little-Nan laughed when Lydia said she'd work with any colour of silk but blue for fear of the story it will tell. "Rest assured, dark blue may symbolize melancholy but light blue is the colour of hope."

She runs her hand down the banister, along the backs of slipper chairs and brocade curtains, past the ballerina who never sleeps either, and outside. The Bed and Breakfast is dark. Little-Nan went into Junko's room every night to ensure the candles were out. Lydia walks into the woods. She stands for a moment to feel tiny and at the mercy of towering pines, humbled, she feels humbled. The low swoop of the trees and hum of night sounds comforts her, the sound of mist and the inside of a shell. She breathes in and out, slips off her sneakers and wiggles her toes into the ground, presses her soles flat against the cool earth. Streams of energy rise up through her legs, her sides, through her arms, her back, her shoulders, her neck, up into her head, through her face and into her eyes. She opens them, breathes in and out, puts her shoes back on, smiles and makes her way to the bridge. The water laps below her, to her side the white house sits peacefully like the sleeping white pony she used to see in the woods. In the morning she'll call Charlie and settle the end of things. She listens for the owl, wills it to call out to her. The low hum of night is all she hears. She runs her feet through the water and returns to the house to check on her mother. When she steps inside, the phone rings. She runs for it so as not to wake Constance. *Who is calling so late?*

"Lydia?"

"Rosa?"

"Why haven't you responded to the numerous texts I've sent about the success of opening night and the continuous success of the run due mainly to your incredible costumes?"

"Rosa, do you know what time it is?"

"Didn't you read the links to the reviews I sent you, the clippings? They were in the package with *Hope*. Every theatre critic that's worth anything is raving over our costumes, the headdresses, the masks. My God, Lydia, you're a star here, you have to come back. If you don't get a call in the next few days from Desmond or some other name in the industry begging you to come back I'll be amazed. Why the hell didn't you read the messages?"

"I drowned my phone in the river."

"You drowned your phone? Is that river even deep enough to drown a phone? It looks shallow."

"On the contrary, Rosa, the river is deep, very, very deep. The theatre is shallow."

The air between them was hard, distant. "Honey, are you okay?"

"Rosa, those costumes are yours as well as mine, lap it up. Be the go-to girl for us. Let it take you far."

"You're scaring me. This is your big break. This is everything you've worked for."

"No, Rosa, this is my big break, here, away from all that bullshit."

"There's only one week to go. Your apartment is waiting for you and so is the city, the world, for all you know. My God, this is everything you've ever wanted."

"Nobody's called me here."

"How would you know if you drowned your goddamn phone?"

She said she had to go, Constance was calling her for dinner. "Now?"

"We're busy. The guests are a lot of work."

"I'm sorry, but Charlie's been trying to call you too."

"He called me on the house phone once."

"There is never any answer at the house."

"He didn't even ask his mother-in-law how she was doing the one time he called. No apologies. Nothing."

"He needs to speak to you."

"Of course he does, now that I'm a big success. I drowned the phone, Rosa. It's dead. All communication is dead."

"Even with me?"

The last time she'd spoken with Rosa she let it slip that she thought he had moved on. The production was doing so well, the reality of the situation doesn't exist to him. He's in Verona dealing with his other issues. "You made it easy for him," she said. "By leaving."

"I had no choice." She wasn't going to pound the pavement at that point in her career, struggle to make ends meet on an apprentice's or assistant's salary. Rosa was quiet and then she said, "But what about him? What about your marriage? You keep talking about the job."

Rosa's voice echoed in her head like her mother's fragile footsteps on the hardwood floors. A picture of her father gazes back at her. "Have you found the missing link, yet?" Rosa asked. "Because I'm coming back to get you soon."

She doesn't answer. There was nothing wrong with her past. The past was flawless. "I haven't happened upon the crossroad if that's what you mean." Then she gazes into the backyard and says she has to go. "One week," Rosa says. "One week." The phone clatters on the counter.

She runs upstairs and rips open the package Rosa sent, grabs the tin of *Hope*, the newspaper clippings fall to the floor, unread. She couldn't even look at the photographs or read the reviews. Letting go was not something she had ever been good at. She clung to things, clung so tightly even her hands showed how hard. She was barely without a swatch of some kind of fabric like a chain-smoker, or chronic gum-chewer, one who twiddled their hair out of nervousness. Blankets, she realized, all the fabric, all the textiles, every goddamn costume, was a blanket.

She grabs the matchsticks Rosa was thoughtful enough to add in the care package she sent and runs downstairs and out the door. "Lydia, is that you? We're in here, pet, in the lounge, there's someone I want you to meet."

"Mom?" She stops for a second then keeps going. Constance is sleeping, she left her fast asleep. She runs outside, glances up at the closed windows of the guest house, then into the woods to the bridge, plunks herself down and lets the cool river calm the soles of her feet. Instantly her heart slows down, and her head stops spinning. Amidst the trickle of the water and the security of the wall of pines, she feels hidden, not blanketed.

Raiden's backyard is still. The light melody of the *biwa* trickles out of an open window accompanied by a low, smooth voice singing words she doesn't understand. There's no stomping.

She misses Rosa but there was something in her voice that proves she's moving on, a lightness, as if her voice is speaking to her from the sky. That's what city people do. Life doesn't stop there. You adapt, holes close in, you have to carry on. Even though she does miss her, what happened is in the past. Everyone's but hers. It was time to drown it in the Chase. Raiden appears beside her.

"You are up late," he says.

"You are too. What are you doing out so late?"

"The point of the question is dull," he says, "but the answer is intimate. How many people hearing it will open their eyes?" Then he lights up his cigarette.

"Where do you get these lines?"

He laughs.

"From the wise ones," he grabs his knees and pulls them to his chest.

She looks at him. "They don't sound that wise to me, why don't they just say what they mean."

"Like Shakespeare?"

She tries not to laugh.

The water plays beneath them, the music of piano.

"Have you heard of Hélène Grimaud?"

He shakes his head.

"Brilliant, as a child she was so clever she defied all her piano teachers and continued to play and take on pieces everyone would have discouraged her playing. She kept following her instinct, her gift and became hugely successful because of it. Then she left Paris to run a wolf sanctuary in Salem. Imagine?"

"Imagine," says Raiden.

"That's unique, there's nobody like her."

"Do you think she gave up her dream to do so?"

"No, I think she went after a new dream and changed the reason she did the first one. She's doing what she wants, how she wants to, which is how life should be."

He looks out over the water and nods.

"She defied the claws and fangs of the dharma cave."

"Good work."

They both breathe in time with the flowing river. The leaves rustle. The air is smooth and warm, silk skin.

"Did you know J.S. Bach had nine children?"

Raiden looks at her. Raises his eyebrows and smirks. "I did not."

"And five night herons flew around me today. Five. Not just over me, they circled me, landed on a tree, circled again, then flew in the opposite direction they came. Five."

"Five."

"What do you think that means?"

"That there are four more somewhere."

"What?"

He pulls his knees to his chest. Kaito watches from the dark backyard. His instructions are not to speak until the ceremony is over. He needs to stay in his role.

"My father wanted lots of children. He wanted to fill the Queen Anne with them."

"If he'd only known," says Raiden.

"Mom was upset, felt guilty for not being able to give him what he wanted, more children. It's why he taught. Had a school of kids instead. Sophie told me that just after I got married. I was supposed to start having kids. 'I don't want kids, I said,' and she said, 'Not for you, stupid. For dad.' God, all my sister wants me to do is have children for mom and dad. Is that why people have kids, for their parents."

Raiden turns to face her. She pulls away. He keeps her gaze, his mouth tight shut, his face pleading. He got up. There is so much he wants to say. He is supposed to be the teller of truths and he can't get the truth out to save his own mother's life. *Is it better to have been blind and deaf from the beginning?* Lydia fiddles with her shoelaces and pulls on the other shoe. Without looking up, she says, "I don't know why we want the things we do? What's the point?"

"What do you want, Lydia?"

"To be free."

"Of?"

"The things we are supposed to have."

Lydia's lips keep moving and all Raiden can hear is Constance saying, "Please don't tell her, if she can't hear it from me, I don't want her to know."

Kaito hears, "Sometimes I feel my mom is trying to tell me something but she doesn't know how. Is it that I let her down? That she wishes I would have children. It's weird, she's never been so quiet, when I feel she has so much to say."

She needs to reflect even more now. Further than she ever has, Sophie is right, she's selfish, the only thing she ever hated about her work, is that she had to be selfish to do it. Now she has to think more? She isn't one of the schoolboys in Raiden's program, caught breaking and entering and beating up other kids and stealing from Mr. Randal. Her future is not in jeopardy of being spent in a correctional institute, lost in drugs, or at the peril of the many bodies of water that surround the town. She is convinced that if he put her to the test right then, she would achieve her Dragon Staff Certificate. She could do it, faster than any of the damn punks who lose their way in this town. Her breath grows shorter between thoughts. She stares back at Raiden who is nodding his head like he's listening to someone. She wonders if he's heard every word she's thought.

"I knew a man who sat on the bank of a river much like this for one week staring at the end of his nose in meditation."

"Pardon?"

"One week staring at the end of his nose on the bank of a river."

"Wow," says Lydia. "I can't imagine doing that."

"Those who think one's insight exceeds others, has no eyes."

He walks into the backyard, beneath the red lanterns and into the house.

The Emperor

CONSTANCE WAKES LYDIA with a start. Her red cheek has faded to pink. The sun beams into the room. "What are you doing on the floor?" she says. Lydia lurches up. "What time is it?"

"It's noon. I thought you were at the cathedral."

"Noon!"

The room spins. Lydia sits back down again. She asks how Constance is feeling. She says fine.

"No Mom, really, how are you?"

Constance sits on the edge of the bed.

"I know it must be so hard since Dad died. I'm..."

She tells Lydia not to say that word. "He isn't... you know. Dear. He's moved on."

She scuttles out of the room, says she has to hurry; the emperor is coming to tea.

WHEN LYDIA REACHES the cathedral, Raiden and Kaito are on the stage pointing to various spots and nodding their heads. Raiden catches sight of her before she takes off downstairs. She's rehearsed an apology all the way across the path.

"Lydia?" he says.

"I'm so sorry Raiden, I slept in. I..."

He moves toward her. His red and gold *kosode* glimmers in the sunlight streaming through the stained-glass windows. She feels like a schoolgirl who has wronged the headmaster. Feels like she used to when her father would reproach her for something her mother found wrong. Raiden gazes into her face. "You look terrible, like you have not slept. How can you sleep in if you have not slept?"

He was the one with all the answers but this time he seems sincerely without one. She looks past him to make sure Kaito isn't listening and she whispers, "Because I sat up all night by the stream and stared at the end of my nose. I got so cold I had to go in. Then I continued at the end of my bed until my mother waltzed in and woke me up and I realized I had passed out on the floor."

His eyes light up. He straightens himself and claps his hands together and asks, "And what did you discover? What did you see?"

Kaito moves to the front of the stage and stretchs his neck like Mr. Randal whenever he saw Lydia coming and going from the cathedral. Lydia says, "I saw the end of my nose. I discovered it's more red than I thought, and longer and I think I pulled a muscle in my eyes."

The thickness of disappointment oozes down his face. For the first time since being in that abandoned house of God, Lydia experiences the forsaken religion that once ruled the place. A fragment of a larger presence gazes down upon her. She wants to reach up to the very peak of the ceiling and knock and plead with the gatekeeper to let her in. *Let me in. Goddamn it. Come on, open up. The Buddhists are driving me crazy.* No one answers and she's glad. Raiden would have hated that she categorized him. He follows his own path. He takes what he needs from the masters and makes it his own. She let him down. She failed his test. She saw the end of her nose and not beyond it. The man she admires more than anything since losing her father turns his back on her. The cathedral shows no empathy. She calls after him. "That's it?"

"My dear, you are a long way from enlightenment."

Little-Nan isn't the slightest bit annoyed that she is late. She was not obligated to be there at a certain time. She's more concerned by her pallid face and the dark blue around her eyes. She thought she should take the day off to rest. It was fine with her. Thanks to Lydia she was actually getting caught up. "Go," she says, "spend time with your mother, with yourself." But Lydia is determined not to give up, not today. In the little stone room a cool air breathes through the walls. The ceremony is only a few days away; Junko arrives in the doorway with Pipit. Pipit's eyes are blank. There are no words exchanged. Little-Nan picks the white robe off the mannequin and drapes it over Junko's shoulders. She grunts.

Lydia pulls the sleeves to see how they hang. Junko winces. Lydia avoids looking at her fingernails and wonders about her feet. Her breath escapes in short bursts through the slits in her antiquated mask. Masks differentiate the living from the dead. Ghosts wear masks. Each breath hits Lydia's face. Little-Nan hands her the *obi*. She ties it around her waist. Junko lets out a moan. If she squeezes tight enough perhaps she'll snap. Wouldn't that be something, to break her in two. Pipit and Little-Nan call her the *kyojo*, the mad woman.

"Am I hurting you?"

"Sorry to disappoint you, but no. It feels good. Tighter, please."

She releases her grip and backs away. Kaito calls from upstairs and Pipit and Little-Nan say they have to go and will she be alright finishing for now. Junko and Lydia are all alone.

Junko looks around the room, runs her fingernails across the table, silks, up and down the hanging robes in view. She stops and removes her mask and turns to look at Lydia. Her face is pale, white, not a stroke of colour on it, her lips almost invisible. She looks like a child.

"Only a few more days until the ceremony, you must be excited."

"Your tongue does not lash me in the way you desire."

"Junko...I..."

She doesn't move. For a moment she wants to grab her by the shoulders, spin her around and shake her. She's afraid that if she grabs her she'll break. Her sadness is being wrapped up in her white robe like a gift nobody wants. She has four good souls going out of their way to rid her of her sadness so that she can move on. Their attempts evade her. She is unreachable. She lifts her arm to her face revealing a tattoo. An owl, in flight. The owl, elusive, so hard to find, like true happiness. One must never give up the search for happiness, even when they are gone.

"Junko, we're trying to help you."

"We are nothing without family."

"But Junko, we're your family. Raiden just wants you to be happy."

"*Makoto no Hana*, you are so young in your heart. Raiden wants you to be happy. Raiden is fulfilling an obligation. It is his job."

She places the mask over her face, which when maskless is the most beautiful one she's ever seen. She leans close and whispers, "I have experienced true happiness. I've been happy. Everything is impermanent." Junko rips the *obi* from her waist and lets the yards and yards of stark white fabric fall to the floor, drowning

Junko's slight form. She slips her arms out and it crashes to the floor. "I am ready," she says. In just her underdress, light and transparent, silk skin and bones, her bare feet connecting with the ground, hair flat and dry hanging down her back, she walks out.

"Junko?"

Lydia attempts to gather the robe and replace it on the hanger. "Shit," she says, and gives up and runs after Junko. The halls are empty, except for Daniel. "Daniel?" he turns and runs up the stairs.

"Daniel?" Lydia runs upstairs after him and Junko.

THE HAMMERING HAS subsided. Kaito's completed the stage and the bridge that connected the side room to the stage. The cathedral is quiet, but doesn't feel empty. The dark warm wood smells like the outdoors. She drops to her knees. She's alone. She's never felt so alone.

The Owl

LYDIA RUNS OUT of the cathedral, runs like she did as a child, hair flying out behind her, she wonders what she ran from then, what she's running from now. She stops at the river. Her cell phone lies face down in the water, wedged between a rock and the shore. She gathers as much air as she can and she howls. All the buried tears erupt. She pounds the ground. The pines move closer, shadow her like a conscience. If it wasn't for Pipit's delicate hands resting on her back, she'd have shoved her long red nose under the water until she could no longer breathe through it.

"Lydia, you are safe. We are all safe."

Her unflinching black-lined eyes, shimmering hair and the ruby lips that even dolls would want to kiss, pull her back. Lydia's a hillbilly in comparison. Maybe that's what she was and it was time to face it. Born and raised in the country, trying to make something of herself she was never meant to be. Her whole career was a construct; that ego, that role — a construct; married to the biggest construct of them all, Charlie, the actor. She was never Juliet, not for a second, not when they met, not when they married, not when they split. Their whole marriage committed suicide, even if it was accidentally a stupid plot, a bad construct. She was Juliet's dressmaker. She made her beautiful and titillating. She caused the breakup of her marriage and now she's Junko's dressmaker and Pipit's and Little-Nan's and her mother's, all the beautiful flawless women, Lydia works for them.

A PICNIC BLANKET rests on the small patch of grass by the Chase. Three miniature mugs and a bottle of wine rest on it. Pipit shrugs. "Sometimes I come out here on my own."

"There are three glasses."

"One is for my mother; the other is hoping he'll join me, but he never does."

"Raiden?"

She laughs and almost spits out her mouthful of wine.

"Here, you can have this one. I just poured it."

She hands Lydia the cup. Unlike the warnings on booze bottles: don't drink and drive, don't drink while pregnant; don't drink. Does the Kanji on that pristine little bottle of clear liquid say, drink and forget that you spent last night staring at the end of your nose hoping to obtain the key that will break the barriers that lead to beyond — drink and be enlightened?

Pipit twirls a dandelion. In the water, Lydia thinks she sees faces: Charlie's, her father's.

"What do you see?" asks Pipit.

"My father."

"Me too," she says.

"You never talk about your father."

She sips her drink and gazes up at the pines. "I didn't know him."

Lydia sips the wine, "I sometimes wonder if I ever knew mine."

Pipit faces Lydia. "My mother speaks to herself, she is in her own world."

Lydia faces Pipit, the two of them directly opposite one another, mirror images and opposite, light and dark. "Once I heard my mother say, 'Do we ever know the one we marry, the ones who give birth to us, is there any way of truly knowing anyone when we don't even know ourselves?"

Lydia closes her eyes and repeats the words. Then she asks, "Your mother is in the city?"

"My mother is in your house."

The glasses fly out of both their hands. Lydia leaps over them and runs off. "Lydia?"

She stops in front of the signposts her and Sophie had made for Henry's birthday, then she runs into the house and calls Rosa. "I'm so tired, Lydia. There's too much for one person to do. Desmond is exhausting, everyone's morale is down. Lady Capulet had a mini-breakdown. Her understudy is two sizes smaller than her. All her costumes had to be altered. Imogen is looking tired and thin. More alterations. Her and Charlie are living their parts. They have no idea who they really are to each other. "I'm reaching the end of my rope. The apartment is good but it's becoming too painful to be there. Your absence is everywhere." She inhales from her stick of *Hope*. Lydia listens, just lets her speak until she stops.

"I found the crossroads. You know the place that I was searching for, where I may have gone the wrong way? I found it Rosa, the missing link."

"No."

"The signposts that Sophie and I had made for our father. To Town was etched into the one pointing left, the one pointing right reads, To the Owl." Rosa remains silent, smoking, sipping red wine on the fire escape overlooking the temple. "Sophie and I spent hours in the woods searching for owls because Dad said they are impossible to find, elusive. 'Kind of like true happiness,' he said."

"Okay," says Rosa.

"I had been going right. I always went right, right into town, right to the grocery store, right to the cathedral and right to the river. They were alright. And when I break that down, I was always trying to do the right thing, always wanted to make sure I was doing the right thing. But there is no right thing, Rosa. You have to follow your heart, you have to go for the happiness. It's just about being happy. Not the fancy job. You just have to do whatever makes you happy by nobody's standards but your own."

Rosa gulps her wine and rolls her eyes.

"I hadn't gone left, To THE OWL. One should never give up the search for true happiness, even when they're gone. I found the crossroad, Rosa. I hadn't gone left to the owl in order to find true happiness. Something I am realizing occurs in tiny increments, like sand. But a grain of sand is often as illuminating as a full moon."

"You sound like a flake," she says. "But I think that's really good. Now you can come home."

"No, Rosa. I am home."

Lydia drops the phone and runs back out to the signposts. She turns left. She walks across the path, through the trees, smells the warmth of the fast-approaching summer and the spiciness of the pines. Birds flitter from tree to tree. She wonders why she thought the owl was this way. There was a shimmer through the trees. It was the little stream making its way along to wherever it comes out. She steps over branches and fallen trunks, tangled vines. She follows the stream to an opening. A bright green, well-manicured lawn. She looks closer and sees the red lanterns on the long lagging clothesline and hears the tinkle of the *biwa* and the stomping of feet. Raiden approaches her from the side of the house. "Ah, you have come full circle. I'm so proud of you."

"How did you know I was going to come here?"

"You always end up at the bridge."

Pipit keeps her head down. She looks small, sad.

Raiden approaches Lydia, holds out his hand. Lydia backs away. She looks up at the sky, he was here too, her father. She looks at the white house. This was where he found true happiness.

"What is this about?"

Constance appears through the trees. "Wait," she says to Raiden. "Wait."

Raiden backs away and Pipit drops her head. Kaito closes the curtains to his room. "Maybe there is no such thing as the truth," he whispers. He stomps his feet, once then twice, then kneels and touches his forehead to the floor.

Constance takes her daughter's arm. "Come on, let's go home."

"Better to have been blind and deaf from the beginning," says Pipit.

The Dragon Staff Certificate

RAIDEN ARRIVES FOR his final fitting. He looks worn out. Lydia drapes the black silk over his thin frame. He is stiff, every muscle bound and held. "Raiden, you're like concrete." He laughs but there is no joy in his laughter. She places her pincushion on the table, gazes into his eyes and asks what is wrong. "You're about to marry one of the most intriguing, albeit insane, women I've ever met and you don't look happy."

"I made a promise, Lydia, and I cannot go back on that promise."

"But why? You don't love her, Raiden. How will that help?"

"Not everyone marries for love, Lydia. You should know that."

Red, lots and lots of red. The needle in the eye of the red poppy. The room spins. Raiden stares at the wall like he is concrete. He has hardened, he's cold. Not the man she's learned from who spewed proverbs at her for her own good. She stares at him, at his deep thin eyes that lead to God knows where. He avoids her stare. His eyes move like fish, gliding back and forth in their black sockets. Raiden removes the black silk and places it across the chair where it hangs like the skin of a panther. He pulls out a cigarette, offers Lydia one. They walk outside and sit on the swing set by the side of the cathedral where Sunday School kids played before the bishop left town.

"Junko is a not a widow, Lydia. She lost the man she loved too soon. They were never married. They had two children." He stops.

"She sees ghosts. She's not well. She's dying. She dreams of connecting with him again one day and I know it is hard for you to understand this, but she has to let go or else she won't move on."

"We came here for her to face what she cannot let go of. We all came here to face what we can't let go of."

"Why here?"

"Because this is where her memories are."

"She does not love me any more than I love her. I did love her, but I can't anymore. I have to let her go. For her to let go of her grudge, we have to conduct this ceremony... we have to bring her in touch with the dead."

"To escape the claws and fangs of the dharma cave..."

"She must move on, she must..."

"To possess the key to break the barriers that lead to beyond."

"Or else she will never reach enlightenment."

"And she will float over the earth draped in a white kimono with her long black hair and no feet. She'll never be with the man she loved."

Mr. Randal waves from his front porch and asks how everything is going. Raiden waves back. "You know Lydia, letting go is not hard, people hang on for the wrong reasons."

"For fear they'll forget, or feel that if they move on they'll let the person down. Do they hang on out of guilt?"

"Your father is being clung to by many. We all have to let him go."

"My father?"

He takes the tin of *Hope* from his pocket. If he were dressed in blue jeans and a T-shirt he'd be regular, an ordinary person, a layman. She worries about her own mother being stuck on earth and never able to connect with Henry. Her dreams, her forgetfulness, her visions. "My mother still says she has tea with the emperor. Only she sees him. He comes to tea, she looks forward to it more than anything."

His breath was soft and calm. "Perhaps your mother's emperor is your father."

Raiden gets up and walks over to Mr. Randal's.

Pipit sweeps up scraps from the sewing room floor. Kaito pops in to ensure everything is on track.

"What did Raiden tell you?" asks Pipit.

"That I need to let go."

She rubs her hand up and down Lydia's arm.

"He is a good man, he's made many sacrifices."

"But why make this one?"

Pipit keeps her head down and drapes the individual *obis* over each mannequin.

She half expects Junko to appear in the window, crazed eyes peering through a porcelain mask, long fingernails like daggers. *What on earth would she be like during the ceremony?*

CONSTANCE HAS BEEN baking the wedding cake and dyeing the fondant to the exact colour she wanted, dusty pink, with tiny pearls pressed around each layer, then she'd place the wisteria around it that the girls would pick on their way to the church in the morning.

It was hard to believe the ceremony was one day away. Lydia was unsure if she wanted it to be over, she was only just beginning to enjoy the process. Only just getting to know the counsellors. Constance and her ate in silence. Looking up and smiling at each other every so often, then back into their thoughts.

After dinner, Lydia was restless; she decided to go back to the cathedral to go over all the garments. "Mom, do you mind if I stay on for a while? I think I might help Raiden with his programs."

She said, "Darling, you need to follow your..."

"Don't say heart, Mom, please."

"Then what does one follow?"

"Their feet."

They had to be up early. Alarms had been set for days. The weather called for sunshine, record high temperatures. Too hot for spring. It didn't feel like the evening before a wedding. Lydia rummaged through the various bolts of fabrics and ends that Little-Nan had organized across tables and in boxes. She picked out pieces of fabric decorated in horses, and streams, falcons, peach trees, monkeys and even rabbits, which she learned symbolized fertility and rebirth. She didn't feel like this was a rebirth but simply growing into the person she was meant to be. Starting from scratch, a rebirth would mean not using everything she'd learned and growing from it. Her hands were drawn to a steel blue fabric embroidered with wisteria.

"A symbol of long life, prosperity, and good fortune," said Little-Nan.

She stood in the doorway smiling. A good choice in her eyes. The pale green symbols were family crests, *Ka-mon*. "Ka" means family, "mon" stands for emblem or crest. Family is of great importance. Junko's whisper blew through her ears, "We are no one without family." The weight of this fabric was best suited for a *katabira*, an unlined summer kimono. The fabric was ramie. She'd never worked with it before. The fabric caught the light, making it look like water, like a little stream. Deep blue vines, pink delicate blossoms, yellow leaves and the pale green of the family crests and red, lots and lots of red. This was her story. She sought the right colour of thread, fed it through the eye of the needle. Lydia flipped over the fabric to ensure the symbols lined up. It was important that everything connected in the right place.

LYDIA WAS SCHEDULED to be at the cathedral early. Kaito would drive Constance and the girls over, then come back for Junko at the last minute. Before she walked out the door, Constance said, "The emperor is very proud of you. For everything you've done, everything. He wants you to know that."

"Mom, there is no . . ."

Kaito arrived at the side of the house, asked if they could talk for a moment. Lydia nodded and her mother grabbed her arm. "He was human, Lydia."

She stared at her mother. "He was real."

She didn't understand.

"People make mistakes and we have to forgive them."

"Even monkeys fall from trees."

She looked in her palms. *What is she looking at?* thought Lydia. Kaito bit his lip, motioned for her to come. She lifted her hand to him, "Hold on," she mouthed.

"Mom, what do you mean?"

THOUGH KAITO WASN'T there, notes of the *biwa* sifted through the cracks in the upper floor, seeped into the walls, had become part of the structure. Black wigs rested on the heads of the mannequins. Lydia runs her hands across her own robe. She removes it from the mannequin and drapes it across her shoulders. Places her arms in each arm and attempts to gather the material to fit her shape, she ties the red *obi* around her shrinking waist. The white pancake makeup felt like playdough against her skin. She lines her brows with black, then the inner rims of her eyes. Outlines them like a panther's. She dusts deep purple shadow over the lids and coral on her cheeks, crimson on her lips. The *getas* slide between her split-toed *tabis* and elevate her. She grabs her hair and places a net around it. Fits a black wig. Ties in a bun on her head. She is afraid to move. Her limbs feel boneless and hang loosely at her sides like *peau de soie*.

She walks upstairs to the little stage. Red shimmers through the stained-glass windows, the only light glistens in from the moon. A few of the candles remain lit from earlier and are dispersed around the room. She senses someone and scans the pews. Feels like she's being watched. Lingering at the top of the aisle a too-familiar silhouette. She sees red, lots and lots of red. The suffocating fabric. The thick floral brocade salvaged from a dead woman's couch.

"Charlie?"

"Lydia?"

He says, "You look breathtaking."

"This is not a character, Charlie. The kimono brings out the true self."

"Oh, for God's sake, Lydia."

She glances around to see if Little-Nan or anyone is around. They're all resting for the big day tomorrow. Their work is done. Lydia's nails dig into the railing of the handmade bridge. She looks up at the spot where the statue of Jesus used to hang. She wills it to appear and crush Charlie for his sins. *Come on, God, you must have left a piece of yourself here. Just do away with the infidel. No one will know. I won't tell a soul.*

Charlie walks toward her dressed in his brocade pantaloons over orange trunk hose and his suede low boots. It all looks so cumbersome to her now.

"What do you want Charlie? Did you come here to pray, to seek forgiveness, to go to the confessional? Go ahead, get down on your knees and beg for forgiveness."

Something red catches her eye. Silk. Red silk swaying like two flags. Raiden stands off to the side of the stage. He is moving his arms in the air, swaying his long flowing sleeves like flags. Charlie's face is wet with tears.

"I never meant to do it," he says.

Raiden disappears.

"It was an accident. I didn't mean to hurt you."

"An accident?"

"Lydia," he shakes his head, cries. "I want a divorce. Will you grant me a divorce." The words stun her. She stomps her *getas* on the stage. She stomps and stomps. She wants to drive him away like the spirits. "A divorce? I should be asking for the divorce. I'll have you locked up for what you've done," she says.

"For what?"

"Breaking your vows, getting me fired from my job."

"They can't put me away for that."

"Tell the truth, Charlie, it's all the evidence I need. Tell me the truth then I'll get divorced."

Charlie throws a yellow envelope at her feet. "Just sign it," he says. "You never gave me the time of day when we were married. You were so caught up in your goddamn costumes and fabrics and 'the job,' what difference does it make? I mean, look at you. You are so consumed by what you do. You *are* a costume."

She glances down at her elaborate robe; he had no idea how far she'd come.

"Just sign it, Lydia."

"You take responsibility for your actions and I will take responsibility for mine. I'm sorry. I'm sorry that I wasn't loving or attentive. I'm sorry that I was so driven. And you are wrong, the kimono is not like our costumes..."

"Look, it's okay...I..."

Kaito appears at the foot of the stage. He rounds his arms in front of him, joins his hands and bows. His long deep-green robe is embroidered in hawks and lions. His hair is piled up on top of his head and his eyes are lined in black. Charlie jumps back. By stomping his feet in quick succession, knees bent and singing an indecipherable song, he chases Charlie onto the stage next to Lydia, they stand close but the distance between them is visible.

"Face each other, please."

Lydia's shocked and refuses at first. Kaito places his soft hand on her back and twists her to comply.

Kaito claps his hands once. "Sit," he says.

Charlie looks around. "This is crazy, where?"

"On your knees."

They do.

Kaito slides in front of them, claps his hands together again and says, "Pay heed to the words of master Hakuin, his Precious Mirror Cave..."

Lydia pictures Junko, her room, her cave of mirrors. "The mirrors," she whispers. Charlie looks at her and shakes his head. Kaito continues to dance and sing in front of them. She feels dizzy but light and thinks back to when she started working in the basement with Little-Nan. *The kimonos are not like costumes.* "Hakuin believed that those with the essential mind liken it to a mirror of perfect clarity that reflects all things that truly are." She looks at Charlie looking at her. They are not mirror images of each other. They are not seeing their true selves, or are they?

Kaito continues to sing the words of Hakuin's beliefs, all part of his role in the program, this is his moment.

"The sudden appearance of an enlightened figure in the mirror cave..."

She watches Kaito, thinks of the figure on the bridge, Junko.

Kaito leaps from one foot to the other and continues, "...illuminates the darkness and reveals the true self."

Lydia stands up; she can't look at Charlie anymore, he is the farthest thing from her true self.

Charlie sees himself, the enlightened figure before him, dressed in robes and a mask painted on with precise lines and colours, and expressionless gaze; he wonders if he has ever been his true self.

"One day you will reach the great mirror of wisdom illuminating all things with blinding brightness..."

He moves around Charlie. Charlie bats him away and attempts to step aside. Kaito raises his arm, his voice, he takes his beat, closes his eyes, stills his feet, breathes in the confidence he has honed to perform one of Old Granny's songs; Hakuin epitomized his beliefs to keep striving; Granny appealed to all people, classes, that no matter who one thinks they are — samurai, priest, sage, shopkeeper, milkmaid, artisan — we are all common people. In the text he has memorized and felt and lived, and stared at the end of his nose for, Granny believed that those who think they are better "may appear quite splendid in their fine surplices and robes, but they are in fact a truly sorry-looking lot."

*"... But don't think I'm some passing fling
I'm not your, 'flower of the night!'
Scary, those notions in most men's minds,
As for good looks, that's no blessing,
Always hearing 'What a pretty face;'
Men aren't my cup of tea; I sleep alone..."*

Charlie pushes past Kaito. "That's enough," he says. "I get it."
Kaito doesn't falter in his lines. He raises his voice.

*"They may whisper I'm a 'man-killer'
But I'm not the one who'd take your life."*

Kaito stops. He bows and says, "Old Granny's Tea-Grinding Songs."
Charlie runs off the stage and seeks solace in a hard, cold pew.
"It's not Imogen," he says.
Lydia watches him, his hands gripping his tousled hair. His soft hands, hands that have never suffered. She knows. Sees it in his white knuckles. She removes the wig from her head, slips out of her *getas*, unties the red sash around her waist, letting it all slide off her.
Lydia grabs the envelope. He'd even placed a pen inside it. She glances at numbers, dates, she signs and throws it up the aisle to Charlie. As he goes to grab it, Raiden appears and places his foot on it.
"I did not hear the words my eyes can already see," he says.
Kaito joins Lydia on the stage and sits next to her.
"He confessed. I heard it. All the gods heard it. All of them."
"The gods aren't reliable witnesses, Lydia."
She laughs, the kind of laugh one does before bursting into tears.

She can't cry. Junko glides down the aisle. Her skin translucent, mother-of-pearl. Her black hair almost blue. Her red lips and black-lined eyes stand out against her royal blue and gold kimono. She is undeniably beautiful but for the devil that lurks inside. Junko's voice drifts closer to them. She approaches Raiden and peers into his eyes, raises her long bent fingernails and whispers, "'tis death to marry you."

Charlie grasps the yellow envelope and backs out of the cathedral. Junko follows him.

"I did not hear the words my eyes can already see," Raiden repeats.

Kaito says, "Amen."

Raiden was right. She didn't need to hear him say what she already knew. She wasn't without blame for what happened. She filled her life at the time with what she thought she needed. One of the many nights she spent speaking with Kaito at the stream he deduced that she was not coping with her father's illness. She was young and alone in the city and was afraid of losing her father. There was no other man in her life to replace him so she gravitated toward one and married him. Fathers are the first men in a woman's life, who gaze upon them with love, and if not love, amazement, and throughout their lives they mistake one for the other and that's what causes a lifetime of heartache. She really did think Charlie loved her, she said to Constance the one night that she finally uttered, *"he wasn't worth it"* and she replied: "No, no, honey he was simply amazed — for a spell."

She stood in the backyard and gazed at the sky. There were no skyscrapers to block out stars or utter blackness. The real dark was eerie. Constance's laughter echoed through the slightly opened kitchen window; she thought she heard her dad's whistling. He whistled and hummed, but barely talked the closer he got to the end. He started to let his feelings out at unpredictable times and never consistently. His outpourings of honesty were a little like rainbows and eclipses. *Hearts continue to break but there's good homes to be had. Tomorrow is another day.* A feeling like warm milk floated over her. She glances at the end of her nose, then darkness drew the curtains.

Junko peered through the crack in the door to the bed and breakfast. Through her mask she whispered, "Congratulations waif, you found the key."

WHEN DANIEL APPEARS at Junko's bedside, she wakes slowly, hesitates. He is dressed in the robe with the purse of inexhaustible riches.

"Teito," she whispers, smiling. He takes her hand and leads her through the woods. Kaito holds out his hands to his side, he stomps his left foot, then his right, a slow and deep drum. Teito leads Junko across the bridge, down the riverbank and into the cool and welcoming folds of the Chase.

LYDIA DIDN'T DRAW the curtains the night before the ceremony. She wanted the sun to wake her up, to allow the window to be her connection to nature. Pipit startled her when she appeared in her room hovering like she did the first day she arrived. Her face was not made up. "Junko's gone."

"What?" she leapt up and threw on jeans and the floral blouse that had been laid out the night before. Constance was still sleeping. They ran to the guest quarters. In Junko's room, all the mirrors had been smashed, candles strewn everywhere.

LYDIA RAN THROUGH the woods, ran like she did as a kid, hair like swaying wheat in the wind, into town. Little-Nan was already at the cathedral. The sun was rising. It was too hot already. Little-Nan was pale. She shook her head but never uttered a word. Pipit placed her hand on her back. "I'm sorry," she said. Lydia wasn't sure what she meant. She looked around at the mannequins. One remained naked. Junko's *shikomuko* was gone. She looked underneath the table, ran upstairs to the little stage Kaito spent so much time making, the bridge, the stage, the picture of the pines that Raiden drew to hang above the bridge. They remained intact. All the trouble they took to erect the traditional setting and the bride disappears on the day of her wedding, the day they'd all been waiting for. Lydia couldn't believe the parallels of the situation. How she'd worked so hard to create the costumes for the production and she was fired a month before it opened.

"I've yet to see my costumes come to life."

Little-Nan shook her head "These are not costumes, they are a way of life."

Lydia walked back downstairs and gazed at the kimonos. Kaito appeared in the doorway. He approached Little-Nan and comforted her. She was not peaceful. We tried.

"She will wander this earth as a ghost," Pipit said.

"No dear," said Little-Nan. "She's resting now."

Raiden arrived in black. He asked Pipit, Little-Nan and Kaito to meet him upstairs. "What happens now?" Lydia asked him.

He took her hands and said, "When you understand, you belong to the family."

The stillness of the room felt like silk, *peau de soie*, soft like skin. She packed away the ends of lace and straggling needles, noticed an envelope shoved beneath her antique pin jar. LYDIA is written across the front in ornate brush strokes. She slices it open with her pinking shears. What looks like a bookmark falls into her palm, an ink drawing of a walking stick with the head of a dragon, down one side in calligraphy it says Dragon Staff Certificate.

Lydia runs upstairs, all the candles are lit and the tinkling of the *biwa* fills the hall.

LYDIA CALLS OUT to her, "Mom, are you coming with us to celebrate beneath the pines?"

She shakes her head, "No, dear, you go ahead. The emperor is coming to tea."

Raiden shoots his thin eyes toward her. He drops his head. Kaito dances ahead of them playing his *biwa*. It is hot, too hot for spring.

"JUNKO?"

Constance ran upstairs, smoke billowed from Junko's room.

Lydia wandered through her father's library. She thought how much the gold velvet curtains hung like the backs of weary monks. Beyond the window there was an unfamiliar hue. A white chalky substance coated the sky, not like clouds, planes or satellites. Dust, she swore it was dust. *What a mess*, she thought. She closed her eyes and counted to ten, backwards, then the house went black.

ROSA LETS HERSELF into the house. Lydia lay on the floor, the half-drunk bottle of Scotch at her side, the phone off the hook. Rosa panics.

"Jesus, Lydia. No, no, no. Oh, baby, it's not worth it." She slaps

Lydia's face. She doesn't respond. "Oh My God, don't kill yourself, not for a man, no, no." She calls the paramedics.

Through slits in her eyes Lydia watches two large men dressed in black running toward her carrying a large red bag. They stop and peer over Rosa's bare shoulders. "Rosa?" she whispers. *How rude*, she thinks, when the men in black loom over her friend like hyenas — scraggly and desperate. She swats them away.

"Lydia, Honey? Oh, thank God."

Rosa taps Lydia's face with her little rough hands. She peers into it like she is barely visible, as if she was searching for her. It was comforting to Lydia to think she had disappeared. A flashlight shines into Lydia's eyes. *Oh, thank God*, she thinks, *the light. I can see the light.* She can't feel her body. The men mumble something about vital signs and hospital. Then Lydia notices the emblems on their uniforms and tries to push herself up. "The cops, Rosa? Desmond called the cops?" Rosa hushes her, a sharp sting thrust into her skin. Her head is too heavy, hard like concrete. "What the hell's happening?" The men hoisted her onto a flat surface and the ceiling churns.

Lydia sticks out her arms, protests, screams. "I had a bad dream. It's just a bad dream, put me down. I need to dust the sky! Look at the sky." She wails like a child, cries for her mother. Rosa panics and tells the paramedics to stop. The paramedic reassures Rosa that Lydia's behaviour is normal. In a few seconds the sedative will calm her and they'll take her in. "Take her in?"

"For assessment. In most cases of breakdowns the patients cry out for their mothers, are temporarily deluded, hysterical — perfectly normal," he said. "Textbook."

"Breakdown?" Rosa says.

"What's going on?"

"Sophie, my God I am so glad you are here."

Sophie had been calling and calling. She places the package she'd been holding onto the side of the stairs, she wipes away a load of dust.

"I told you not to come here. It's too sad."

SUN STREAMS IN from above them through the space where the ceiling used to be. The banister lay beside the stairs like a fallen tree in the forest behind the estate. Remnants of smoke hang in the air; it had been a few months now but they say the smell of fire never leaves a burnt-down home.

At Lydia's side is a wooden mask and a half-burnt page ripped from Constance's reservation book, the month of April crossed out and through the middle was written The Counselors. Sophie hands Lydia the package. "This was mailed to me before the fire." Lydia opens it, and pulls out a piece of handmade paper:

Dear Lydia,

I met your father when I had travelled here with mine, he worked for your grandfather. I came back to say goodbye, to join him, to leave my daughter with the family she has never known.

Until we meet again, Makoto no Hana, in the mirror cave.

Junko

She sits up, *where are they?* "The candles," Sophie starts to say, "it's beyond tragic, Lydia. I've been trying to tell you since we lost Mom, but you've not been well."

"I'm sorry, Sophie, I had no idea what to do; she was adamant about coming."

"But I belong here, this is where I belong, the Counselors need me. I'm part of their program now. There's nothing left for me back there."

"Lydia, the production opens tonight, you have to get back."

Lydia looks at Rosa. "Tonight," she repeats.

"I said I'd be back in one hour, Lydia. I shouldn't even have left you for that long."

Charlie stands in the doorway.

Kaito flashes before her eyes, *I'm so sorry, I'm so sorry. I was chasing away spirits but sometimes the stomping lures them closer.*

It's never too late to start a new family, dear.

Lightning flashes, sparks shower, in one blink of an eye you have missed seeing.

The candles.

On the wall the singed ballerina hangs to one side.

The dead wear masks, Lydia.

Do do do dodododo...

Step right up folks and ride the magic carousel.

It's time you got back on the horse.

I've decided to forgive you, Lydia.

For what?

For abandoning me when I lost Daniel.

You're in denial Ms. Templar.

Don't listen to the doctors, Lydia, walk it off.

It's time to get back on the horse, dear.

Where is your mother, in the city?

She's in your house.

When you understand, you belong to the family.

When you do not understand, you are a stranger.

Junko?

"Mom..."

"She's with Dad, Lydia, you know this. I told you not to come."

Sophie picks up her sister and plunks her in the lilac slipper chair. "My God, Lyddy, you are supposed to be in the hospital."

"No, I can walk this off..." Raiden and Pipit hover in the doorway. "I need to be with family," she says.

"You an architect?" says Mr. Randal. "You building something?"

Rebuilding, Raiden thought, *rebuilding*.

"What?" says Lydia. She lifts her heavy head and peers toward the door.

Little-Nan sweeps away the ashes. Kaito stomps his feet on the ground, chasing away the last of the spirits. Henry holds the weathered hands of the woman he loves. The owl. One should never give up searching for true happiness even when they are gone. Shadows on the wall scream without sound.

"What's in your hand, Lydia?" Sophie reaches to grab her sister's fist, but unfolds it gently after seeing her watery gaze.

"The key to unlock the barriers that lead to beyond." Lydia clutches her Dragon Staff Certificate and smiles. Rosa drapes her arm around her friend, lifts her to her feet and leads her outside.

Sophie stands in the ruin of the once elegant front door.

"I don't get it, Lyddy. The key to unlock what?"

Raiden walks through Sophie, touches her arm and turns to look into her sea-green eyes, "When you understand, you belong to the family. When you do not understand, you are a stranger."

Sophie jumps and brushes away the sensation of breath tickling the hairs on her arms.

Lydia stumbles over her untied lace, looks down at her Converse, kicks them off and presses the soles of her feet into the hard ground. Sophie runs to her sister and hugs her like she wished she'd done years ago. Lydia gasps and wants to howl like the wolf, purge her sorrows to the large-mouthed pure god, purge her sorrows to Sophie. Sophie grabs her sister's shoes and helps Rosa take Lydia to the car.

The engine revs. Yo-Yo Ma plays the Cello Suites. "No one plays Bach like Ma."

Sophie and Rosa look at each other, a shock of relief wavers between them. They clap hands. Sophie leans into the back and buckles her sister's seat belt. She glances out the window at the Queen Anne, "I'm glad we're getting out of here."

Rosa pulls out of the long driveway leading away from the once ornate Queen Anne at rest in the valley. She lights a stick of *Hope*. Lydia closes her eyes. "What was in the envelope, Lydia?"

A yellow funnel pierces through the grey. Lydia imagines plucking Constance from the ashes, the fluffy ball of a dandelion, the evanescent stage, dissipating across the corn rows when the wind blows. Lydia opens her eyes and says, "No one plays Bach like Ma." She stares at her hands and through her hands the feeling of the uneven road ahead. *When all the seeds are gone, the bare knob at the top of the stem resembles the tonsured head of a monk.*

[THE END]

ABOUT THE AUTHOR

ALEXANDRA LEGGAT is the author of the short story collections *Animal* (shortlisted for the Trillium Award), *Meet Me in the Parking Lot; Pull Gently, Tear Here* (nominated for the Danuta Gleed First Fiction Award) and a collection of poetry entitled *This is me since yesterday*. Her poetry, fiction, and essays have been published in journals across the US, Canada, and the UK. She teaches creative writing at the University of Toronto's School of Continuing Studies.